The SONG *in my* HEART

Tracey Richardson

Bella
BOOKS
2015

Acknowledgments

There are so many individuals deserving of my thanks over the years, that the list would almost be as long as the novel, so I'll keep things simple.

Readers, you always come first in my heart...without you, the rewards would be few!

Bella Books, thank you for operating such a first-class organization dedicated to books for and about lesbians... I firmly believe Bella is the best at what it does.

Thanks to my fellow writer buddies and supporters, both abroad and those close at hand...you guys keep me inspired, and you help me put out a better product. And speaking of putting out a fabulous product, thank you to the wonderfully talented Elaine Dark (www.elainedark.com) for writing and performing the song especially for this book. Please take time to visit Elaine's web page or Facebook page (Elaine Dark Productions) to listen to more of her work. In the hands of my editor, Medora MacDougall, my work is always vastly improved, and for that I am very grateful. Brenda F., your website work has been awesome over the years, and Karen H., your book trailer videos rock!

My infinite gratitude to my partner, Sandra, for eagerly accepting my early semi-retirement so I can spend more time writing novels, yay!

About the Author

Tracey has written seven other novels published by Bella Books, including Lambda Literary finalists *No Rules of Engagement* and *Last Salute.* Tracey worked as a daily newspaper journalist for more than twenty-five years and lives in the Georgian Bay area of Ontario, Canada, with her partner and two Labrador retrievers. Visit Tracey on Twitter@trich7117 and at www.traceyrichardson.net.

her to stumble. "Why are you spending the summer drumming for a singer nobody's ever heard of? And in front of audiences of like, what, four or five hundred people? Did something happen you haven't told me about?"

Sloane had toured and played session drums for some of the biggest acts—Pink, Katie Perry, Kelly Clarkson, Melissa Etheridge. Playing summer music festivals was bloody amateur hour. Dess had done it when she was young and hungry, and so had Sloane. Playing through punishing rainstorms and mosquitoes the size of small birds, sound systems that sucked and died, audiences that were either really into it or were more into making out under their blankets and smoking pot than listening to the music. But that was years ago, and once you'd done it, you didn't go back. Not unless you were one of those washed-up old dope-addled has-beens whose records were hawked on television in the middle of the night.

"I lost a bet," Sloane grumbled. "I was playing poker with a bunch of other studio musicians I was working with last month outside of Detroit. I lost, and this was the bet, because Erika didn't have a drummer. And I know what you're thinking. Hell, I was thinking it too. But she absolutely fucking blew me away, Dess. And you know what? I'm glad I lost that stupid bet, because I think things are really going to happen for Erika, and it's going to be a blast having a front row seat to it all."

"All right, tell you what. If she's as good as you say, if she plays anywhere in Michigan or around Chicago this summer, I'll sneak in and watch." Even that, Dess knew, was probably a lie. She hadn't been to a concert in years and had no desire to go to one now. It simply hurt too much.

"Oh no. You can do better than that, Dessy-Do!"

"Oh Jesus, did I ever tell you that you were put on this earth just to make my life miserable?"

"Too many times to count. Look. I want you to do more than watch. I want you to join us on the tour."

"What? What the *hell*, Sloane?" Was she kidding? Had she misspoken? Sloane knew Dess didn't sing anymore—*couldn't* sing anymore—and would not go near a stage even if it was jammed with hot, naked women carrying bags of money. She knew damned well this was not something to joke about. "You know you just crossed a serious line with me."

"Okay, look, calm down. I'm not asking you to sing. I'm asking you...Shit. I'd like you to tour with us as Erika's lead guitarist, okay? The guitar player she was supposed to have broke his wrist three days ago and..."

"Absolutely fucking not! Jesus Christ!" Anger and tears throbbed in Dess's throat like a second heartbeat. How could her best friend in the world even suggest something as painful, as horrifying, as her getting up onstage again? Sloane knew damned well what it would do to her, what it would cost her. Christ, she'd be the laughingstock of the entire country! The tabloids would have a field day mocking her. The audiences would dismiss her as a joke, or, worse, skewer her with cruelty. The legendary Dess Hampton strumming a guitar for some nobody in the backwater of the Midwest was a preposterous idea. It was a dignity shredder. Well, Sloane could forget it, because it was never going to happen. And it hurt like hell that she would even think to ask something like this.

Dess ground out the words like they were broken bits of glass. "This is the worst thing you've ever suggested to me, Sloane. And I'm dead serious. I can't believe you asked me this."

"Aw, Jesus. I'm not trying to piss you off or hurt your feelings, okay? I'm sorry, Dess. I really am. But Erika's in a jam, and I—"

"Erika! What about me? You don't even *know* this girl, and you care more about her feelings than mine?" Dess's incredulity rushed out of her in an angry stream. "How could you even think I would do something like this? How could you even ask?"

"Oh, shit. I've really screwed this up, haven't I?"

"Yes, you royally have."

"Okay, how about this. I'm going to email you a link to her on YouTube. Just watch it. That's all I'm asking you to do."

"Sloane, forget it."

"No, please. Just watch it and then we'll talk again."

No, Dess thought, *we won't talk about this again.* She could hear keys tapping in the background. Fine. Sloane could send her all the goddamned links she wanted. It didn't mean she was going to watch a single second of Erika Alvarez. Or anybody else performing. That part of her life was done. Over.

"There was a time," Sloane said quietly, "when you used to want to help young musicians. You felt you owed it to the universe to bring others along, remember?"

Sloane was right, but that was a long time ago. Before cancer annihilated her career. "I'm not that person anymore, all right? I don't have anything to give. Look, Sloane, I gotta go. But good luck with the tour and all that. And I hope Erika Alvarez makes it big some day. Tweet some photos or something, okay?"

"There, done. The link should be in your in-box. Dess honey, I know you'll forgive me when you see how good she is. I'm not letting you off the hook yet."

Sloane's arrogance was legendary, but this! This took the cake.

"'Bye, Sloane. Keep in touch."

"Don't you worry. I'll be in touch real soon," Sloane answered before ending the call.

Dess set her cell phone on the counter, reached down to pet Maggie's head and cast her eyes toward the six-foot-high window in her dining room that looked out on Lake Michigan and Chicago's Gold Coast. While the cobalt blue of the water looked cold, a reminder that winter had only recently released its grip on the city, spring was creeping up on Chicago with its budding trees and shoots of sprouting grass. It wouldn't be long now.

"One more month, Maggie old girl, and we'll be on that lovely island, and you can swim as much as you want, and I can lie around on the screened porch reading novels and writing some songs. What do you think, huh? Doesn't that sound perfect?"

Maggie licked her hand in response, and Dess smiled. Life was simple, but good. She was healthy again—knock on wood. She had more money than she could ever spend in her life. She had wonderful friends and a loving extended family, and she still had music in her life. Not the way it used to be, for sure. She wasn't on magazine covers anymore, wasn't the hottest concert ticket in the land, didn't trend on Twitter. She couldn't get a recording contract anymore even if she wanted one. Which, of course, she didn't. Music had left her behind, but she hadn't left it behind. She listened to it every day—mostly folk, jazz and blues—and she played guitar two or three hours a day. It was simple, unglamorous, but it was enough.

Until her sudden illness a little more than six years ago, Dess hadn't realized how exhausting, how soul-killing the demands of the music business had become. There was the constant pressure of producing hit song after hit song, of recording a new album every year, of enduring the grueling weeks and months of touring, giving interviews and making appearances, attending constant meetings with agents, managers and executives, fulfilling the endorsement contracts, the endless wall-to-wall ass kissing. Oh, and trying to have some kind of personal life at the same time, which she'd failed miserably at. It was a merry-go-round that never stopped, never gave you a break.

No, she thought with satisfaction. She'd left her mark, reached the very pinnacle of fame and fortune and success. Now it was her time to enjoy life. To breathe. To play around with music in a way she hadn't done since she was a teenager. To write songs, to work seriously on mastering the guitar. To maintain her health, to enjoy nice dinners with friends and family, take long nature walks with Maggie. Make a serious dent in the hundreds of novels and biographies that lined her bookshelves. Maybe she'd even start work this summer on writing her autobiography.

Her laptop on the little desk alcove between the dining room and kitchen chimed another reminder. Sloane's email with the YouTube links. Jesus, Sloane could be a pain in the ass sometimes. An obsessive pain in the ass.

Dess stalled, wiped down the countertops for the third time that day, refilled Maggie's water bowl, then washed and dried her hands. *Okay, fine,* she thought. She'd take five minutes and look at the stupid YouTube video so that at least she could say she had. She owed Sloane that much.

Five minutes turned into fifteen. Dess watched the video, then watched it again, then viewed a second video of Erika Alvarez singing in a coffee house. Many things struck Dess at once as she watched, mesmerized. Erika was attractive. Okay, more than attractive. Dark, thick below-the-collar wavy hair—tamed and wild at the same time. Her cheekbones were high and sharp as rock cliffs, and her eyes flashed black and mischievous. Her skin was rich and golden, her lips full and kissable. She was gorgeous—stunning—in an authentic, natural way.

Dess leaned closer to the screen to better study the luscious cleavage exposed by the open leather vest, her lasciviousness giving her a pang of voyeuristic guilt. But only a brief pang. Sex appeal oozed from Erika's sensuous strokes of the microphone and the subtle swaying of her hips in time to the song's slow beat. A beat that matched the rhythm of sex, it occurred to Dess. Erika knew how to use her sex appeal without flaunting it or debasing herself, and the combination of sexy and wholesome was something money couldn't buy.

Her voice too was like nothing Dess had ever heard before—gravel and silk, deep and rumbling, then soaring high and sweet. It was pure, clear, powerful—a light summer breeze one instant, a ripping, thunderous storm the next.

"Goddammit, Sloane." Dess whistled softly and wiped the fine film of sweat from her forehead. Sloane hadn't been kidding about Erika Alvarez. If anything, she had understated her talent.

Dess knew exactly what having a voice like that meant, not to mention having the looks that accompanied it. If Erika played her cards right, the sky was the limit. And then some. With a voice like hers, she could sing any style of music she wanted. Well, except maybe opera, but Dess wouldn't even put *that* past her. She had a face and a body that cameras and audiences would instantly worship. She was the full package, the real deal, as far as Dess could see. Good enough that she should have been discovered by now. But fame and success were fickle. Dess had known countless talented people who went undiscovered or quickly faded away when they were on the brink of greatness. There were others too who, based on their musical talent alone, had no right to the success they enjoyed. None of it was fair.

She wondered how badly Erika wanted this. What her motives were. What lengths she would go to and how hard she was willing to work. And how she would handle it all if she got there.

Dess once thought she knew exactly what she wanted, and she couldn't wait to get there. Of course, in the beginning, she'd only fantasized about the highlights—the adulation, the mammoth and joyous crowds she would sing to, the money, the other artists clamoring to work with her. But there'd been so much more she'd never considered. Things that, had she not been strong and singularly determined, would have broken her. There were the obvious things, but there were more insidious things too, like questioning the genuineness of people and what lay behind their motivations, whether they liked you for yourself. The kind of nagging questions that ate away at the fringes of your life until you began to question everything, to doubt everything, until you withdrew, trusting no one.

If her life-threatening illness hadn't halted all the craziness her life had become, Dess had no doubt she would have self-destructed by now. No one could sustain that level of fame and success without a spectacular fall, and Dess knew, in that regard, that she was no different than anyone else. No, she thought with conviction. She would not watch, let alone help, this young woman drown in the soul-sucking, parasite-infested, exploitative, drug-, alcohol- and promiscuity-infused business that had destroyed so many others.

If Erika Alvarez was even half as good as she appeared to be in her videos, she was a shooting star who was destined for exactly that charming fate. And Dess had no intention of being there to see it happen.

CHAPTER TWO

Erika Alvarez's most excruciating piano recitals—the ones that had had her a half note away from throwing up all over the ivories—were nothing compared to this. Waiting for Dess Hampton—her secret idol as a teenager, her first hot pubescent fantasy—to open the door was pure torture. Erika wanted to melt into the walls of the cavernous hallway on the top floor of the spectacular Gold Coast condo building. She wanted that big oak door never to open, and yet she was breathless and weak-kneed with the anticipation of it.

Sloane, grinning beside her, gave her a friendly nudge that seemed to say, "It will be okay, you're going to love Dess, she's just a regular person." Meeting Dess Hampton was beyond cool, but the truth was, Erika had absolutely no desire to beg for her, or anyone else's, help. Drool over, flirt with, definitely, but that was it. Dess had been out of the business so long now—six or seven years—that she'd all but been forgotten by her worldwide legion of fans, the media, her record company, concert promoters, the Broadway stages, the corporate world, radio and television and even social media. The disappearance of one of the world's most bankable singers had been astoundingly quick, shockingly final and seemingly irrevocable. Dess Hampton had simply slipped away like day yielding to night. Throat cancer had stolen her career, the news stories said.

Though, had she wanted to, Dess certainly could have profited from her illness, Erika supposed. Plenty of famous people had turned illness or some other personal trauma into a success story. Not Dess Hampton. She had chosen to ride into the sunset without a look back. The rumor mill said she couldn't sing worth a crap anymore, that she shunned even the tiniest shred of attention, had outright rejected any sort of work in showbiz. She had become a recluse, as far as Erika knew. Even the paparazzi had long ago abandoned any interest in her, and that was no simple accomplishment for a star of Dess's stature.

There was nothing Dess could do for her, Erika was convinced, save for perhaps an autograph and a selfie for her Facebook and Twitter profiles. Really, she'd begged Sloane, there was no point to this. But Sloane, a little bit crazy, a lot independent, had ignored her.

The door opened with a heavy thud, and in its shadow stood the legendary singer—smaller than Erika had imagined, youthful, trim, glowing. She didn't look at all like a cancer survivor nor even someone in her, what, early forties? No makeup, hair the color of honey that just touched her shoulders. The phrase "natural beauty" sprang to mind. With growing apprehension she watched as Dess's slate-gray eyes lit up at the sight of Sloane, then narrowed shrewdly and suspiciously at Erika. Clearly, Dess Hampton wasn't particularly thrilled with her presence here. *Well*, Erika thought, *that makes two of us.*

Sloane and Dess traded a secret look, Sloane aiming a follow-up shrug at Erika that hinted of a shallow apology.

"Come in," Dess said neutrally.

She probably gives the IRS a friendlier welcome than that, Erika thought.

She and Sloane followed Dess and her happy, tail-wagging, wiggly chocolate Lab, whom Dess introduced as Maggie. *Forget the dog*, Erika thought, as her eyes helplessly gravitated to Dess's tight little ass, all curvy and filling out her designer jeans perfectly. She amused herself with the fantasy of firmly cupping that ass, pulling it into her body…oh yes! There was plenty she could do with this woman that entailed not a single note of music or even talk. She had no doubt she could melt that icy demeanor in about two minutes flat. Two minutes *naked*, that is.

"So, you're Erika Alvarez?" Dess said, turning sharply, not offering her hand.

They were standing before a massive leather sectional in a great room with ceilings the height of a European cathedral. Massive windows looked out over the lake and there was a fireplace that took up an entire wall. Erika could imagine sitting here watching a thunderstorm, or even a snowstorm, as the fireplace warmed them. A bottle of wine wouldn't hurt. Maybe some soft music…

"Ahem," Sloane mumbled at her to draw her attention.

Erika swallowed, nervous again. Was she supposed to sit? Kiss the queen's feet? Make a beeline for the baby grand in the corner and start playing? It was, after all, an audition of sorts, thanks to Sloane and her meddling plan to enlist Dess's help. She had been instructed to impress, though to what end she wasn't quite sure yet, and the prickle of pressure brought back memories of her mother dragging her to auditions before brow-furrowed strangers in starched suits, pens poised over clipboards. Her mother always had caustic words of advice for her. "Sit up straight, Erika, breathe, breathe!" Or, "No, no, nina, not *that* song, the other one!" And, "Ay Dios mio, do *not* look at the keys, hija!"

"Yes, this is Erika," Sloane answered on her behalf. She looked innately pleased, like she'd just discovered the cure to a particularly unpleasant social disease. Sloane was clearly enjoying her role as broker. Or star maker. Whatever. She would indulge Sloane, because Sloane had been good to her and would be indispensible to her on the tour this summer.

"Well, then," Dess replied, her tone as cool as the lake outside.

A pity, Erika thought, *that someone so beautiful, so successful and full of talent, had become so imperious, rude even.* As if that were the only option left to her now that her career had disintegrated.

I can't sing anymore, but I can still play the part of queen if I want. Queen Bitch, that is. I can still act like you're wasting my precious time.

"I'm going to make a pot of tea. Why don't you play something for us?" Dess gestured at the baby grand piano, so shiny it looked wet. Clearly it was an order because there was no accompanying smile, no hint of a question or that it was a friendly suggestion. She might as well just have said, "Do it."

Erika ground her molars, hard, and took her time getting to the piano. She was used to performing on demand. Had grown up rushing to the piano at the snap of her mother's fingers. Fine, she decided. As with her childhood recitals, she'd get this over as quickly as possible. It would make everyone happy—well, Sloane anyway—and then she could catch a flight back to Minneapolis and start some serious prepping for the summer circuit. The first festival was five weeks away, and she had at least a dozen more songs to learn with her band, such as it was. So far it was only herself on keyboards and bass or rhythm guitar and Sloane on drums. They still needed a lead guitarist, and she could kick Sloane's butt for not securing someone yet, like she'd promised. They were cutting it damned close.

At the piano, Erika flexed her fingers, stretched her wrists and admired the gorgeous Steinway & Sons instrument. Antique and top of the line, by the look of it. With rancor, she wondered if Dess even knew how to play it. She'd been in a few rich peoples' homes before, knew it wasn't uncommon for them to have an expensive, rarely played piano as a display of their wealth. Same thing, in her mind, as hanging an original Warhol or a Picasso. *Look what I can afford to own!*

Without a word, she launched into the opening notes of Adele's "Set Fire to the Rain," having decided to play something she liked instead of trying to guess what might appeal to Her Majesty. She closed her eyes, gave herself up to the words and the beautiful notes. She went to another place when she sang, a place somewhere between heaven and earth, where everything else fell away and the only emotion was pleasure. No, more than pleasure. Joy. And it came from her innermost being and reverberated through her entire body, pulsing a hot glow in its midst. It was almost like an orgasm, only longer and, more often than not in her experience, more fulfilling.

She was belting out the chorus, feeling it course through her from her gut and up into her chest with hurricane-like force, shimmering past her vocal cords and out of her mouth, when she became aware of the distant shattering of a dropped dish. The intrusive noise took a moment to register, like awakening from a dream, and it was another bar of music before she stopped playing.

Sloane leapt up from the sofa and ran to the kitchen. "Dess, you okay?"

Erika turned and saw that Dess was bent over, picking up pieces of a china cup from the floor.

"Shit," Dess huffed. "Clumsy, that's all."

Sloane had begun hopping around, looking panicked. "You didn't cut your hands, did you?"

"No, I don't think so."

"Thank you, God!"

"Jeez, Sloane." Dess stood, hands on her hips. "What's the big deal if I did? It's not like I'd need stitches or anything. It's just a cup."

Sloane fumbled with the broken pieces, leaving Dess to turn her full attention to Erika. She strode purposefully toward her, but when she stopped, she seemed wary, unsure.

"Y-you," Dess stammered. "Your voice."

"Yes?" This was going to be fun.

"Where did you learn to sing like that?"

"Like what?"

Jaw muscles clenched, relaxed. A tiny glint ascended in Dess's eyes. "Like you're the offspring of Gladys Knight and Karen Carpenter. With a little Whitney and Wynonna thrown in for good measure."

Erika shrugged. Even from someone as famous and talented as Dess Hampton, the compliment meant little. For most of her twenty-eight years, praises for her singing and musical talents had been heaped on her, but they simply didn't satisfy anymore. She wanted to be known as one of the best. Wanted to be *known*. Like Dess. Or the legendary singers Dess had mentioned. She not only wanted to perform before thousands, tens of thousands, but to have those thousands prostrate themselves before her.

She wanted to transform peoples' lives, to influence not only the music business, but popular music itself. And not because she was insecure about herself, but because she was completely secure in her talents and in what she had to offer. She dreamed that her voice, her playing, her songwriting, her performances, would be the vehicle by which those transformations might take place. She wanted never to be forgotten. Wanted her music to set a new standard. Of course it was arrogant to think that way, but if she didn't believe it could happen, it never would.

"Church?" Dess was saying. "Did you grow up singing in a church or something?"

Erika shook her head.

"Voice lessons since you were four?"

"Nope, but piano lessons since I was five."

"Then where…"

"I sang whenever I could, which was almost always in private until I went away to college. Then I joined a garage band, earned some pocket money singing in bars. Sang at weddings, birthday parties, open mic nights. Any place I could."

Dess stared at her as though she were an apparition, and Erika resisted a smart-ass retort.

Sloane rejoined them and set down a tray on which sat a teapot, three intact cups, sugar and milk. "Erika's parents weren't exactly supportive of her wanting to grow up to be a singer," she said, rolling her eyes. "Wanted her to be a master pianist or something. Isn't that right, Erika?"

"Something like that." Erika didn't want to talk about her parents and their obsession to push her onto the world stage in an honorable career in the arts that would elevate her and her family past the stigma of immigration and how that career would not—*could not*—be something as common and ignoble as singing. She didn't want to think anymore about the endless hours at the piano, her cramped hands, her sore back, her mother snapping at her with her whip-like voice.

"Could you sing another song for me?" Dess asked, polite this time.

Erika began playing "September in the Rain," softening her voice to a warm, intimate tone that spoke of a broken heart still stuck on someone. Inexplicably, the emotions of lost love came easy to her, even though she'd never known the kind of big love that people wrote novels and songs about. *But I will*, she knew with certainty, which was why she could sing about it being spring while it felt like a rainy September in her heart.

When she'd finished, she stole a moment to enjoy the look on Dess's face—the distinct, momentary melting of the Ice Queen. It was, strangely enough, more gratifying than a screaming audience. Or at least what Erika imagined a screaming audience before her would feel like. There was serenity, rapture, on Dess's face, like she'd just had a religious experience. Erika sucked in her breath, her lungs tingling at the pure beauty emanating from Dess. *I did that to her*, she thought, and it filled her up with something she couldn't name. She never tired of how people physically reacted to her music, because it was far more genuine and spontaneous than verbal compliments. It was the reason she sang.

Sloane poured tea, asked Erika to join them on the sectional. "So," she said, looking every bit the director of a colossal business deal, "I have a proposal for you both."

Dess's features had once again taken on a pinched, annoyed look. "Why am I not surprised?"

Sloane plowed ahead, ignoring her friend. "I propose that we work together. The three of us."

"Work together how?" Erika asked, confused. She was expecting Sloane to ask Dess to offer guidance, advice, maybe make a few calls on her behalf. Endorse her, somehow.

Sloane grinned like it was already a *fait accompli*. "It's simple. Me on drums, Erika on keyboards or bass or rhythm guitar, whichever the song requires, and Dess on lead guitar. Maybe backup vocals too… Just for this summer tour of music festivals we have lined up, of course. Nothing more."

As swiftly as a light being switched off, the color drained alarmingly from Dess's face. Silence stretched out, Sloane looking less and less like the genius she thought she was, and Erika shifted uncomfortably. Clearly, the idea was not going over well with the Ice Queen.

"It's brilliant, Dess, it really is," Sloane said, her tone less certain than her words.

"No," Dess said with asperity. "It's not brilliant at all. First of all, you *know* I don't sing anymore, even backup. Second, I have no desire to be back on stage, let alone a circuit of outdoor festivals. Third, my presence would only ruin things for Erika because it would become all about the washed-up Dess Hampton and not about this emerging, wonderful talent here that deserves all the attention."

Erika blinked. She was wonderful? *Okay, wait. Dess's compliments don't mean anything to me… No sir. Not. One. Single. Thing.*

"It could work, Dess. In fact, nobody would even have to know it was you. You could go by a stage name—just another anonymous band member wearing tie-dye, a big floppy hat and oversized sunglasses. And your presence would help Erika. Having that experience, that guidance, along for the ride would be priceless. Joining us would give Erika that foundation that could push her career to a whole new level."

"And I should do all this because why? Because I need the five hundred bucks a week I'd earn? And the adulation of three hundred people sitting on lawn chairs stoned out of their minds?"

Ouch! Okay, thought Erika, she didn't have to be mean about it. It was a crazy idea to have her join the band, though. Dess was right about that. And it rankled that nobody had asked her opinion. Christ, could Dess even *play* the guitar?

As if on cue, Dess and Sloane gazed questioningly at her. Erika shrugged, her confidence deserting her. These two women had played on stages all over the world, had amassed more awards than Erika could even guess at. Who was she, after all, to offer an opinion when something this big was offered to her? Could she afford to say no? Did she have the right to? She was in a jam. She needed a guitarist, and right now she'd take anyone who knew at least six chords.

Her attention back on Dess, Sloane said, "For you, my friend, the reason is simple. It would be good for you. Because music feeds your soul. And you've been away from real music for too damned long."

Dess crossed her arms over her chest, the tea long forgotten. "*Hmph.* Kale and quinoa are good for me too. Doesn't mean I want to eat them three times a day."

"No, but this is something you'll thank me for one day. Just you wait." Sloane and cocky were no strangers to each other obviously.

"And I should believe you because why?" Dess said suspiciously.

"Because I know music is still the most important thing in your life. And this is music, and musical talent in its purest form. It's about people playing and singing for the love of it and not for the money or the accolades. Or the drugs or the pussy."

Erika gasped, unsure how Dess would react to that last part, but she only laughed. And what sweet, warm laughter it was. It softened the faint lines around her eyes and immediately humanized her.

"Well, damn," Dess said. "I was looking forward to the drugs and especially the pussy."

"*Pfft*, as if, Ms. Pure-as-the-Northern-Michigan-Snow."

So the Ice Queen didn't do drugs and didn't play around. But she did like pussy. That was good to know, although Erika couldn't say why, just that it gave her a tingle in her southern regions. Dess, by the sounds of it, was serious about music and was the antithesis of a party girl. Erika wasn't so sure about Sloane, however, and that gave her pause. She didn't want destructive distractions around her. To her, it was all about the music, about striving for perfection. Erika was all business in her pursuit for greatness. She didn't want high-maintenance people around her who were more interested in fun than work. The other thing they all needed to be clear about was that she was the boss here, in spite of her youth and her thin résumé.

"Well?" Sloane looked at Erika for acknowledgment. *Finally.* "Do we have a deal?"

Dess was looking at her too with an unreadable expression.

Mustering a brand of bravado she reserved usually for the stage, Erika flicked a thumb toward the limited-edition, mahogany Taylor acoustic guitar she'd earlier noticed nestled in a stand in the corner, next to the grand fireplace. "Why don't you play something for *me* this time?"

Amusement flickered in those liquid gray eyes, and the barest hint of a smile spilled from the corners of Dess's mouth. But she did as she was told, fetching the guitar and plunking down on a high leather stool beside the window. Quickly, she ran through a few scales, her comfort with the instrument evident in the smooth grace with which her fingers moved. She adjusted the tuning as she went, then plunged into the opening notes of "While My Guitar Gently Weeps," arpeggio style.

Erika's attention was riveted on Dess's fingers—long, sure, adept, sensuous—moving quickly yet deceptively, the guitar as one with her body. The notes rang out clear and true, yet Dess's unique musicality bled through in the subtle movements—the pauses, the hammerings, the bending of notes, the transitions. She was putting her own signature on the song, and clearly the woman knew what she was doing. Dess Hampton was every bit as talented with a guitar as she'd once been with her voice.

With magnetic force, Erika could not take her eyes off Dess. Her eyes were closed, and there was an angelic smile on her lips as she continued to play the guitar. Erika could no more resist joining in the song than a child could resist a sprinkler on a scorching day, and she took her place beside Dess at the window.

"I don't know how someone controlled you, they bought and sold you," she sang. They fell into a groove together, neither outshining the other, but rather complementing each other's gifts perfectly—a true equilibrium of give and take. Dess flashed her a look of silent acknowledgment that the impromptu duet was fine with her, that it was working. And it was. It was lightning and thunder merging to produce an immeasurable power, and it felt and sounded more natural than any duet or collaboration Erika had ever been a part of. An uncanny instinct had them fitting their music around each other, joining, separating, merging seamlessly again.

The song's end was met by silence. Sloane's mouth hung open in what Erika assumed was approval. She glanced at Dess and was rewarded with a nod. Both of them, it seemed, had passed each other's test. And Sloane's.

"My God!" Sloane said, breathless. "Do you two have any idea how incredible that sounded?"

Two shrugs, both playing it cool, like two champions sizing each other up at the finish line.

"Well, I sure as hell do," Sloane answered herself with an enthusiastic clap of her hands. "You two are lethal together. Spectacular! I can't wait for us to get started."

Hmm, thought Erika. *Lethal, huh?* An interesting choice of words.

CHAPTER THREE

It took only a few strides for Dess to regret confiding in her sister that she was joining Sloane and Erika for their summer tour. The sisters were running along the path parallel to the lake, dressed in matching Adidas nylon pants and jackets. To outsiders they probably looked like twins, except Carol was two years older and two inches taller. And didn't have a musical bone in her body.

When Dess had also confessed she was having second thoughts about the tour, Carol began verbally kicking her ass, promising that if she *didn't* do the tour, she was going to kick her ass for real. Dess sparred back, expounding on all the negatives— living out of an RV, keeping late hours and being subjected to an exhausting pace that could negatively impact her health, having to find an alternate place for Maggie to live (and she didn't want to be separated from Maggie!). There were other things she didn't bring up, like her terror of getting back on a stage, fear of her identity being discovered and, worse, that she'd be ridiculed.

Carol, as usual, had an answer for everything. She was an executive with a pharmaceutical company and more than expert at debating, arguing, selling, manipulating. It'll be fun living out

The music had noticeably relaxed Dess, acting as some kind of salve to her. Or maybe it was a form of bloodletting, Erika thought. She could relate to that. Music was her savior, her drug, her lover. It was something she'd go to any lengths to create, to enjoy. And creating it now with others who worshiped at music's altar every bit as much as she did gave her a warm glow in her belly. It was going to be fun making music with these two, as long as personalities didn't get in the way.

Breaking the spell, Dess replaced the guitar in its holder. "Well, I think we've successfully broken the ice. But let's wait until tomorrow before we really get to work. You guys have had a long day and you need to unpack and get settled."

"All right," Sloane said hesitantly. "But we're going to really be under the gun, and it's totally my fault."

Dess looked at her questionably.

"I just got the call last night or I would have told you both sooner. I've been asked to fill in for Taylor Swift's drummer in Detroit this week. Just for two nights," she said, holding up a hand against any forthcoming protests. "He's down with pneumonia, and I can catch a plane out of here the day after tomorrow and be back in forty-eight hours."

"But we haven't even figured out our set yet," Dess complained, the pulse at her neck throbbing visibly. It occurred to Erika that Dess was far more frazzled than she should be, given her stature and experience with this sort of thing. She was pacing now too, and Erika had to tamp down the urge to grab hold of her.

"Dess," Sloane said with one raised eyebrow. "It's Taylor Swift."

Dess halted, a fleeting look of bewilderment on her face before she broke into a pained smile. "You're right, what was I thinking? Taylor Swift or..." She spread her arms, not finishing the thought, but Erika guessed it would have been something sarcastic. *Taylor Swift or the three of us. Like that was a fair choice.* "Okay, look. After dinner we'll sit down and work on our set list. Then tomorrow we can get working on the songs and then tweak the list."

Erika should have bristled against Dess's commandeering tone, given the fact that this band, this summer gig, was hers and not Dess's. But all she could think about was Sloane's coming absence for two days. And two nights. Sloane was the buffer, the mediator, the court jester. *How in the hell am I going to stay here alone with Dess without one of us killing the other?*

CHAPTER FOUR

Dess's hangover shrouded her like a wispy morning mist rising from a lake, but without the awe and beauty. She suspected Sloane's hangover, by the look of her, was more like a raging thunderstorm. Not her problem if her friend couldn't hold last night's wine, she thought wickedly. Of the three of them, Erika seemed the least affected, but she was young, so her body probably metabolized alcohol much easier. *Her body. God, I don't want to think about her body*, Dess thought with irritation, rubbing her temple. If she rubbed hard enough, maybe all thoughts of those athletic thighs, tight waist and full, round breasts would disappear. Last night over the kitchen table, she couldn't stop herself from stealing guilty little glimpses (dirty little glimpses!) of those luscious attributes. She had then spent half the night tossing and turning in bed, wondering what the hell had come over her. They had work to do, she reminded herself. A lot of work to do. There was precious little time to indulge in or even think about whatever midlife crisis might be trying to invade her life and make it hell right now.

To Dess's disappointment, they'd failed to come to an agreement on the dozen or more songs they would need to perfect in the coming week. Badly failed. To the point where they'd only managed to agree on a couple of songs so far. Erika had made the grave mistake of asking if they could play one of Dess's hit songs, which had nearly sent Dess through the roof. Not only could she not fathom someone else singing one of her songs while she stood only a few feet away, but it was much too risky. She didn't want anything to give away the fact that it was really her up on that stage, masquerading as a nobody. She would die from the humiliation. No. The Dess Hampton the world had come to know was happily retired and wanted to be left in peace. Any suggestion to the contrary would imply that she was out to try and prove something. That she was a coward trying to slip in through the back door or, worse, that she was trying to recapture her earlier glory on the coattails of this talented up-and-comer. It was absolutely imperative that her true identity be kept a secret.

Dess swallowed back the annoying tears gathering in her throat as she watched Erika go through her piano scales and wondered—again—how the hell she'd been talked into joining this little road show. She was largely doing it for Sloane and Carol, to get them off her back. But mostly it was because she owed them for their loyalty and friendship during her battle with throat cancer. They'd stuck with her, pushed her through the radiation treatments that ultimately destroyed her livelihood and crushed her spirit, then helped her pick herself back up again. She'd go to the ends of the earth for them, including doing this summer concert series, since that was what they seemed to want. But she didn't have to like it, nor was she yet convinced it was a good move for her. Once October came, however, she'd never have to step near a stage again.

"We need to cover a bit of everything with Erika's voice," Sloane suggested. "Rock, blues, jazz, R & B, you name it."

Dess didn't agree, and she and Sloane had been arguing all morning about the set list as Erika fiddled at the piano, ignoring them. Dess argued that Erika should stick to a couple of genres rather than spreading herself too thin. Better she make a name for herself as a rocker or a blues singer, a country singer, whatever, she'd urged, and then she could branch out after she'd established herself. Sloane thought Erika should try everything and see what stuck. Or simply be great at all of it and dare people to try and pigeonhole her.

They were about to ask Erika to weigh in when the first instantly recognizable piano trill of the Carpenters' "(They Long to Be) Close to You" floated through the air.

Dess stopped talking. Stopped moving. Stopped hearing what Sloane was saying. Every nerve in her body danced on the head of a pin, painfully alert and riveted on each note taking flight from Erika's fingertips. It was an iconic song, the opening piano riff like nothing else that had ever been written. But it was Erika's voice that instantly set her nerve endings ablaze, made her catch herself from her weak-kneed stumble. It was a voice every bit as uniquely talented as Karen Carpenter's—deep and tonally clear and perfect in depth and pitch and range.

Sloane had finally stopped talking too, and both women stared at Erika, who seemed so absorbed in the song that she had completely tuned out everything and everyone else in the room. *God, I remember what that's like,* Dess thought on an intake of held breath. There were moments and songs when a singer reached a zenith of immersed perfection, where flawless met the transcendental. It was a high that was better than any alcohol, opioid or orgasm. Dess could reach those perfect moments playing guitar sometimes, but it wasn't the same as simultaneously playing an instrument and singing, where the two coalesced into a synchronicity that soared on the wings of angels. The way Erika was doing now.

"Goddammit, she's good," Sloane whispered.

Yes, Dess thought. *Goose-bumpy good.* It was almost frightening to think of the possibilities that awaited such a talent. Erika Alvarez could be one of the greatest singers of her generation if she wanted it badly enough and the stars all aligned. The summer concert series would give a good indication of her drive and ambition, how she coped with demands both on-stage and off, how audiences received her. As for the stars aligning, who knew? Luck remained the biggest determinant of success, followed by hard work and then talent. The jury was entirely out on Erika

Alvarez's future, but it was going to be one hell of an experience to see it all unfold.

As Erika played the final notes of the song, Sloane clapped, then dourly said, "I hope you're not including that song on the set list. Much as I like it, it's too saccharine and not the kind of thing—"

"Don't worry," Erika said with a self-deprecating laugh. "I wouldn't dream of it, unless I'm playing to a bunch of old ladies."

Ouch, thought Dess with a wince. *I like that song, dammit!*

"Anyway," Erika continued, "I was only fooling around so I didn't have to listen to you two bicker about my set list."

Dess and Sloane traded a look. Erika was right. They were being rude and overbearing about the damned list, and it was time to give Erika some control. "Point taken, Erika. It's your set list. Why don't you decide what you want, and we'll back off."

Dess ignored Sloane's raised eyebrows. If Erika was going to grow as a musician, part of that growth included being assertive and making her own choices.

Erika, still at the piano, shuffled some sheet music and cleared her throat nervously as if she were preparing for a speech. "I want the songs to be bluesy, with a bit of R & B and folk thrown in. I haven't decided on all the songs yet, but mostly they will be new takes on old covers with a couple of originals mixed in."

"All right. The originals," Dess said, zeroing in right away on what could be the strongest—or the weakest—part of Erika's concert set. "Pick your best ones and let's hear them."

Erika's face colored. "I don't want to use my stuff. It's not good enough. I'd like to write something new. With your help, that is."

Oh hell, Dess thought. *Not only do I have to play guitar, shepherd the young pup away from all the pitfalls in the music business and give her whatever sage advice I can, but now I have to help her write some bloody songs? Why don't I just do everything and dub somebody else's voice over mine?* Her eyes shot daggers at Sloane, as if to say, you got me into this!

Sloane gave her a needling wink but directed her remarks at Erika. "Fabulous idea. You and Dess can work on writing a song while I head off to Detroit tomorrow."

Dess's imminent protestations were quickly and strategically preempted by Erika's enthusiastic gratefulness. She'd look like a snotty bitch now if she said no.

"There's something we can work on now," Erika said. "With Dess on guitar and you, Sloane, on the hand drums. I want to do a really bluesy, soulful rendition of 'Ain't No Sunshine When She's Gone.' And then I want to do a full acoustic version of 'Sweet Child O Mine.'"

"Now you're talking," Sloane said, racing to the conga set.

Okay, those songs she could do in her sleep, Dess thought as she retrieved her best acoustic guitar.

* * *

The grueling hills slicing through the center of the island, forcing Erika's legs to pump harder and harder to propel her bicycle along the path, were exactly what she needed. An exhausted body left little energy for the mind to nervously ponder being alone with Dess for the next couple of days, although it occurred to her that her burning lungs didn't need quite this much exertion.

Over breakfast, Dess had relented on writing a song or two together, more out of debt or deference to Sloane than anything else, Erika supposed. But she wasn't so proud that she wouldn't take a gift, even if it was half-hearted. They'd started their morning exploring the island on bicycles, and Dess was inarguably kicking her ass, as she zoomed past her at every opportunity.

Jesus. More than a dozen years older than me, and a cancer survivor too, and I can't keep up? Erika was more amused than annoyed that someone a dozen years older was far superior in the fitness department. She appreciated that Dess could out-cycle her, that she had the kind of body that was fit enough to leave her in the dust. Stamina, strength. All good things to have in bed, Erika thought wickedly.

After bisecting the island, they navigated its circumference, which was mercifully flat, but the stiff breeze off the lake was providing a challenge. It was Dess's theory that they'd be more open creatively later if they burned some energy first, but Erika wasn't sure there'd be any reserves left. The problem wasn't in exerting herself, but in the manner in which she exerted herself. She'd be happy to use up her energy on Dess. On top of Dess. Underneath Dess. Inside Dess. *But not on this frigging bike!*

Erika pushed on the pedals as they hit yet another hill. The Grand Hotel rounded into view and she stopped to enjoy its grandeur. *Yes, that's it, I'm enjoying the view and not stopping to pick my lungs up off the ground!* Dess looked back, stopped and gestured at the restaurant directly across from the hotel, a place called the Jockey Club.

"Lunch?" she shouted.

Oh, there is a God! "Yes, great."

They took seats at an outdoor table, the golf course a carpet of green straight ahead, the Grand Hotel looming on their right. It took several excruciating moments for Erika to catch her breath, and when she did, she said, "It's gorgeous here."

Her eyes raked appreciatively over the hotel's massive six-story white structure. A quick Google search had told her its porch overlooking the straits, adorned with crisp wind-whipped American flags hanging before every balustrade, was six hundred and sixty feet long. It was built in 1887 and had been made famous over the decades in a handful of movies. It was easy to imagine how little the hotel had changed over a century, and it made sense that it had been the setting for the famous time travel movie, *Somewhere In Time*. If she didn't know better, watching the bicycles and horses pass by, Erika would swear she had traveled back to the late eighteen hundreds.

"It's a real sanctuary here," Dess replied, accepting a soda and lime from the waiter. "Well, not so much in July and August when it's nuts with tourists. I keep my distance then. Spring and fall are my favorite times here."

Erika twirled the straw in her tall glass of Long Island ice tea. Alcohol was what this torture called a bike ride needed. "It'd be awesome to sit on that Grand Hotel porch on a chaise lounge with a fancy cocktail." A couple of girls waving palm fronds over them wouldn't hurt either.

"Funny you should say that," Dess said with a laugh. "Sloane had the same crazy idea late one night. She was drunk. She hopped over the fence, her flask in her back pocket, snuck up onto the porch and plopped herself in one of those very chairs and fell asleep. One of the workers found her at dawn and kicked her out."

For all Sloane's wildness, she struck Erika as a savvy musician. An expert who knew her way around the minefields in the business. And she seemed to know how to surround herself with great talent, which was a useful skill. She knew talent when she heard it, and she didn't seem to waste her time with imposters. Erika, however, didn't allow herself to feel too flattered at Sloane's—and Dess's—attention. There was simply too much work to do to keep earning that attention, to keep in her mentors' good graces. If not much else, Erika could thank her taskmaster parents for instilling a hard work ethic in her.

"Sloane certainly has b—guts, doesn't she? Listen," Erika ventured, wanting to revisit the topic of writing a song together. Dess hadn't seemed altogether thrilled about it earlier, and if she had no intention of giving it her best effort, Erika didn't want her help. "I'm sorry if I was a bit presumptuous in suggesting we write a song together. If you don't want to…"

"No." Dess's mouth solidified into a hard line as her gaze drifted over the empty golf course before them. "If I were in your shoes, I would have suggested the same thing." Her eyes swung back to Erika, revealing the barest hint of vulnerability that shifted something in Erika's heart. "But what makes you think I can help you write a good song? I only had a couple of hits with my own songs. Most of my songwriting has happened since my… illness."

Erika brushed her thigh against Dess's as she leaned closer, wanting the physical contact to reassure Dess. "I know you're a great talent, Dess. And I trust that you can take me places with my music that I can barely allow myself to imagine. I trust you completely. And I trust that we will come up with something way better than I could ever write on my own. If you're willing to try, so am I."

Erika held her breath. It was the first real crack she'd seen in Dess's confidence, and she worried her words would fall short. She needed a sharp, confident Dess if they were to write anything good.

After a long pause, Dess grinned at her as the waiter, dressed in jodhpurs and knee-high boots, delivered their chicken and vegetable wraps and side salads. "No pressure, huh?"

"For me, lots of pressure. For you?" Erika said, bravely raising an eyebrow. "This'll be a walk in the park."

They chatted about the charms of the island as they devoured their lunch. After their plates were cleared away, Dess laid down the gauntlet. "If we're going to write a good song and trust each other, as you say, then we'll need complete honesty between us. And that means getting to know each other better. Strangers writing songs together doesn't work in my experience. Deal?"

Erika didn't have to give it a second thought, even as her palms began to itch. The thought of getting better acquainted with the enigmatic Dess Hampton was both terrifying and electrifying. "Deal."

CHAPTER FIVE

It was too chilly to sit on the porch to hatch ideas for a song, so Erika and Dess moved to the cushioned rattan sofa in the glassed-in three-season room off the back of the house. Dess didn't normally take up residence on the island until late May, but she found herself enjoying the crisp air, the buds on the trees and the ubiquitous lilac bushes, and the smell of fresh earth on the cusp of giving birth to another season of greenery. It was a clean, invigorating time of year that was full of promise. Not only for the coming season, but perhaps for something greater, Dess thought with a prescience that was disconcerting. There was no doubt that Erika Alvarez had come swooping unexpectedly into her life for a reason. Dess hadn't entirely decided if that was a good thing or not, but for now she would bravely ride this wave and see where it took her. Because her sister Carol and Sloane were right—her life needed some shaking up right now. But more important, helping a neophyte like Erika might be Dess's chance to right a long-ago mistake that still haunted her. She hadn't told anyone, but she hoped Erika might answer her need for redemption. That Erika might be the key to finally securing the universe's forgiveness.

"This song," Dess said. "A ballad? Rock? What pace and feel do you want it to have?"

"Definitely something bluesy," Erika said without hesitation. "And a bit mournful. Plaintive, like I'm longing for something. That's the sound I want to go for."

"How does a girl from Texas become such a student of the blues? Because you have a great bluesy voice, by the way. It's just that I would have expected country and western out of you, given your geographic roots."

"I love the blues because it's so old and it's such a melding of so many other styles. Gospel, rock, country, soul. It's all there. And it's so raw, so full of feeling. It's about life's best and worst, which really means it's about the good and bad in all of us. I think it's the root of all music, and that's where I want to be. At the root of it all."

Erika's obvious passion for the blues was impressive. "So the blues is big in Texas?" Dess asked.

"Oh yes. There's an incredible amount of blues talent in Texas, and playing blues makes you a better musician in a hell of a hurry. There's a gunslinger mentality in Texas." Erika's dimples rose with her smile. "It's simple. Be the best or be gunned down."

"Well, then. You're used to pressure." *And wanting to be the best.*

Those damned dimples were unnerving, the ghosts of them lingering after Erika's smile faded. They're lethal, Dess thought with a spark of concern for the effect they were having on her. "You only have a trace of a Texas accent, but you grew up there?"

"My parents immigrated to Texas from Mexico before I was born. So, yes, I grew up there, but there isn't much about that time I like to remember." Her eyes darkened into black stones shimmering at the bottom of a crystalline river. "I went to the University of Minnesota, so that's where I've made my home the last few years."

Dess resisted the urge to press. Pain was always the perfect, powerful source of inspiration for a musician. For her, the pain had mostly come later, long after fame had ripped her from the pedantic, pastoral life she had known growing up outside Chicago. Erika, it seemed, was ahead of her on that score. Just don't let the pain take over your life, no matter how much it advances your career, Dess wished to one day tell her. Too many artists thrived on their pain, then capitalized on it, so they got caught up in a vicious circle. She'd seen too many of them pay for it with their life.

"All right, something bluesy then. Let's start with what's been on your mind. What's been consuming your thoughts lately?" Dess poised her pencil over the pad of paper on her lap and watched as Erika's finely shaped, dark brows dipped in concentration.

"Honesty, right?"

"Of course."

Erika flashed a smile that left no room for ambivalence. "You."

There was a quickening in Dess's veins. *Oh God*, she thought, mostly unnerved, only a tiny bit flattered. *I don't want to be at the center of anyone's thoughts, the inspiration for a song. Especially not from someone as eager and as hot as this young buck.*

She was afraid to think about what this sexy, beautiful, talented young woman actually thought of her. Sloane had already told her that Erika was a lesbian, and Dess imagined she could—and probably did—have any woman she wanted. She certainly wouldn't want some washed-up old broad like herself, Dess was sure. On the extremely slim chance that Erika did harbor designs on her, it was a moot point, because she was finished with that nonsense. She'd never been able to make a relationship work for the long haul, and she wasn't about to try again anytime soon. Especially not with someone more than a dozen years her junior. And never again with someone in the music business. Oh no. That ship had sailed a long time ago.

"Care to elaborate?" Dess said, her mouth impossibly dry, as she lobbed the topic back in Erika's court.

Erika caved with surprising rapidity. She blinked a couple of times, and her Adam's apple bobbed up and down. The cockiness was gone, and what was left in its place was adorable.

"I—it's pretty straightforward really," Erika stammered. She spread her hands out, and Dess noticed they trembled the tiniest bit. "I want what you have. The crazy ride to the top. The massive audiences, the hit records, the awards, the influence and power to create what I want. I want it all."

"But why?" Dess said, louder and with more bite than she'd intended. This foolish ingenue didn't know what she was up against. Audiences and record buyers were fickle, managers and music executives were ruthless in their demands, and some were even crooks. Awards were a joke, because too often the best songs and the best musicians got ignored after the orgy of ass-kissing was over. As for influence and power, there was no guarantee you would acquire it, no matter how famous you became. Dess knew from experience that the negatives more often outweighed the positives. What she didn't know was how she was going to convince Erika of that without snuffing out her hopefulness, her ambition, her dream. As much as Erika needed to hear some of these things, Dess reminded herself that dreams needed to be nourished, guided. With a strong hand, yes, but not with a fist.

"Why not?" Erika countered. "I think I have the talent, and I think I have something to offer. And if I'm right about both those things, then I deserve to be at the top. And at the top is where I can really leave my mark. Where I can prove..." Her voice trailed off, her gaze wandered.

Dess didn't want to argue about this, but Erika's motives raised a red flag. Who was she trying to prove something to? Her immigrant parents? Teachers and childhood friends who never thought she could do it? Well, those were pathetic reasons, and they wouldn't cut it.

As if reading Dess's mind, Erika shot back, "Why did *you* want it?"

"I didn't. Or at least, I didn't think I wanted any of it. I was young, barely out of high school. I started winning some talent contests, and before I knew it, I was signed to a record deal and started doing concerts."

Erika grinned. "Sweet."

Dess's pulse quickened at the sight of those damned dimples again, but her temper escalated too. "It wasn't all it's cracked up to be, okay? There's a lot more to it than you think. And you need to do it for you and for the sake of the music. Because at the end of the day, if you're not true to those two things, you have nothing." Not the awards, not the magazine covers, not even the platinum and gold records hanging in her music room.

Erika's breezy shrug was typical of a twenty-something. "I will. But I still want what you've got."

Dess shook her head and stood abruptly, her pad of paper thudding to the floor. The girl clearly didn't know what she was saying. "Honey, all I've got is a rearview mirror."

"Oh my God. That's a perfect line for the song. Maybe even the title." Erika began writing furiously on her own pad of paper.

Dess stormed off. She needed to collect herself.

* * *

Erika remained in the three-season room, so engrossed in writing her song that she barely registered Dess's absence. She was satisfied with her first draft of lyrics, but the more difficult part lay in the writing of the music, as she knew from experience. Marrying the two together was both the fun part and the most challenging.

She tiptoed to Dess's music room, Maggie approaching her with her wet nose and her happy tail.

"Hi, Maggie, old girl, where's your mama hiding?" she whispered, letting Maggie lick the back of her hand. "Think she'd mind me using her piano?"

Erika sat down at the piano and propped her sheet of lyrics in front of her. *Hmm, something kinda bluesy, maybe a little raunchy and plaintive too.* She banged out a riff, then another one until she found one she liked. What she really needed was Dess on guitar laying down the rhythm and contributing ideas for blues licks they could roll into the song. Dess was supposed to be helping her with this, dammit, not storming off in a snit because Erika had dared to suggest that she led an enviable life. Jeez, why should a little idolizing bother her anyway? It couldn't have been the first time somebody had said that kind of thing to her, and it was flattering. Wasn't it?

Erika stopped playing, questions about Dess buzzing through her mind like a swarm of angry bees. She had so many questions, but she didn't dare ask. Not yet. What bugged her most was why Dess seemed so bitter about the music business. It gave her the life she had, after all—this house, all these awards on the walls, infinite adoration. Yet she acted like it had been some kind of curse or nightmare that she'd had to endure. Her anger made no sense.

"You're making progress," Dess said, stepping into the room. Startled, Erika jumped. "I think I've stalled, actually."

Dess plucked a Les Paul electric guitar off the wall and plugged it into a nearby amp. "Play me some more of what you were just doing."

Erika obeyed, and Dess joined in, improvising some licks on the spot. They each made adjustments until the two sounds melded, fitting together like seamless slots. It reminded Erika of whipping up a gourmet meal without a recipe. Trying a little this, a little that, until it began to taste just right.

"Can I see what you've written for lyrics?" Dess asked.

Erika handed over the sheet of paper, bracing herself for the nuclear explosion she was sure would follow. She watched Dess read the words, watched as the line between her pretty gray eyes deepened, then smoothed as she reached the end.

"It sounds a little on the cynical side," Dess said. "A bit harsh."

"It's the blues. It's supposed to be sort of angry and cynical. But it's plaintive too, I hope. The feeling of wanting something you can't or don't have."

Dess still hadn't indicated whether she liked the song, and her omission hurt. Erika had laid bare her feelings on that wrinkled piece of paper. She did want what Dess once had and now so casually didn't give a shit about anymore. What was so wrong with wanting what tens of thousands, perhaps even millions, of other people wanted? She'd thought long and hard about it for years, had worked her ass off since going away to college. This wasn't some fly-by-night fantasy that she would discard in a few months. She was no longer a kid with stars in her eyes. And whatever was haunting Dess was not her fault.

She pounded out a few bars on the piano.

"Whoa there," Dess yelled over the racket. "That might be a bit heavy for the song. Okay, look." She squeezed onto the piano bench next to Erika, their thighs and shoulders touching. *Damn.* The contact electrified the air around them, and Erika's heart pounded. Maybe it was the mix of anger and reverence toward Dess that put her breathlessly on edge. But something else, too, something much further south, was stirring.

The urge to bend Dess over this piano bench, peel off her clothes, kiss every inch of her skin, plunge herself inside her, strangled the very breath from Erika's throat. She hadn't felt such a thunderous rush of desire for anyone in a long time. Years, in fact, and she had to squeeze her legs together. Shakily, she wiped the back of her hand over her moist forehead, and tried— *please God!*—to think of something else, anything else. The birds outside, the freighter out on the lake that looked the size of a toy, the storm forecast for tomorrow night…

When she allowed herself a moment of clarity, she knew this attraction made little sense. Half their time together was spent at odds with each other, and the other half, well, they weren't exactly good friends. Friendly strangers, maybe. And yet there it was, a physical chemistry that had the power to shake the ground beneath her and to instantly decimate any walls she might erect for self-preservation.

Dess, completely oblivious to the hormonal eruption next to her and Erika's struggle to tamp it down, began reading the first verse and chorus out loud;

> *I want what you got.*
> *You say all you got's a rearview mirror.*
> *But that rearview mirror's got a highway full of memories.*
> *Memories I'll never know.*
> *'Cuz I want what you got.*
> *I want where you lived,*
> *Who you loved, what you did.*
> *I want what you got.*

"Okay," Dess continued. "I like it. It's good. But I think we can improve the writing. Then we can layer in more music, though I like the riffs we've done so far."

"Really?" Erika said, a starstruck kid all over again.

Dess rose from the piano bench, her absence like a cool, unwelcome breeze against Erika's skin. She flipped some switches at a bank of electronic equipment in the corner.

"Let's record what we have so far for posterity, then get something for supper, okay?"

"Oh shit." Erika glanced at her watch, saw that it was after six thirty. "I didn't realize it was so late."

"Another half-hour of this before dinner, then I think we should pack it in until tomorrow."

Erika couldn't keep the mischief from her voice. "What if we're struck by inspiration late tonight?"

Dess smiled. Damn, her smile was alluring, almost heartbreaking in its vulnerability. *Makes you want to hold her in your arms and never let go. Protect her, nourish her, adore her, kiss away all those sad things she has inside her. God, what's happening to me? Am I trying to write some schmaltzy ballad now?*

"We'll see about that, but I wouldn't count on it. Maggie and I are usually in bed by ten thirty every night."

Boy, would I ever like to change that, Erika thought with renewed lust. While the strength of her attraction to Dess still surprised her a little, she felt no guilt. She loved women, loved sex, and Dess—a beautiful, sexy woman—was here in this big house, alone with her. In her mind, it could be that simple, although she'd been brought up well enough to mind her manners. A little fun in the sack with Dess Hampton was nothing more than a harmless, masturbation-inducing fantasy that she had no intention of trying to make happen.

Dinner consisted of pizza and a tall glass of beer at the Rebel Yankee tavern, and Erika quizzed Dess about the island—its history (she'd had no idea it had played a role in the War of 1812), its people (fewer than a thousand inhabited it year-round) and its charm. The cab ride back to Dess's house was the most interesting—and the most enchanting—cab ride Erika had ever taken. The cab was a horse and buggy, because motorized vehicles weren't allowed on the island. Another charming quirk about the island—all the bicycles and horses, Erika thought, her nose twitching at the earthy, not unpleasant smell of horse sweat permeating the air. She inched closer to Dess to ward off the evening chill.

"How come you don't have your own horse and buggy?" she asked. It would be fun to take a ride like this, just the two of them.

"Are you kidding? I don't trust myself to be able to handle one of these poor beasts. I'm sure they'd raise a fuss if a city slicker like me ever tried to command one. A bicycle works just fine for me most of the time."

"Well, I think it's incredibly cool. And romantic. I've never been on a horse and buggy before."

Dess simply looked at her with a raised eyebrow.

"What?"

Dess smiled, shook her head teasingly. "Romantic, huh? You're going to be writing love songs by the end of this visit here, aren't you?"

"With any luck," Erika mumbled, hyper-aware of the fluttering sensation between her thighs. She wasn't especially into casual flings, but she'd be happy to make an exception. Nothing complicated, nothing full of entanglements. A mature, sexy, smart and talented woman like Dess would be the perfect choice in making this a summer to remember. A smile rose to her lips as she envisioned slowly unbuttoning Dess's blouse, slowly tasting what was inside.

It was just as well that Dess, staring blankly at the driver's back, was oblivious to the lustful thoughts charging through her mind, Erika supposed. While she enjoyed a good challenge and had no shortage of confidence in herself, she had to admit she stood little chance of melting the Ice Queen. Not that she had any intention of trying. *No, uh-huh, no way.*

CHAPTER SIX

Maggie trotting happily between them, Dess led Erika down the sharply descending stone path that zigzagged like a drunken sailor down to the water's edge.

"This is your own private access? And your own little beach here?" Erika asked, awe in her voice.

"Yup, all mine. Well, and Maggie's. And my mother's when she stays here with me in July and August."

"It's nice and private. Ever do any nude sunbathing down here?"

Dess cut a quick glance at Erika, but her eyes were unreadable behind her wraparound sunglasses.

"Every day," Dess answered dryly. "Sometimes twice a day, matter of fact."

"Wow, really?" Erika lowered her sunglasses, her astonishment like two full moons. It was comical the way her mouth opened too, like a fish gulping air, and Dess could no longer keep a straight face.

"Of course not, silly. But go ahead if you want to do it. Maggie and I won't look, I promise." Dess tried to maintain her grin, but she quickly regretted kidding about something as forbidden but as insanely alluring as seeing Erika's naked breasts. She could only imagine those mounds of young, firm flesh with nothing between them and the sun but the warm caress of a breeze. *And maybe the warm caress of my hands. God,* she thought, *what is happening to me? I haven't looked at a woman or even thought about sex in months. Longer, even. And yet now, with Erika, I can't seem to stop thinking about…sex sex sex! Well, it's not my fault. This woman practically oozes sex with all those curves and tight-fitting clothes and low-cut tops, skin as smooth as silk and that unmistakable swagger that says "I'm a fuck machine." Not to mention dark eyes as big as dinner plates and those spectacular dimples. I'm going to fucking kill Sloane!*

"You okay?" Erika stopped her with a hand lightly on her arm.

"Of course, why?" Dess asked around her suddenly dry throat.

"You look a bit pale suddenly. Do you feel sick?"

Dess strolled to the water's edge, where she spotted a foot-long twig in the sand. She picked it up and hurled it into the lake and watched as Maggie, with a quickness that was remarkable for her stocky frame, leaped into the water after it without a care for the water's chill. The air, at least, was beginning to warm, with light jackets or a hoodie enough to keep the dampness out. Summer, and its waves of tourists, wouldn't be far off now, and it occurred to Dess that it would be the first time in six years that she wouldn't be spending the summer on the island.

"I'm going to miss this place," she said, pitching her voice out to the horizon as Maggie, her prize between her teeth, turned for the swim back.

Erika had silently stepped beside her. "There'll be time for a visit or two between our gigs. And Maggie will be with us, right?"

"Yes. I just hope this old minstrel is up to all this traveling and hauling instruments around. And the late-night performances."

"Sloane and I will be doing the heavy lifting with the hauling and the driving. But it's going to be a big change, having all of us crammed into a thirty-foot trailer for months. You sure you're up to it?"

"Not really, no," Dess said plainly. She wouldn't lie and pretend she considered this was going to be the best summer adventure of her life. It was going to be a hell of a lot of hard work for very little in return. Sure, it would help hone Erika's performing skills, get her some publicity and perhaps get her noticed by someone in the business who could really help her. For Dess, however, it only meant one thing—a chance to pay it forward. She'd been lucky in her career as well as dedicated, and she certainly didn't owe anyone anything for that. But if there was one thing she'd left unfinished in what was otherwise a stellar career, it was helping someone else achieve their dreams. And helping Erika might, she prayed, alleviate the shame she'd carried around inside for well over a decade. A shame that even her self-exile and fall from grace had done little to mitigate.

"Can I ask you something personal?" Erika said cautiously.

Dess picked up the stick Maggie had dropped at her feet and tossed it into the water again. "Sure."

"You seem, if I can be blunt, awfully bitter about the music business. I get the feeling sometimes that you don't think I should go for it."

Dess turned to face Erika. She deserved the truth. "You're right. I've been pretty obvious about it, and it's not fair to you. Jesus, Erika. I don't even know where to start. There are so many landmines in the business. I don't want to see you hurt. Or worse, destroyed. And I don't know quite how to teach you what those obstacles are without...without leaving you dispirited."

"You could never do that, Dess. You could never kill my dream, okay? And you're going to help me so those things won't happen to me, right?"

They began walking down the beach, Maggie trotting ahead of them with the stick clamped tightly between her teeth, her brown fur dripping a wet trail behind her.

"It's not that simple," Dess replied. "I can't protect you from everything. It can be a soul-eating business, Erika, and you'll need to be careful. And strong. You'll need a very solid moral compass and you'll need to stay true to it. Which, believe me, won't be easy."

"It didn't destroy you, though, right? You're strong."

Dess thought about that for a moment. No, it hadn't destroyed her, and yes, she was strong, but it had come close, and it had sometimes turned her into someone she wasn't proud of. Some of the people she had thought were in her corner were really only out for themselves. Like Dayna. Dayna's betrayal had hurt her the most. The rest—the late nights, the killer travel schedules, the pressure of producing hit song after hit song—she'd learned to cope with while managing not to get hooked on booze or drugs. The years of self-centeredness and hard work had stolen the chance to make lasting friendships and to build an enduring relationship with a woman. Those were years she could never get back.

"No, it didn't destroy me, but that might have been more by luck than anything else. Look, I don't mean for it to sound all bad, because it's not. But surviving cancer, it changes your perspective. It makes you focus on what's important, makes you take stock of things so that you can make the kind of decisions you need to make, for the sake of your own survival."

"Is that why you left the music business? Because of the cancer?"

Dess focused on a distant fishing trawler. "I left it, and it left me. Because of the cancer, yes. I needed to focus all my energy on fighting for my life, because that's all that mattered. Not the awards, not the records, not the money, not the crowds." She swung her moist gaze back to Erika, the subject more emotional than she would have expected, given that she barely knew Erika and typically didn't confide in strangers. "And then I discovered that the radiation had killed my voice. So that sealed my fate. The business didn't want me anymore if I couldn't sing."

"But you didn't need to disappear completely from the music business, did you? I mean, you still had your fans. You still had other things in the business you could do?"

"I'd given it all. There wasn't anything else I could contribute that filled me up the way singing did."

"But look at your guitar playing, your songwriting. All the experience and knowledge you have. You could have reinvented yourself. You still can."

Dess smiled to lighten the mood. "I did reinvent myself. For *me*. And I am contributing to the business again. I'm joining you this summer, remember?"

Eyebrows rose from behind the dark sunglasses. "I don't know what to say. Except thank you." Erika placed a hand on Dess's forearm and squeezed lightly. "It means more than you'll ever know. It's an honor, Dess."

The genuineness in Erika's touch, in her voice, brought Dess back to her own youth, when all that mattered was the dream. And the dream's fulfillment. She stopped, faced Erika, and clutched Erika's hands in hers, squeezing harder than she intended, before letting go and dropping her hands to her sides.

"Then promise me you will trust me. Question me, yes. Argue with me, sure. But don't doubt me, okay?"

"Of course. Anything."

"There'll be temptations, you know."

"I already know about those. Especially lately." Her smile was slightly wolfish, enough to indicate that she'd perhaps had a fantasy or two about Dess, and the soft flesh behind Dess's knees tingled in response.

"I'm serious."

Erika raised her glasses onto her head. Dess expected a cheeky expression, more of the predatory grinning, but what she got was dead-eye seriousness.

Barely above a whisper, Erika said, "So am I."

Oh shit, Dess thought, without any clear idea why she was so scared of the many layers—the many wants—within Erika Alvarez's walls. Those wants, Dess was sure, came with a very intensely spirited determination. A determination that might be hard to rebuff. And there wouldn't be much, she suspected, that would derail Erika from the things she desired.

"C'mon, honey," Dess said to Maggie, bending to pet her drenched head. She couldn't look into Erika's eyes anymore because they were web-like in their silky pull. "Let's get you back to the house and dry you off."

* * *

Erika marveled at how effortlessly they were able to put the finishing touches on the song, "I Want What You Got." It was clear Dess was a pro at this. She knew exactly where to make the adjustments—when to add a guitar lick, when to change the tempo, how much emotion to put into the words, how to tweak the words themselves for a better fit. On her own, it would have taken Erika four times as long to write the song and it would have been only half as good.

The business of completing the song behind them, Erika needed to burn off some steam. Burrowing so intensely into music left her energized, like a runner still jazzed after the finish line. There was a residual mischief streaking through her, and, if she were honest, she was a little horny too. The music had set all her nerve endings on fire, and she didn't want the night—nor her connection with Dess—to end.

As they roasted chicken for a late dinner and killed a bottle of chardonnay, Erika pulled her beat-up Martin acoustic guitar from the floor beside her. They were sprawled on the area rug in the great room facing the glowing fireplace, their glasses of wine an arm's length away on the glass coffee table. Erika was no master guitarist the way Dess was. Hell, Dess made *love* to the guitar when she played it. But Erika could competently play most chords, and she could play bass or rhythm more than adequately. Slowly, she began strumming a C chord, then a D minor.

"*The first time…*" Erika began singing in a voice so low and rumbling, it rattled her own shoes, "*ever I saw your face.*"

She lost herself in the Roberta Flack song, the way she always did when she sang something meaningful or something vocally challenging. Time stood still as her eyes closed to everything but the visions behind them. And the visions that danced before her were of Dess touching her face. Dess closing her eyes, waiting to be kissed. Erika poured her heart into the song, imagining herself kissing Dess, touching her. Dess was a woman so layered with emotion. So richly complex. So bright, opinionated, worldly, strong, accomplished. So damned smart. She was nothing like the college girls Erika had played around with. No. Dess wasn't the kind of woman you *played around* with, much as Erika's fantasies tried to suggest otherwise. Dess was a woman of substance, a keeper, a woman to journey through life with. The others, well, the others were merely…fuck material. And fuck material, Erika realized with startling clarity, was no longer a productive way to spend her time. Her eyes fluttered open,, the words of the song continuing to flow from her mouth and meaning more to her than they'd ever meant before.

Dess was staring at her, eyes wide and moist, lips parted in a look of mesmerized anticipation. A tear slithered down her cheek, and Erika's voice foundered.

"No, don't stop," Dess pleaded.

Erika had sung ballads to women before to get into their pants, and the tactic rarely failed. Was that what had motivated her to choose this song to sing to Dess? Oh, she was singing it like it was the last song she'd ever sing, like Dess was the only and last woman she'd ever be with. And it seemed to be having the desired effect, melting Dess, stripping away her defenses. But did she want Dess spread out before her, free for the taking? For using? To fuck and forget? No, Erika knew with conviction. Absolutely not.

Through the slits of her eyes, she secretly studied Dess. She was so beautiful. So vulnerable right now. So in need of touching, of loving, of appreciating. And not because she was the famous Dess Hampton, but because she was a good woman. Erika ended the song, and for a long moment they simply stared at each other, speechless.

"You," Dess breathed. "Your voice. I don't know what it does to me, but…"

Without thinking, Erika reached a hand to Dess's cheek, palmed it softly, trailed a finger along her jaw and caught the tear before it dropped. Dess's eyes flickered shut. Her body leaned toward Erika, her muscles like a guitar string, taut with desire. Erika's eyes drifted down to the silky skin of Dess's cleavage, so tantalizingly exposed by her blouse. Oh, how she wanted Dess. She thrummed with desire for Dess. Nearly exploded from desire for Dess. All it would take now was a kiss, a few strokes, a few whispered words of coaxing, and Dess would be hers.

But she couldn't. Instead, she pulled her hand away as though she'd touched something hot. She shifted to create distance between them. Cleared her throat to drown out the voice in her head that said she must be nuts. *No*, she thought. *I'm not nuts. I'm doing something smart for once.*

Dess scrambled to her feet, the color still high in her cheeks. "More chicken?" she asked with false cheerfulness. "Wine?"

Erika shook her head. "Honestly, I'm a bit tired. Long day today. Long day tomorrow, too." *Christ, I can't believe I'm doing this!*

"You're right, and tomorrow's going to be even longer. Sloane will be back in the afternoon and we've got a ton of songs to learn yet. I think we should get started first thing in the morning." She reached above her head to stretch, then yawned. "I'm going to turn in. Goodnight, Erika."

Erika rose and had to suppress the unmistakable need to hug Dess. Her arms hung loosely and inadequately at her sides, like they didn't know what to do with themselves. "Goodnight, Dess."

CHAPTER SEVEN

Dess had never before slipped her guitar on her back and cycled to a private place on the island to play, as she and Erika were doing now. It had been Erika's idea, and the absence of tourists was the only reason it was possible. They'd have been mobbed if it were summer, which was why during the busy months on the island, Dess kept mostly to her own property. The islanders knew who she was and left her alone. But the "fudgies," as the islanders called the tourists, would most likely recognize her, hound her for autographs and photos and lob uncomfortable questions at her like grenades. Like why hadn't she returned to her career and why had she removed herself from the public eye. She barely discussed those topics with people she knew and loved, let alone with strangers.

The sun on her face, the wind sending her hair in six different directions, Dess felt a remarkable sense of not-giving-a-shit. There was nothing to care about, outside the fact that it was a gorgeous day to be outside playing her guitar. The sense of freedom lifted her, made her feel ten pounds lighter. Although it wasn't enough to make her forget how badly she'd embarrassed herself in front of Erika last night.

God, she thought with a cringe, her heart as heavy as a rock in her chest. She'd practically thrown herself at Erika, looking at her with puppy dog eyes, nearly begging to be kissed. And more. She'd acted like a groupie without any boundaries, and she should damn well know better. She did know better. She'd had plenty of men and women throw themselves at her when she was famous, having lost count at more than four hundred of the little come-on notes that had found their way into her pockets, her luggage, under her hotel room doors over the years. There had been many brazen propositions too and a few admirers who had even become pesky stalkers. It got so exhausting, so predictable, that there was nothing at all flattering about a stranger's—or even a near-stranger's—propositions. Erika, she figured, must have had a good laugh last night at her expense, and she didn't know how, or even if, she should address what had happened. She wanted Erika to know it wouldn't happen again, that they were professionals and that Dess would never act so ridiculous again.

It's that damned voice of hers, Dess decided. Deep as a still river, soulful as an angel's, smooth as a weathered stone. And the knack Erika had for making it seem like she was singing only to you, that the words were meant only for you, that very special listener, was the *coup de grace*. Singing was more effective than alcohol as a panty remover, and she was sure Erika knew it too. Was sure, in fact, that Erika had seduced many women with her voice.

The only thing Dess couldn't quite square away in her mind was why Erika had backed away from what she had been on the cusp of offering. Erika had made enough flirty jokes, had many times looked at her with obvious desire. Had Dess crossed up the signals? Or maybe Erika wasn't single. Or she'd changed her mind about Dess. Or maybe she was one of those people who was all bark and no bite when it came to seducing. A tease.

Jesus, Dess thought. *I'm spending way too much emotional energy on this.* It was going to be a long summer if she didn't immediately drop this entire subject. It was time—way past time—to move on.

"How about this spot?" Erika called out from a few yards ahead. She'd stopped her bike at a rock formation beside a bend in the road, pointing toward a narrow trail that dropped down below the road and wound through some bushes for a few steps before, as near as Dess could tell, it opened up to a private spot on the beach.

"Perfect," Dess replied. "Let's bring our bikes with us so they're out of sight." *So we won't be bugged*, she almost added.

On the sand Dess spread out a large blanket she'd stowed in her bicycle's basket and pulled her windbreaker tighter around herself. She'd packed a couple of sandwiches and a couple of Cokes in a cooler bag for later, remembering how immensely guilty she'd felt this morning at Maggie's big brown, pleading eyes. "I'll take you for a long walk later," Dess had promised her.

They sat down and pulled their guitars onto their laps. Erika had said she wanted them to perform an acoustic version of the Guns N' Roses song, "Sweet Child O' Mine." Dess would play the lead, Erika would play the rhythm chords and sing. Dess set the sheet music on the blanket between them, pinning it in place with a few well-placed stones. After a couple of stumbling starts, they transitioned smoothly enough into the song, Dess surprised that they were so handily able to turn a hard rock song into a folksy ballad.

"I like it," Erika announced. "It's different from any version I've ever heard. And it should satisfy any rock fans in the crowd."

Dess fetched the cola and sandwiches from the cooler bag and spread them out between them. "We haven't really touched anything jazzy yet. Or bluesy, other than the song we wrote. Got any ideas?"

"Yes, since you asked." Erika grinned, her dimples locking Dess's gaze onto them, her eyes like missiles on their target. "I want us to do 'Don't Cry Baby,' although most of it will be piano accompaniment. And I want us to do 'How Sweet It Is (To Be Loved by You).'"

Dess whistled. "The old Marvin Gaye song? What do you want to do to that?"

Erika waggled her eyebrows. "Make it so sexy and soulful that all the women in the audience will be creaming themselves."

Dess nearly choked on the mouthful of Coke she was about to swallow. "Um, okay. Though that part is entirely your bailiwick, not mine."

"Oh no. Even in your wig or hat or big sunglasses or whatever disguise you're going to use, you'll be a lady charmer, trust me."

"Not with anything near the voltage you've got, young lady. You could sing nursery rhymes and still have women creaming their pants, as you so artfully describe it." *Me included.*

Erika somehow managed to look embarrassed, though it couldn't possibly be genuine, Dess figured. Erika had to damn well know how her voice affected people. She was a smart girl and had been doing this too long to play dumb. Dess decided to challenge her on it. Mostly because it might clear the air about what had happened—or almost happened—last night.

"So. Tell me. How many women typically throw themselves at you after an evening on stage?"

Erika's eyes widened reflexively. "W–what?"

"C'mon, you know what I'm talking about." *The way I did last night*, she was too cowardly to say. "You must get phone numbers, out-and-out propositions. And if you claim you're not, then you're blind and deaf."

After a moment, Erika shrugged. "Sometimes, yes, but not as often as you think."

"And what do you do in the face of all that temptation?" *Please tell me you're not promiscuous*, Dess silently pleaded. Sloane was bad enough; she didn't need Erika behaving that way too. She couldn't admit to herself that she cared about the answer for other, more personal reasons, too.

"Nine times out of ten, I go home alone."

It was an honest answer, judging by the absence of any hesitation, and Dess heaved an inward sigh of relief. Then another to ground herself. "Look. About last night…"

Erika had the good grace to look uncomfortable. Like the blame was on her. "Yes?"

"I…" *Oh, shit. I don't even know what I want to say, except that I'm supposed to be the adult here.*

"You did nothing wrong," Erika interjected before Dess could wrench something intelligible out of herself. She could have kissed Erika for letting her off the hook so easily.

"I let the mood of the evening get to me," Erika continued. "No, wait, that's not quite right. I let my emotions get the best of me, and it was inappropriate of me to touch you the way I did. I apologize."

"I appreciate the apology, Erika, but there's no need. I think I let the mood of the evening get to me a little too, and I'm sorry if I gave you the wrong impression." *There. Now she knows in no uncertain terms that I'm not looking for anything other than a professional relationship.* "I can promise you it won't happen again."

Dess meant it too, but she felt a pang of sadness at the thought. It was a hard thing for her to admit, but she got lonely sometimes. Not only in the absence of someone to talk to, to share with, to hang out with, but very much in physical terms as well. A hug, some snuggling, holding hands. And…okay, Carol was right. A little sex now and again would be nice too. But there was no place in her mind for connecting the dots with Erika. For a number of reasons, and all of them very good, Erika was not the woman to fill any of those voids. Erika, she reasoned, simply served as a reminder that some of the things she missed sharing with another woman were still important to her.

Erika flashed a grin that was far too playful. "Well, I wouldn't hold it against you if you wanted to break that promise."

Dess shook her head, not buying the act. "You're an incorrigible flirt, you know that? Although I am flattered, so thank you for that. Now let's get back to the music before you get yourself into trouble." *And before this conversation strays into more dangerous territory.* "What else is in your repertoire that you'd like to play on the tour?"

"What about another original piece?"

"Like?"

Erika swallowed visibly but never took her eyes off Dess. "I know you don't want me singing one of your hit songs from the past, and I respect that. But Sloane said you have binders full of songs you've written that have never seen the light of day. Why don't we change that?"

It was a long moment before Dess could move her mouth. Shock gave way to outrage at the suggestion. There was no way in hell anyone was going to see those binders of songs, never mind sing anything in one of them. They were much too personal, harkening back to some of her darkest days—the breakup with

Dayna, her battle with cancer, the loss of her career, the unspoken emptiness that too often filled her days and blackened her mood. The songs were a form of journaling, and even suggesting that she share her personal pain in the form of those songs felt like a betrayal.

Her jaw clenched. She could barely grind out the words. "Absolutely not. And I don't ever want to hear that suggestion again."

"But I don't understand. Those binders could be a gold mine."

"No," Dess said in a voice sharp as a razor. "You're right. You *don't* understand, and I hope to God you never will."

* * *

Erika could no longer maintain her mask of cheerfulness. The day with Dess had been an unmitigated disaster. Or at least it had become so as soon as she'd stupidly suggested using one of Dess's compositions in her set. Dess's freak-out had stunned and shamed Erika, and even now, hours later, she couldn't jettison the memory of Dess's clenched face—and her voice, which had sounded like ground-up glass—as she unequivocally nixed the idea. For the rest of the afternoon, they maintained their distance, with Erika retreating to a separate corner of the house until Sloane sauntered in after dinner like the prodigal daughter returning home. She regaled them with the highlights of her two-day Detroit gig with Taylor Swift, and her timing couldn't have been more perfect. Sloane was the glue that kept them together whenever things became strained, and that was never more apparent than now, Erika thought dismally.

Dess slipped off to bed early, which was just the impetus Sloane needed to retrieve two glasses and a bottle of Jack Daniels from the cupboard. She poured herself and Erika healthy glassfuls, and they sat down at the kitchen island. They clinked glasses companionably before Sloane's jovial mood dimmed.

"Tell me I'm imagining some frost between you and my best buddy."

Erika shrugged. "It's fine."

Sloane raised her eyebrows but said nothing.

"All right. It *was* fine. Until earlier today when I suggested we use one of her songs that she's got squirreled away in those famous binders of hers."

Sloane sipped her drink, shook her head lightly.

"What?" Erika asked. "How was I supposed to know it was a stupid suggestion?"

"It's not your fault. Dess is extremely private, that's all."

Private was one thing. But practically hostile? What the hell was that all about? "Sloane, I'm sorry if I'm prying. And I know you're very loyal to your best friend. But I don't understand her."

Sloane held up her glass in a silent salute. "God knows, it's no easy accomplishment getting to know Dess. Took me more than a decade, and even then, there are corners of her nobody is allowed to get near."

Erika swallowed the fiery liquid and considered Sloane's observation. "But we're going to be working closely together for months. It's impossible to do that and remain strangers."

"Yes, and that means you're going to have to figure out pretty quick what she's sensitive about, what's off limits, if we're to have peace in this little marriage of three."

A weight settled on Erika's heart that not even the bourbon could lighten. Dess was so talented, so full of wondrous gifts. She was beautiful, funny, smart, had a wealth of knowledge and experience and possessed a generous heart. That she carried so much pain troubled Erika.

"It's like she's carrying a mountain on her back," Erika finally said. "Why? Why is she so bitter? So closed up like a fist about certain things?"

"It's a long and complicated story. And it's her story to tell, not mine. But I can tell you that she's a bit damaged, if you want to know the truth. And for good reason." Sloane studied her glass and its waning contents. "Promise me you'll go easy on her, okay? And that you'll be patient? Because she really is worth it, kid." Sloane drained the last of her bourbon. "And on that, you'll just have to trust me."

Erika drained her own glass. She was going to have to figure out how to gain Dess's trust. And she would, by God, no matter how long it took.

* * *

Dess lay in bed, tossing and turning. Maggie's snoring from her bed in the corner did little to soothe her, the way it usually did. She was still rattled by the way she'd gone off on poor Erika earlier. She had ripped her a new one over her suggestion that they use one of her secret songs, and she was sorry now for overreacting. Erika probably thought she was a spoiled, selfish diva. Or terribly insecure. An apology was needed, she knew, but it wouldn't explain her behavior. The explanation was going to be the impossible part.

Plain and simple, Dess didn't discuss personal stuff with anyone but Sloane, her sister Carol and her mother. That was her inner circle, small as it was, and it was the only circle that mattered to her. They were the only people privy to her pain and her deepest thoughts, just as the songs she'd written were like her own private diary entries. With a foreshadowing threaded more with relief than worry, Dess knew she would need to let Erika inside—at least a little. And they would have to trust each other. If they didn't, it was certain their little tour would be doomed. *And we'll be miserable with each other.*

All right, she decided as she stared into the yawning black of the ceiling. *First chance I get for some private time with Erika, I'll share some things with her. Not everything. Not by a long shot. But I'll need to start treating her like a friend instead of a stranger.* There wasn't much time to make things right between them, and it was Dess who needed to set things on the right course. She'd been naïve, she realized now, in thinking through all the angles involved in joining Erika's tour, because creating music together had become the least of her worries.

As sleep finally embraced her, Dess's last thought circled back to Erika's earlier comment about going home alone nine times out of ten. She wondered with far more than simple academic curiosity what that one woman in ten—the lucky one who went home with Erika—was like.

CHAPTER EIGHT

Their luxury Lincoln pickup truck gobbled up the interstate miles like they were nothing, even with the heavy, thirty-foot rented fifth-wheel RV bumping along behind it. They were heading for their inaugural gig, a two-day weekend festival on the outskirts of Indianapolis, and Erika had offered to drive as a way of calming her nerves. "I'm a Texan," she'd told Sloane and Dess. "Of course I know how to drive a rig!"

In the back seat that was the size of a small living room, Sloane and Maggie snoozed, Maggie's snoring snout resting on Sloane's lap, while Sloane's arm limply cradled the dog. Erika would never have imagined herself in this situation just a few short weeks ago—RVing to music festivals with a bona fide but forgotten music sensation, a highly sought-after concert and studio drummer and an adorable chocolate Labrador retriever. This, she thought with a smile that threatened to bubble into full-throated laughter, was her family for the next four months. Hell, it was a lot more than that. It was the only family that mattered to her these days.

In Erika's jaundiced opinion, her real family meant a genetic bond and not much more. An only child, she was united with her narrow-minded, socially and economically struggling parents only in blood and in name and in their singular desire to be accepted by society at large. Their means of achieving social acceptance was not only diametrically opposite hers, but full of friction. Erika's escape to college had been her one-way ticket out of an existence that saw her parents wield her as their biggest weapon against their subjugation. They never saw her for who she was. Never asked her what she wanted. Never gave her an ounce of freedom to explore who she was and what she wanted, and Erika would never forgive them for that.

"You okay?" Dess said from beside her.

Erika slid a sideways glance at Dess, caught the concern in her eyes and felt, for the first time in more than a week, that Dess was sincerely trying to reach out. Things had been tepid between them since Erika's ill-advised suggestion that they use one of Dess's secret songs in their set. Apology aside, there'd been no real thaw between them until now.

"You looked a bit…troubled," Dess added.

"I'm fine," Erika snapped. "Happy to be on the road, as a matter of fact." Moving, that was the ticket. Erika was always moving forward, because if you moved forward, you could outrun your pain, she believed. She didn't know how Dess could stand wallowing in hers. Sitting around by herself these last few years, brooding, bitter, writing songs nobody would ever hear. It sounded like one hell of a depressing existence.

"Can I ask you something?" The question was out of Erika's mouth before she could stop herself. She didn't wait for permission. "Why do you write all those songs with no intention of them ever being heard?"

Dess paused before answering.

Well, now I've done it, Erika thought, as she waited for the outburst she was sure would follow. Outburst or not, something needed to be said if they were to warm to each other.

Dess's voice was surprisingly gentle in reply. "Therapy, I guess. Music is the best way for me to express my deepest feelings, whether anyone hears it or not."

Erika hadn't thought of it that way. She was so hungry to perform, to put her talent out there in front of people. If she had Dess's songwriting ability, she'd be singing those suckers all over the place. Or begging others to sing them all over the place.

"But if you shared them," Erika suggested, "maybe it would help others who've felt the same way."

Dess seemed to consider this. "I suppose. After all, music is about souls connecting, about shared human experiences. The songs we feel the most connection with stir something in our soul. But my songs...they're so personal. Autobiographical. For some musicians, it's no big deal. But for me? It's tough to share my deepest pain, my deepest thoughts, with the world."

"I would like it if, someday, you would share some of them with me, Dess. Just us, no audience."

Erika knew she'd thrown down a gauntlet of sorts, and she took a deep breath, steeling herself for Dess's answer.

"All right," Dess whispered so quietly that Erika nearly missed it. "Someday."

Erika smiled. It was progress, at least.

* * *

Dess, who knew next to nothing about camping, let Sloane and Erika hook up the RV to the campground's power and water supply. They were supposed to be at the festival grounds for a sound check in an hour. Then, as probably the least known act in the lineup, they would open the show.

Dess was unreasonably nervous. This was small potatoes compared with what she was used to—sold-out football stadiums, packed Broadway theaters, intimate concerts with some of the world's richest and most powerful people. But it was her first time on any stage in more than six years, and she wasn't convinced, as Sloane suggested, that the years would melt away with the first note of music. She prayed she wouldn't make mistakes or perform stiffly, but at least it would be Erika in the spotlight, doing the heavy lifting. All Dess had to do, she reminded herself, was be the anonymous guitar player, shuffling around in the shadows.

She pulled Erika aside as Sloane went to unpack their instruments from the large steel box bolted onto the back of the RV.

"How are you feeling?" Dess asked, keeping her own nervousness in check.

Erika pushed a strand of her wild hair behind her ear—a little habit Dess found perpetually endearing. "A little nervous. But excited too."

"Can I give you some advice?"

"Please."

"Focus on one person in the audience. Pretend you're just singing to her. It will keep you from getting too nervous or too excited, okay?"

Erika nodded. "Thanks. And Dess?"

"Yes?" God, the way Erika looked at her sometimes. Those dark eyes full of fire never failed to spark something in Dess.

"Thanks for being here with me. I couldn't do this without you."

Dess smiled, rubbed Erika's arm. "Yeah, you could. But I'm happy to be here. Well, until I have to actually get up on that stage."

"Maybe I should be asking *you* if you're nervous?"

"Nah. Like a walk in the park to me." It wasn't, but she didn't need Erika to know that.

The sound check complete, they waited backstage for the signal that it was time. The announcer asked them if they had a name, like a real band, to which they'd lamely shaken their heads. Now it made Dess cringe as she heard the emcee introduce them as "Erika Alvarez and her, um, band. Give it up for them, ladies and gentlemen."

There was a smattering of light applause. Barely a ripple of anticipation or excitement, which was disappointing. It wasn't for herself that she cared—she actually preferred a small, disinterested crowd for her first foray back to the stage—but for Erika's sake, it was disheartening. They looked warily at each other. Sloane shrugged—for her, this summer tour was a vacation interwoven with the occasional high-profile gig like the one she'd had in Detroit with Taylor Swift. Erika smiled gamely, but there was no joy in it.

"They'll come," Dess whispered. "Be patient. And remember what I said earlier."

Erika nodded and grabbed the mic, Dess and Sloane taking their places behind her.

"Good evening, everyone!" Erika yelled into the mic. "It's so nice to be here with y'all. Thank you for having us. Are you guys ready for a little action?"

Barely a murmur acknowledged her remarks. A few people were stretched out on the grass before the stage, the picture of disinterest. Others were coming and going, finding their seats or wandering off. It was supper time, though. A bad time slot. They'd have to grind through it and act like they were having fun, like they were singing to a thousand people on the edge of their seats, Dess told herself by way of a pep talk. They'd need to find their own energy, because they sure as hell weren't going to get any from the crowd.

Dess put a hand to her beret one last time to make sure her dark wig remained in place. The wig, the beret and the sunglasses were, she hoped, enough of a disguise that nobody would ever recognize her. Dora Hessler would be her stage name for the summer. It would be fine as long as all the attention remained riveted on Erika, which was the whole point of this exercise.

Dess took deep breaths to still her suddenly pounding heart. It was like a piston on overdrive, leaving her light-headed. Being onstage again sure as hell didn't feel like riding a bike again (Sloane's advice!). Her hands were trembling—not good for a guitarist, she reminded herself. *This is not about you*, she told herself over and over again. *This is for Erika*.

Sloane had launched into a beat on her drum kit. Dess missed her cue, and Sloane threw her a withering look as she kept the beat going. A few more beats and Dess jumped in this time with the beginning electric guitar licks of "Anyway You Want It." It was the perfect high-energy song to launch their set. Erika's voice rang out—so powerful, Dess decided, that everyone on the entire property would feel it in their bones whether they were actively listening or not. Erika gave the song its gritty, raunchy due, and slowly heads looked up, bodies sat up straighter, empty seats began to fill up.

Yes, Dess thought as she flashed an acknowledging grin at Erika. *It'll come, baby, just keep going; it'll come.* A tickling sensation bloomed in Dess's stomach as she watched Erika relax into the song and her confidence take hold. Her tentative steps around the stage began to resemble a strut. Then, as they launched into Mary J. Blige's "I Am," Erika's sex appeal exploded like a bomb. She stomped around the stage in her leather boots, offering up a spirited leg kick on the occasional downbeat, stood still to caress the mic like a lover as her voice dripped into it, all sultry and soulful, then she pointed challengingly to faces in the growing crowd. Dess, like she imagined others in the audience did in that moment, truly believed Erika when she sang the words "*Ain't nobody gonna love you better than I am.*"

Oh yeah, Dess thought with satisfaction, *she's got it.* She was a natural—something Dess herself had to struggle much harder to accomplish in the early days of her career. Erika had charisma and presence by the truckload—two things that would take her further and faster than most aspiring musicians.

By the time they finished their six-song set (they'd been promised more but were cut at the last minute) with their bluesy piano-guitar rendition of "Ain't No Sunshine When She's Gone," the crowd was fully involved and hanging on their every note. Most were on their feet, and most were cheering and yelling for more.

The three women high-fived their victory backstage, then shook the hand of the sheepish stage manager, who didn't waste any time telling them he'd move them into the eight o'clock slot tomorrow night. And that they could perform two extra songs.

Sloane sidled up to Dess as Erika made small talk with a musician who was tuning his guitar. "Isn't this a blast? Being in on the ground floor like this? Things are really gonna take off for Erika one of these days." Sloane bumped Dess's shoulder. "And we can say we knew her when."

Dess studied Erika from afar as she thought about that. She remembered her own meteoric ride to the top. How one day it was roadside motels and smelly buses, then almost overnight, private jets and penthouse suites at five-star hotels. It was like rocketing to another time zone or perhaps to another planet altogether. It was nothing and everything like she'd imagined.

And now, watching Erika idly run her fingers through her thick hair, oblivious to Dess's scrutiny, she had the unmistakable urge to wrap her arms around Erika in a protective hold, keeping her here, where things were still simple, forever.

* * *

Erika peeked around the stage curtain one last time. It wasn't at all like the meager start to last night's concert, thank goodness. This time, throngs of people sat patiently waiting for them, their necks craning, their eyes darting about in anticipation. Word about Erika, Dess and Sloane must have spread, because this time, the shouts and squeals drowned out the emcee's introduction. Dess was giving her a thumbs up, Sloane was grinning like a kid. Erika smoothed her hands down her leather vest one last time—it was warm enough tonight not to wear anything beneath it—and checked that she was showing enough cleavage to be tantalizing, but not so much as to be obscene or cheap. She'd been around the block enough times to know that sex helps sell the music.

One last deep breath and she was running onto the stage, her guitar slung over her shoulder. The crowd cheered and wolf whistled as she greeted them, and she had to yell into the mic to be heard. The audience collectively laughed when she teasingly asked them where they'd been last night when she needed them, then Sloane and Dess launched into the high-energy "Anyway You Want It."

Dressing the part—the tight leather vest, the form-fitting jeans, the leather ankle boots—helped Erika act the part of sexy rocker-blues chick. It also made her feel the part in those moments when she swaggered across the stage like she owned it, like she owned the audience too. The stage wanted to be possessed, shown who's boss, and so did the audience, she firmly believed. But she didn't want to think about it more deeply than that, about where it came from inside her, because too much self-examination might be self-defeating, she feared. What she was doing seemed to be working for her. In spades.

Heeding Dess's advice from last night, Erika focused her attention on a young woman dancing on the grass below the stage. They locked eyes as Erika sang only to her, swayed and shimmied and strutted only for her. She was so immersed in singing and feeling the music, she couldn't even remember what the woman looked like once the set was over.

Later, as Sloane and Dess packed up their instruments in the backstage area and Erika lingered over a bottle of water, the dancing stranger approached her.

"You were awesome, Erika," she gushed, introducing herself as Hailey. "I swear, it was like you were singing just to me! Oh my God, will you pose for a picture with me so I can post it on Facebook?"

"Sure," Erika said lightly and let Hailey lead her a short distance away. She put her arm around Erika, pointed her phone at them and snapped a photo.

Hailey prattled on about the warm, beautiful night, about what the music—and specifically Erika's voice—had done to her. Her voice was low and breathy as she tactlessly whispered how turned on she was, how wet Erika had made her. Her perfume was the scent of mango on warm skin, her touch against Erika's arm promising that she was a sure thing. *Jesus*, Erika thought, *could this woman be any more obvious?*

Hailey leaned closer and dropped any pretense of decorum. "Please. I want you so much. Outside. Under the stars, up against a tree. Just like that, baby, I want you to do me."

Yep, apparently she could *be more obvious.* From the corner of her eye, Erika thought she caught a disdainful glance from Dess. Of course Hailey and her pawing proposition was crass and crude and so predictable. But as ridiculous and unprincipled as the idea of fucking this stranger was, there was a forbidden, alluring quality to it too. Erika was still keyed up from the performance, and what performer didn't like to hear nice things about her music, especially from an effusive, sexy young fan? And who didn't want to feel desired? The truth of it was, she was a bit turned on too—not just from the energy of the performance and Hailey's detailed proposition, but from the last couple of weeks of being near Dess. Dess and her frustrating push-pull behavior. Dess, the queen of hard to get. The sexual tension inside her needed an outlet and soon.

"Let's go for a little walk," Hailey whispered, and Erika found herself being tugged along a stone path that led away from the backstage area.

Just off the path, in the shadows, Hailey unceremoniously pushed her up against a tree and stuck her tongue down her throat. The idea of getting off as quickly as possible, so she could get rid of Hailey, held particular appeal. Although being groped by a young woman against a tree wasn't her proudest moment.

"Whoa," Erika murmured. "You don't waste any time, do you?"

"Hell no. I like it hard and fast."

Hailey's lips locked onto hers again, their mouths joining unromantically like two locomotives hitching together. Hailey came hard at her like a train too, her hands all over Erika's thighs, her waist, her breasts. So hard, so fast, that Erika figured the train was going to jump the tracks any minute. And strangely, she began to welcome the idea of a derailment, because the appeal of a quick fuck was fast losing steam. She could do better than this. Deserved better than a five-second orgasm with a young stranger in the shadow of a tree.

An intake of breath, sharp as steel, caught Erika's attention. She cast her eyes toward the noise, saw that it was Dess who'd halted in her tracks a couple of yards away. Her eyes were wide and so was her mouth before it snapped shut like a gate. *Aw, shit*, Erika thought, not really sure why she should feel guilty, except she did.

She jerked away from Hailey as Dess turned on her heel and stalked off. Sloane slid into view, her hands in her front pockets. "We were just going to tell you we're heading back to the trailer. Dess…I mean Dora, wants to let Maggie out." Her wink was her way of giving Erika permission to have her few minutes of fun. "But since you're busy, don't feel you have to join us."

"No, wait, I'll catch up with you in a minute."

Sloane melted into the dark, and Erika created more distance between herself and Hailey, whose mango perfume now smelled more like sickly sweet bubblegum.

"How old are you, anyway?" Erika blurted out.

"Twenty. Why?"

Hailey looked up at her like a shiny new penny, her eyes eager and her smooth skin almost translucent.

"Forget it," Erika said, shaking her head dismissively. "Look, I'm sorry, but I've got to go, okay?"

Hailey pinned her with an unforgiving death stare. "You're into that older chick, aren't you? You like cougars or something? That it?"

"Maybe I do." Erika turned and picked her way back to where Sloane and Dess had emerged from, refusing to give any more thought to Hailey or her cougar comment.

CHAPTER NINE

"Want to tell me what's going on between you and Erika?"

Sloane sat across from Dess at their trailer's cramped dining table, the remnants of breakfast omelettes pushed to the side. Erika had set out on a long walk with Maggie.

"I don't know what you're talking about, Sloane, and if you're trying to turn something into a soap opera, you can forget it right now." *Yeah, that's it, the best defense is offense*, Dess decided. Besides, there was nothing to say on the subject, because there was absolutely nothing going on between her and Erika.

Sloane laughed as she cradled her coffee cup in hands made knobby and swollen from decades of pounding on drums.

"I don't find any of this amusing, in case you're wondering."

"Oh, the only thing I'm wondering, doll, is when you started getting that groupie look in your eyes over our hot, studly singer."

The blood rushed to Dess's face, instantly warming her cheeks. Sloane couldn't be serious. She did *not* look at Erika like some infatuated teenager. What a horrifying, embarrassing and ridiculous thought that was!

"Yeah, you heard me. Close your mouth before you end up swallowing a fly."

Hot needles prickled her cheeks. "Are you on something? Because you're imagining things that aren't happening."

Sloane leaned closer across the table. The teasing twinkle was gone from her eyes. "Look, I don't mean to get you all riled up. Hell, part of me is ecstatic that you're hot for Erika, but the other part of me is worried, because I know this isn't like you. And I don't want you to get hurt."

"Sloane, you're reading something into this that isn't there, okay?" *Please, please don't let it be there.*

"No. I don't think I am. I saw how shocked and pissed off you were when we stumbled across Erika making out with that groupie last night."

"Well, of course I was. A little. I don't want you and Erika tomcatting around all summer. We're here to work, not to play around."

"Yeah, I get that. And so does Erika. Doesn't mean we can't have a little fun now and again. But you looked like you wanted to kill that girl, the way she was mauling Erika. And Erika looking like she was enjoying it a little too much. Man." Sloane leaned back, spreading her arms along the back of the bench seat. "You sure looked some pissed off."

Indignant, Dess swore under her breath. "I was not pissed off. And I don't have a thing for Erika, so you can get that thought out of your perverted little mind."

"Well, you *should* have a thing for Erika. Christ, she's like sex on a stick, walking around in those jeans and boots. And that vest!" Sloane whistled. "Notice how she spills out of that goddamned thing on stage? Woo-ee! What red-blooded dyke wouldn't be salivating over her?"

Sex on a stick? Is she kidding? "Sloane, you're nuts, you know that?"

"Of course I know that. And you're finally hot for someone for the first time in years. Admit it. And tell me you didn't have a wet dream about her last night, after seeing her up against that tree."

Oh, fuck. Dess needed cold water on her face. Now! "Oh, God, you didn't...hear something last night, did you?" She had the trailer's small bedroom to herself, while Erika and Sloane slept in the two narrow bunks at the opposite end. There was a good amount of distance between the two sleeping areas, but Dess *had* had a sex dream last night. And it *did* involve Erika in that damned leather vest of hers, leaning over her, kissing her, pushing her thigh against Dess's crotch.

"Ha, I knew it!" Sloane leapt up for a little dance and a fist pump before sitting back down.

"C'mon, I never said I had a wet dream about *her*. And besides, you're making her out to be nothing more than a sex object." Erika was much, much more than that. She could sing, like the goddess herself had blessed her throat with a golden caress. She seemed kindhearted too. She hadn't pushed Dess too far into sharing her most painful memories, and Dess was grateful.

"I know she's more than simply hot. I wouldn't be on this tour if there wasn't substance behind it, and neither would you. I just don't want you to fall for her and get hurt, okay? You're not exactly, you know, very experienced in all this dating stuff."

Dess rolled her eyes. "So one minute you're saying it's okay if I have a thing for Erika, and the next you're saying stay away from her because I'm too naïve and might get hurt?" It was a rhetorical question, because she certainly had no intention of having any kind of "thing" with Erika, serious or not.

"Dess, honey. If I thought you could have a simple fling with Erika without any complications, I'd be the first one to tell you to go for it. But I know you. You don't do simple, uncomplicated flings. You put your entire heart into everything you do. And that can be risky sometimes, that's all."

Sloane had a point. She had been with Dayna for five years, lived with her for three. There'd been nobody to speak of since. And before Dayna? Dess could count on one hand the number of women she'd slept with, including Dayna. I'm a loser, she thought, momentarily ashamed of her innocence. *Not only in terms of experience, but when it comes to love as well. I do a crap job of choosing women.*

To Sloane, she said, "You're right. I don't do simple flings. I don't do any kind of flings or relationships these days, so there's nothing to worry about."

"But I do worry." Sloane covered Dess's hand with her own. "Dayna hurt you badly, and I don't ever want to see that happen to you again. Not that Erika is Dayna—I'm not saying that. But she's young. And she's got dreams."

Yes, Dess thought, *she's got big dreams. Dreams like I once had.* Erika deserved to try for that brass ring, even if it didn't turn out in the end the way she hoped. If Dess could help guide her a little, protect her a little bit from the worst of it, it was as much as she could hope to do. She certainly wasn't going to hold Erika back by trying to start anything romantic with her.

"I hear what you're saying Sloane. Loud and clear. And you've got nothing to worry about. I promise."

Through the window they could see Erika and Maggie striding toward the RV. Maggie's tail was wagging with joy, and Erika…*Mmm-mmm*, Dess thought before clamping down on the thought and banishing it from her mind. She'd have to stop thinking of Erika that way. Immediately.

* * *

With three days to get to Des Moines for the next music festival, they meandered through Indiana and Illinois. Erika was hoping to use the time to pen another song with Dess, something a little slower, more contemplative this time.

The evening air was laced with a damp chill, not unexpected for May. They'd lit a huge campfire that sprayed sparks like raindrops, to keep them warm while they shared a bottle of merlot. Erika's old guitar was on her lap. She'd been quietly picking a few notes, trying to find a melody that fit together, while Dess and Sloane gossiped quietly about people Erika didn't know and didn't care about. Maggie lay languidly on the edge of their circle, her eyes glazed over and half-lidded as the fire warmed her nose.

Moments later, Dess motioned for Erika to hand over her guitar. She didn't even know Dess had been listening to her.

"How about trying it this way?" Dess said, plucking a pattern as she alternated between an A chord and a B minor, followed by a C-sharp minor, then a D. There were no words to the melody so far, so Dess hummed quietly. *I wish she'd try singing*, Erika thought, remembering how Dess sounded on her hit song "Try Harder." Her voice had been so powerful and clear, spanning several octaves. She sang ballads like she'd been born to it, her voice soulful and mournful and delightfully hopeful at the same time. It was nothing short of a tragedy that she would never sing like that again.

Erika couldn't fathom not being able to sing anymore. The very thought was like a fist around her throat. *Poor Dess, my God, how did she ever cope with that?* Erika stole a glance at her, her face a picture of concentration in the orange glow of the flames as she effortlessly strung notes into a melody that sounded sweetly anguished. Erika swallowed against the urge to go to her, put her arms around her and simply hold her. *I would die if I couldn't sing*, she thought. She almost did die before singing saved her. But she couldn't think about that right now.

"That sounds beautiful," Erika said in a voice rough with feelings she didn't want to explore. "Don't stop."

"I'll keep going if you can think up some words," Dess replied with an encouraging nod.

Sloane's eyes lobbed back and forth between them, as though she were watching a tennis match. Her silence was awfully un-Sloane-like.

Erika began to hum the melody along with Dess, closed her eyes and let the words bubble to the surface without thought. "Last night I had the sweetest dream," she sang. "You were here just loving me. It must be written up there high, so high among the stars. You're the muse when I need you, you are the song in my heart."

Sloane set her glass between her legs, began clapping. Maggie's ears perked up in approval. And Dess. Dess's smile was nothing short of triumphant. Erika wanted to cry.

"Wow," Dess said. "Where did those words come from?"

Erika simply shook her head. She had no idea.

Sloane erupted from her seat. "Ladies, that sounds like a number one hit to me. Seriously. Let's perform it."

"No." Panic throbbed in Erika's throat. "It's just words, it's—"

"It's perfect is what it is," Sloane said. "Dess?"

Dess shrugged, but the smile refused to leave her lips. "It's a good start."

"Then let's work on it. Now." Sloane disappeared and returned a moment later with a bongo set, which she set on her lap.

"I don't know if I can write a song on demand," Erika confessed, panicking a little. It usually took her weeks of solitary struggle and included lots of swearing, hand-wringing and trashcans full of balled-up paper. A love song was the hardest of all. Not only to write, but to analyze, to think about the words and where they came from. A love song told a story from the heart, and heartfelt stories were the hardest to express.

Dess reached over and placed a reassuring hand on her arm. "I'll help you every step of the way. We'll do this together. Do you trust me?"

That was easy to answer. Whatever Dess's faults, Erika knew without question that she was reliable, trustworthy, more than capable. It was herself she didn't quite trust. Not only did she not entirely believe in her own talent behind the smokescreen of bravado, but she feared Dess didn't trust her either. *And why should she?* Erika admonished herself. She was young, unknown, raw and given to wandering off with young, horny groupies, she reminded herself. *God, Dess must think I'm a total flake.* Dess hadn't said anything to her about the other night, but she didn't need to. Erika had seen the disappointment in her face at catching her with Bailey or Hailey or whatever the hell her name was. The look had said far more than any words could have, and Erika didn't want to ever be the cause of her disappointment again.

"I trust you completely, Dess."

"Kid," Sloane said with a grin. "I don't know if I'd go *that* far."

Erika kept her eyes on Dess. "Anything you want me to do," she whispered to her and saw the slight surprise, then the quiet acknowledgment, in Dess's eyes. Dess clearly understood that anything meant…well, anything.

CHAPTER TEN

The Des Moines festival promised to be more demanding than their first gig, with a schedule of four separate performances for their group over three days. Sandwiched between those were the extra workshops and jam sessions the musicians were encouraged to sign up for. *Oh well, what the hell*, Dess thought as she eyed the list of volunteer opportunities. *If I'm going to be kept busy, it might as well be crazy busy.* She signed her name—or rather, the name Dora Hessler—to lead a guitar workshop for kids.

She kept her dark wig snugly affixed and her sunglasses firmly in place every time she stepped out of their trailer, but fearing that her true identity would be revealed, Dess stayed intentionally aloof from strangers, including other musicians. When she did talk to them, she said as little as possible without being rude. She was careful not to make up things that would trip her up whenever anyone asked about her background. She hated all this lying business and figured the less she talked about herself, the fewer lies she'd need to make up.

Tonight's set came in the third slot of the evening lineup. As smooth as their performances had become in such a short time, Dess had pronounced earlier in the afternoon that they weren't yet ready to perform the love song she and Erika had been working on. The level of emotion Erika had exhibited with the song, tentatively called "The Song in My Heart," had surprised Dess. She'd been unfair in pegging Erika as primarily an upbeat, raunchy singer who thrived on the grittier stuff. Oh, how delightfully wrong she'd been! Erika gave her goose bumps when she sang their ballad with those powerful vocal cords of hers—vocal cords that seemed directly linked to her heart when they sang about joy or despair. Watching Erika belt out a song onstage beside her now, Dess wondered just how many layers, how deep were the depths in this talented young woman who was still such an enigma to her. She'd probably never know the answers to those questions, would never be let far enough inside, but she did know with certainty that the sky was the limit for Erika Alvarez's music career if she kept working at it and if luck shone its capricious light on her.

The crowd, generous in its appreciation, exuberant in demanding more, barely let them off the stage after their final song. The whistles and shouts of "more" continued as they rehydrated backstage and scurried to put their instruments away to make room for the next band.

Cutting a path through the backstage chaos, a long-haired young man with a guitar slung behind his back marched up to them and bowed deeply, like a subject before his queen. Erika grinned at the display of deference.

"You dudes were sick!" he enthused, and Dess laughed out loud at his choice of words. She couldn't remember a time she'd ever been called "dude." Or "sick" when she wasn't ill.

He was trying to look cool, but he couldn't find the off button for his grin. "No, I mean, you guys were *fucking* awesome, man. Hey. My band's up after this next set. You ladies like to join us for a song?" His anxious eyes darted between Dess and Erika, Sloane having already wandered off.

Dess started to back away. Time to play it safe. "Afraid I can't, but thanks for asking."

"You? Please?" Puppy dog eyes implored Erika. "Your acoustic version of 'Sweet Child O' Mine' was, like, the sweetest thing ever! Sing it with me at the end of our set. Electric, though, not acoustic, okay? That'd really be the bomb!"

Erika shot Dess a questioning look, and Dess nodded back. The guitar player's group, called Sun's Up, was a bit heavy metal, but they were popular. And good. Exposure from appearing onstage with them would help Erika gain recognition much quicker and with a young audience, which was always a bonus. "I'll be right out there, watching," she whispered to Erika, jerking her head toward the audience. "Go get 'em."

Secretly, Dess relished the opportunity to watch Erika perform from the vantage point of the audience, and the anticipation vibrated through her body like a tuning fork. It was a chance to analyze Erika's talent more objectively. And to see firsthand, at ground level, the kind of effects she had on the crowd. *Yeah, that's it*, she told herself. It would be an appraisal, an adjudication. As Erika stepped onstage to the opening riff of the Guns N' Roses song, the vibe of the crowd was one of urgency, blatant sexuality and a devil-may-care happiness. It zapped Dess like an electrical shock, catching her up in it, giving her the slight sensation of floating above the crowd, yet being at one with it too.

The pure charisma and sexuality of Erika kept Dess's eyes, ears, all her senses keenly riveted on the young singer. Without her own guitar playing to concentrate on, she was caught like a pinned butterfly as she watched Erika pour every ounce of her energy into the duet with the long-haired metalhead. It wasn't long before she ruled the stage like it was her kingdom, like the band was *her* band, like this was *her* set. She gyrated with the lead guitar player, effortlessly out-dueled her singing partner, teased the crowd with every movement and expression. At times she gestured to the crowd to come closer, planting her legs apart like she was ready for them to rush the stage, and in the next instant she was stomping around with her face to the sky or giving the audience her back. They were eating out of her hand, begging for more, and she gave it to them, launching into a Linkin Park rock song.

Sweet Jesus, Dess thought, as she watched those tight, denim-hugged hips gently, then sassily, sway and grind. And that leather vest—barely containing those gorgeous breasts that looked like fruit you could reach up and pluck. Dess's hands itched. Her breath fluttered in her chest like she was a teenager who'd never been laid before. She hadn't felt this sexually hot for anyone in years, maybe decades. Even Dayna hadn't made her feel this way—like she wanted to grab Erika by the wrist and thrust her hand where she knew she needed release. It was crazy. Shocking in its intensity and inappropriateness. Maybe she was in some kind of perimenopausal craziness—a sort of last-ditch onslaught before the old hormones dried up. That smart ass Sloane would undoubtedly agree with her.

She glanced quickly around her and noticed how men and women, all ages, not just the younger ones, were clamoring for Erika, looking much the way she supposed she herself looked— sweaty, breathless, on edge. And it wasn't only because of the way Erika looked and strutted around, but also because of her voice, which was not of this earth. Dess tingled as she realized that those around her had also recognized that Erika was something special.

God, had Sloane ever been right. Erika Alvarez had it, whatever exactly *it* was. She was a star in the making, and the thought both thrilled and frightened Dess, because she knew every high, every low of the sweetly agonizing journey to fame. Oh yes, she could attest to all the financial rewards, the endless accolades and compliments, the promises, the demands, the attention from all the *important* people. Even the little things, like walking unannounced into a five-star restaurant and being given the best table in the house, became a gratifying expectation. She also knew all too well about the pressure, the exhaustion, the people who did nothing but take and then take some more until there was nothing left to give. Fame came with a price. A price that, for some, was more than they could pay. Dess hoped with every fiber of her being that Erika would not be one of those, that she would be able to shoulder the awesome burdens that came with what she so desperately craved.

Once the show ended, Dess made her way back to the trailer and collected Maggie for a walk. Sloane and Erika hadn't appeared, and it wasn't a stretch to imagine that they were hanging out with some of the other musicians. She steered Maggie closer to a cluster of trailers other musicians were camping in. She told herself she simply wanted to check on her friends, make sure they were okay. She was not, she reassured herself, being a mother hen. Sloane and Erika were adults and could handle themselves. Or at least Sloane could. She'd take a passing glance and be on her way.

In the distance, a group of eight or ten people sat around a campfire, drinking straight from bottles of hard liquor. Marijuana smoke choked out the campfire smoke, and there at the center of it were Sloane and Erika. Grinning, laughing, sharing a toke, completely oblivious to Dess and Maggie's presence a couple of dozen yards away. Maggie perked up her ears, then her nostrils. Then she let out three staccato barks, like rifle shots, in the direction of the gathering, as if to warn the group that Erika and Sloane were her people and that nobody had better hurt them.

"Shh, I know, Maggie. They'll be okay. They'll be home soon, I promise." *They'd better be*, she thought with rising concern. And Sloane damned well better look after Erika.

* * *

Preceding Erika, Sloane unceremoniously entered the trailer, launched herself into her bunk and began snoring almost immediately. Erika was still juiced from the performance—her one drink and the few hits of a joint had done little to settle her down. She opened the fridge and pulled out a bottle of water.

"Thirsty after your partying?"

Startled, Erika turned sharply toward Dess, sitting in the dark at the dining nook. "A little."

She unscrewed the lid and took a long drink. Even though it was dark, she could see a crease the size of the Grand Canyon etched on Dess's forehead.

"Maggie and I saw you and Sloane a little while ago. Looked like you were having a good time." Disapproval was evident in Dess's voice, if not her words.

Erika thumped the bottle of water on the table, some of its contents sloshing over. Dess was not her mother, nor her boss. Or even her big sister. She didn't need the third degree from her.

"Look," she whispered, not wanting to wake Sloane. "You got something to say to me, then let's go outside and talk."

She spun around and stalked out of the trailer, unsure if Dess would follow. She did.

"Before you ask," Erika ground out, "I only had one drink and I shared all of one joint with Sloane. That's it."

Dess relaxed considerably. "Okay, fine. But just so you know, I wasn't about to accuse you of being a pothead or an alcoholic or whatever."

"No, but you feared I'm setting out on that path, didn't you?"

Dess leaned against the trailer and crossed her arms over her chest. "No. I didn't. But I was a little worried, yes. I've seen too many promising young talents go down that path of excess. First it was just for fun, then it became an addiction. And then, for many of them, it became a one-way ticket to an early grave. And that was after it had already destroyed their career and any meaningful relationship they'd ever had."

Erika blew out her breath. *Wow, she sure isn't holding anything back.* "Fine. I understand. But I'm not like that. And I'm not some kid you have to watch over constantly. Or that you have to lecture about every little possible thing that could happen, okay? You're going to have to trust me to learn some things as I go along. And right now, I don't think you trust me worth a shit."

Dess's eyes flashed in temper before softening considerably. "You're right. You're not a kid, and I don't want to be anybody's mother. I'm working on the trust thing, okay?"

Erika stepped closer. "Every day, I wake up hoping that this is the day you start seeing me as a woman. A woman who's much more than a fledgling, desperate wannabe kneeling at the great Dess Hampton's feet." Moving another step closer, Erika placed her hands against the trailer alongside Dess's head. "I want you," she whispered, "to see me as a grown woman with my own thoughts, dreams, ideas, opinions, experiences. And desires."

She leaned her head down, her lips an inch from Dess's forehead, their bodies only a finger's width apart. She wanted to prove to Dess that she was a woman, a contemporary in every way. And she wanted Dess to acknowledge it with more than mere words. "Do you accept that I'm a woman and not a child who needs to be coddled and corrected all the time?"

Dess trembled ever so slightly, and it took all of Erika's willpower not to wrap her arms around her.

"Tell me," Erika quietly urged.

"I…"

Dess's eyes closed, and she tilted her chin up. Blood pounded in Erika's ears as she waited for Dess to make the next move. God, how she wanted Dess to throw all of that damned caution of hers to the wind, to pull down the barriers she had planted firmly between herself and the rest of the world. But that was unlikely to happen.

Lips brushed suddenly against Erika's mouth, tentative at first. And then Dess began kissing her hard and with desperation, and their mouths were on fire, their need for physical connection overriding everything else. The flames ignited by the kiss scorched Erika's soul, leaving her breathless and desperate to hang onto her self-possession, her sanity, because the intensity of their mutual desire was stealing all sense of reason. She rocked into Dess, her body pushing, fusing into Dess's body, wanting nothing more than to take and be taken. Their unified heat melded with the heat of the kiss, which deepened with every racing heartbeat. Dess moaned from deep down, and her voice released something that had been knotted up inside Erika. She wanted to melt with this woman. Wanted to spill everything that was inside her into this capable woman, where she knew she would be sheltered, nurtured, cherished. Maybe even loved.

"Oh, Dess," Erika whispered urgently, pulling her mouth away and sliding it along Dess's jaw. She planted delicate kisses on the soft skin. "You undo me, do you know that? I can't think right now, I can only do. And I want to touch you. All over."

Dess placed her hand on Erika's chest and gently pushed her back. It was the tiniest move, but it felt like a giant fissure had suddenly opened between them. "I started this, I need to stop it," she said in a breathless stream. Her eyes were shining, and Erika imagined they were shining with desire. Or perhaps something greater.

"No," Erika whispered, her body quickly making up the distance between them.

"Yes."

I did that, Erika thought with satisfaction as she watched Dess's chest rapidly rise and fall, saw that her cheeks were flushed pink. Dess couldn't really want to stop, in spite of her words to the contrary. *Could she?*

"Why do we have to stop?" We're just getting started, she wanted to add, picturing the dozens of pleasurable things she'd love to do with Dess right now.

Dess shook her head, more determined this time. "No, Erika. We can't. We're working together. We have to be—"

"What? Professional? Perfect every minute? We're human, not machines. And we have feelings for each other."

"No, we don't. We're friends. Friends who also work together. I don't want to do anything that's going to upset the working relationship between the three of us."

Erika leaned close enough to whisper in Dess's ear. "I know you have feelings for me. Feelings that go beyond a professional relationship. Just as I have feelings for you." Softly, with one finger, she traced along Dess's jaw and silently celebrated the responding tremor. "We can at least be honest with each other about that."

"You don't understand." Something in Dess's voice alarmed Erika, and when she looked into Dess's eyes, there were tears.

Oh God, she thought with a quiet gasp that sent a shockwave through her. *Somebody's hurt you. Hurt you so badly that they've wrecked you for anybody else.* She stepped back, took Dess's hands in hers. "Okay. Fine. But I'm not giving up on you, Dess Hampton."

Erika walked back into the trailer and hopped up into her bunk, sliding the curtain across for privacy. She laid back and, frustrated but keyed up, finally smiled to herself. *If Dess Hampton won't sleep with me, maybe Dora Hessler will.*

CHAPTER ELEVEN

The hour-long workshop teaching kids how to play guitar flew by and was far more fun than Dess would have predicted. The dozen youngsters were all very eager and attentive, all of them little sponges anxious to learn the three chords and three simple nursery rhymes she showed them. Their fingers were so tiny, but so nimble on the fret board, and she envied their lack of fear. And the music! How refreshing it was to break things down to their simplest root notes and strum patterns. When the kids played back what she taught them, Dess nearly danced with joy at the magic of it all, at the kids reminding her of the pure joy of making music.

Equal to her pleasure with teaching was her relief at having a temporary distraction from thoughts of Erika. And, above all, from that sizzling, mind-blowing, knee-buckling kiss last night. She hadn't planned the kiss. Hadn't thought of anything before she'd leaned in and done it. She had simply acted. Or perhaps it was a reaction to all that chemistry sizzling between them, like a hot frying pan full of oil. Being alone with Erika was increasingly full of temptation. If she broke it down, she couldn't pinpoint exactly what was drawing her like a magnet to the singer. She was gorgeous, yes, her body was exquisitely sexy, yes, her voice…her voice was ethereal and out of this world, for sure, and her eyes were fathomless and full of a thousand different emotions. She was talented, she was funny, she was smart, she was warm. But hadn't Dess met a thousand women like her over the last two decades? Ten thousand?

Clearly not, because she couldn't stop thinking about Erika. And her control? Her control was increasingly in tatters. *Ha, what control?* At this rate, just weeks into their four-month tour, they'd wind up in bed any day now and would probably be married by the end of it if she didn't get a grip.

Packing up her guitar in its hard-shell case, Dess thought about the two words rolling around in her head. "Bed" and "married." Two words that couldn't be more incongruous with her life at the moment. She'd never wanted to marry anyone, not even Dayna (*thank God!*), having long ago concluded that if it was going to happen, it would have happened by now. As for bedding women—the idea of it was alluring, but it just wasn't in her to go off and have transitory sex with someone. The fact that she'd just now linked "bed" and "married" with thoughts of Erika had no significance whatsoever, she reassured herself. It was just the hormones and the loneliness talking.

"Ah, there you are." Sloane marched up to her, looking uncharacteristically concerned.

"What's up?"

"I'll walk you back to the trailer."

"Why, do I have a stalker or something?"

"Nope. But we do have a pesky reporter who's started asking questions about you."

Dess rolled her eyes and let Sloane carry her guitar case. Sloane and Erika had been scheduled to meet with a magazine reporter earlier this morning—Dess had opted out, of course. The festivals, anxious for any press coverage they could get, encouraged reporters and performers to cooperate with each other. It was a win-win for Erika, because a mention in a national music magazine, no matter how small its circulation, would boost her career.

"Was this reporter asking general questions about me? Or should I be worrying that my cover has been blown?"

"No, she doesn't know who you are," Sloane answered. "She was curious about you because of what she called your 'exciting' guitar skills. Actually…" Sloane bit her bottom lip, but a grin still leaked out. "She said it was like you make love to the guitar when you're playing."

Dess made a face. "Thanks. I think."

"We made some stuff up to keep her off your trail."

"Now you've got me scared. Made up what kind of stuff?"

"That you have a crazy ex-husband who doesn't need to know where you are right now."

Dess pulled her sunglasses down so her eyes could shoot daggers at Sloane. "You didn't."

"Yeah, actually we did. And that you've spent your career being anonymous because that's the way you want it. That you have no desire for fame and recognition. That you simply play for the love of it and all that bullshit. I think she bought it. Then we steered the conversation back to Erika."

"So I'm safe?"

"For now, yes. But she's covering a lot of our festivals this summer, including that big one in Wisconsin in two weeks. Let's hope she forgets about you by then."

Dess shrugged, perplexed as to why this reporter would be more interested in her than in Erika. Or Sloane. Both of them were supremely talented and didn't mind giving interviews. Either way there wasn't much she could do about it, and worrying wasn't going to help. Besides, she had more pressing things to think about. Like the fact that Sloane was flying to Seattle for a week as soon as this weekend gig was over. She was ditching them to play a few shows with Melissa Etheridge. Which was fine, except it meant she'd be spending more time alone with Erika. And on Erika's turf. They would spend the week of Sloane's absence at Erika's apartment in Minneapolis, then get ready for the Wisconsin festival. What tormented Dess was how she was going to be able to resist Erika while alone with her in a two-bedroom apartment. *Christ*, she thought, as her stomach began a gymnastics routine.

"Hey," Sloane said softly. "It's cool, okay? I didn't mean to worry you."

"It's okay. I'm not worried."

"Well, you *look* worried."

"Sorry. Just thinking about that ballad Erika and I have been working on. Sloane, I don't know if we're going to be able to get it done anytime soon. Or if it's going to be good enough."

Sloane stopped walking, forcing Dess to stop too. "What are you talking about? That song's already fucking great. And you two have a whole week together to perfect it. Hell, you've got nothing else to do but write songs together. And take Maggie for walks."

Dess turned and started walking. *Easy for you to say, Sloane. It's going to be a little hard to write songs if we can't keep our fucking hands off each other!*

* * *

"You're sure our trailer's okay to park in your building's parking lot?" It was the third time Dess had asked the same question, and it was beginning to annoy Erika.

"Yes, I'm sure. I checked with the building superintendent."

"And they're okay with Maggie staying in your apartment? Because she and I can get a hotel r—"

"It's absolutely fine to have Maggie here. And I have lots of room, before you ask about that again." *Jesus.*

"Okay, okay. You don't have to get short with me."

"Sorry. I'm not trying to be short with you," Erika said. "Look, we need to work on our music, so it'll be easier to do that if we stay together while Sloane's away. I thought we all agreed to this?"

Dess sighed as though she were making some great sacrifice, and Erika nearly blew her top. She'd had it with the cold shoulder. Had it with Dess being dismissive and aloof since their kiss. As much as the kiss had unraveled her like a spool of thread, she wished it had never happened. Not if it was responsible for creating this gulf between them.

Erika forced herself to stay calm as they deposited their bags and guitars in her apartment. She showed Dess around, noticing that Dess practically collapsed with relief when she was shown her own bedroom. They settled Maggie in, fetching a bowl of water for her and placing her toys around the apartment so she'd feel at home. Maggie sniffed the perimeter of each room, then happily lay down in her doggie bed in the corner of the living room. Her eyes lazily watched them.

"Now," Erika said, as Dess sat down on the couch. She tried to keep her voice level, but it was nearly impossible. She wanted to shake some sense into Dess, then kiss her madly. "You want to tell me why you've been acting like being around me is such a hardship? Like you'd rather be just about anywhere else?"

Dess's mouth hung open, and for a long moment she didn't say anything.

Erika dropped onto the sofa next to her, keeping a cushion between them. A demilitarized zone, she thought with fleeting amusement. "We need to talk about this, because I can't spend the entire summer acting like we can barely stand each other. Not when…"

Curiosity flickered in Dess's eyes. "Not when what?"

Okay, fine, Erika thought. She steeled herself. The truth was going to be painful, but so be it. "Not when I think I'm falling in love with you."

Dess's eyes were like floodlights being switched on. If she was flattered or pleased about Erika's confession, it quickly became buried in a streak of denial. "That's absurd. We don't even know each other. Six weeks ago, we hadn't even met!"

"Well, I've got a newsflash for you. People can fall in love a lot faster than in six weeks. And I do know you. Not as well yet as I intend to, but my heart knows you."

"Oh, come on. That sounds like a line from the song we're writing."

Dess's words and tone bruised Erika, and it took tremendous effort to keep her voice from shaking. "If you weren't so afraid of everything, you might actually realize that I'm someone worth falling in love with."

"Erika, I didn't mean—"

"Why is it so hard for you?" Erika said, wanting to hurt Dess the same way Dess had hurt her. "Why is it so hard to follow your heart? To take a chance? To give in once in a while?"

Dess shook her head slowly, but she couldn't look at Erika. Her voice was hard granite. "You don't understand."

"You're right, I don't. And you sure as hell aren't going to explain it to me, are you?" Erika jumped up from the couch and stepped into her shoes. She couldn't sit here anymore and stew in her hurt and anger without saying something she'd regret. Or before tears materialized. She would not give Dess the satisfaction of seeing her cry.

"I'll be back," she said over her shoulder, stalking out the door before Dess had a chance to reply.

* * *

Dess accepted Erika's peace offering of dinner at Lola's, a popular pizzeria on Xerxes Avenue that featured a menu of dozens of wood-fired pizzas to choose from, all served on a charming array of dinnerware that had clearly come from auctions or thrift shops. Dess went for the Hawaii Pie-O: house-cured bacon, fresh pineapple, mozzarella, provolone and serrano peppers. Erika chose the Forager: crimini, shitake and portabella mushrooms, taleggio, fontina, tarragon and truffle oil. They agreed to share a bottle of California cabernet.

They edged into conversation by talking neutrally about the tour, about music, about anything but the topic that had tossed them into such a tailspin.

"The time you played half-time at the Super Bowl," Erika said as she sipped her wine, waiting for the food to arrive. Her eyes flashed with deep interest and admiration. "That must have been one of your career highlights?"

Dess smiled at the memory. It was eleven years ago. She'd been at the peak of her career, selling out concerts in a matter of hours. Everybody was demanding her time and attention— her fans, the record companies, concert promoters, television talk shows, Broadway show producers, companies wanting her to endorse their products. A Saudi prince, shortly after the Super Bowl concert, paid her three million dollars for a one-off private concert at his palace in Dubai. It was all so crazy as to be almost unreal. The time, she realized now, had flown by in a blur punctuated by exhaustion and an insanely arduous amount of obligation that had made it harder and harder to stay true to herself. She could hardly even remember what kind of person she'd been then or even whether she'd been happy.

"I guess it doesn't get much bigger than playing before almost a hundred thousand people and all those viewers at home watching on television," Dess agreed. "So yeah." She shrugged, opting for the quick answer. "You could say it was a highlight."

"I watched it on television. I was in high school," Erika said dreamily. "I remember you looked so...so *hot*, but so sure of yourself and humble at the same time. I was so envious, so full of admiration. I thought, yeah, one day I want to do that. I sure as hell never thought I'd actually be sitting in a restaurant with you." Erika lowered her voice. "Or that I'd kiss you."

The timbre of Erika's voice sent a surge of excitement through Dess's veins.

"What was it like singing in front of that many people?" Erika asked.

Dess pressed her legs together. Her physical reaction to Erika continued to surprise and shock her. "About like you'd imagine. Scary as hell, but incredibly exhilarating too. There's nothing better than the joyous energy of all those people coming together, and knowing you're at the center of all those good feelings. But it's a two-way street. As much as I'm giving them, they're giving to me too."

"How so?" Erika was leaning forward, as if to absorb Dess's answer with every cell in her body.

"You already know what I'm talking about, just on a smaller scale. It's an exchange, a sharing of the love of music, a mutual appreciation of the joy music gives. You see, it was not me they were worshipping up there, but the music. It always comes back to the music. Music is one of the most emotionally moving things people ever experience, and you're sharing that moment with them. They're remembering things and at the same time creating new memories. And it's an honor to share that with them, to be that bridge between them and music."

"Yes, but people did worship *you*, Dess. I did. I saw it in others too. It wasn't only the music, but the person delivering the music too. You must admit, the messenger can become bigger than the message."

"Yes, but it's ultimately the music—what's coming out of that person's mouth on stage—that speaks to them deeply enough to set off all those endorphins. If they're enjoying that moment, that song, their energy needs a place to converge, and that's on the person on stage. It's like they're transferring all that love to you, but you can't forget where it comes from. You, the singer, are only the vehicle."

"I agree with you, but I also think it's more complicated than that. I think the connection the singer is making—the energy they're bringing—influences the crowd too. Like if the performer is getting off on the music too or if they're just going through the motions. Audiences can tell the difference, and they identify and appreciate the one who's giving it a hundred percent."

"Yes, that's true. And that's why you have to find a way to bring it each and every time you get up on stage, no matter what your mood is that day, what you're feeling inside. You have to be consistent every time in giving them your best. You owe the audience that."

Man, this felt so much better than arguing with Erika. She watched Erika mull over their conversation as their pizzas arrived. The aroma alone quickly put an end to any more thinking. Or talking.

"God, this smells so good," Erika said as she sliced off a bite with a knife and fork and stuffed it in her mouth. "Oh my God, I think I'm having an orgasm."

Dess nearly choked on her own bite. She did not need visions of Erika having an orgasm right now.

It wasn't until the quiet and darkness of the drive back to the apartment that Dess thought back to Erika's simple declaration earlier that she thought she was falling in love with her. She hadn't wanted to consider that it was true, because she was too hellbent on rejecting the notion as being ridiculous. But was it? Love was about chemistry, not math. It was about feelings that welled up all on their own from a deep place where there was no sense of time, no excuses for why it couldn't or shouldn't happen. Love was about honesty between two souls before doubts, fears and rationalizations got in the way. Dess knew that, and yet she'd fallen into the trap of immediately throwing up obstacles. "We don't even know each other," she remembered telling Erika.

Well, she thought as they pulled into the parking lot of Erika's apartment building. *Perhaps it's time to change that.*

They greeted Maggie, and Erika moved to switch on the lights.

"No," Dess said. "Not too many lights."

"Okay." Erika turned on only a stained glass lamp on the end table. "More wine?"

"Only if you're having some."

"Oh, I'm definitely having some." She returned with two glasses and a bottle of merlot. She poured wine into each glass and sat down in an easy chair, opposite Dess this time. Dess didn't blame her for not sitting closer. Didn't blame her either for the slightly defensive posture she took now. Erika had earlier put her heart on the table, and Dess had all but stomped on it.

"About earlier," Dess ventured, her throat suddenly parched. She took a sip of wine. "I'm sorry I jumped all over you. That I acted like your feelings weren't valid. It was wrong of me."

"Thank you for saying that. And I'm sorry too," Erika said quietly. "I said some harsh things to you."

"I think there's a way to resolve this."

"There is?"

Dess smiled to herself at Erika's eagerness, and at the glint of hopeful flirtatiousness in her eyes. *She probably thinks I'm going to suggest more of that incredible kissing.* Dess's eyes zeroed in on those full, soft lips, and she had to suppress the dizzying desire to launch herself into Erika's lap. She wanted to kiss Erika. Had never stopped wanting to kiss Erika, she realized with growing acceptance. The thought of kissing Erika made her wet, made her heart gallop like a wild horse, and she could no longer deny the physical sensations that simply looking at Erika or remembering something about Erika, unleashed in her. Kissing, however, wasn't going to advance their issues right now. Well, it would, she thought wickedly, but only in physical terms. There were other, more important things they needed to get out of the way first.

"I want us to know each other better," Dess said evenly. "And you were right, I have been guarded with you. But I want to change that. Immediately."

CHAPTER TWELVE

Talking openly with Dess was much easier, so much more natural, than Erika had expected. Nothing held back her desire to be completely open, and not only because such honesty between them signaled that their relationship was deepening, but because it felt so right—like a lock clicking open.

Dess's gaze was bold, unsettling in its scrutiny. "You're incredibly talented, Erika. Talented enough to reach the very top echelon of the music business. But what I need to know is why you truly want it so badly."

Erika had a stack of answers she spewed out whenever she was asked that question. "I want it because I have the talent and the ability." "Because I'm willing to put in the work it requires." "Because I want to give to others what music has given to me." "Because I love music so much and I'm determined to be the best at anything I do." "I want to share my gift with the world…blah, blah, blah." It was all true, but she knew Dess was after something much deeper than that. Something nobody else knew about her. The truth.

Erika swallowed and drew a deep breath. This wasn't going to be simple or quick or easy, but she wanted Dess to know the truth.

"My parents groomed me from a very young age for a career on the stage. But as a pianist. All their energy, any money that wasn't needed for food or housing, went to my lessons. Piano consumed two hours every day, six days week. That's how much I was supposed to practice. And that doesn't count lessons three times a week, recitals, private performances."

"Wow. That's a lot for a kid."

"Too much." Erika took a sip of wine to keep her voice steady. "I began to resent it. Not because I was afraid of all the work or the pressure to perform, but because it wasn't my choice. I never got a say." Her voice began to shake, the intensity of her emotions surprising her after all these years. She hadn't played a serious piece of music on the piano in at least five years, and she hadn't seen her parents in more than seven.

"I'm sorry," Dess whispered, and now Erika wished she were sitting beside Dess instead of across from her.

"The toughest was in high school. The kids." Erika shook her head. "They were mean because I was different. I was the geeky kid who played piano in all her spare time. The kid the teachers all raved about as being so talented. And I was the weird kid who came from a home where English wasn't spoken as a first language, where my parents kept to themselves and worked like dogs in their minimum-wage jobs to support my music."

The school memories still stung—the vitriol from her peers, their scorn, their mockery. Teachers who were so awed of her talent that they treated her differently.

"At what point did you rebel?"

"College. I finally was able to escape my parents and their dreams that felt like a prison to me. I mostly stopped playing the piano, started singing. And my parents, well, they pretty much disowned me for that. Singing to them was as classless as being a whore—their words, not mine. And then when I told them I was gay, well..." Erika shook her head, unable to go on.

Dess held out her hand. Erika reached out and clasped it like a lifeline, let Dess gently tug her until she was sitting next to her.

"I'm so sorry," Dess said in a voice thick and warm and comforting.

Still holding her hand, Erika confessed, "I wanted to sing because that's who I am. And I want to be the best at what I do because that's what my parents instilled in me. But I am doing this for *me*, Dess. For me." Her voice caught, and Dess squeezed her hand. "It's because I love to sing, and I am nothing without it."

"You're a very strong woman to have survived what you went through."

Erika wiped a tear from her cheek and shook her head miserably. "You don't know the half of it."

"Will you tell me? Please?"

It was a big step to trust Dess. To tell her something only her therapist knew. "I don't know if I can. I'm sorry, but that's the truth."

If Dess was stung, she didn't show it. She glanced away, still holding Erika's hand, and when her gaze returned, there were tears in her eyes.

"There are things, hard things," Dess said, her voice quivering, "that you don't know about me either."

For a long time they didn't speak in the near darkness. A clock ticked from the kitchen. Maggie occasionally sighed or snored from her place on the floor.

"When I got sick..." Dess's voice, after such a long silence, startled Erika.

"Go on."

"When I got sick six years ago, everything changed. And so fast. I wasn't even sure the throat cancer was survivable at first. And then, once I realized the odds were in favor of beating it and that I was going to be okay, I began to realize the total devastation it had done to the rest of my life."

"Your career? Because it destroyed your voice?"

"Yes, my voice. The radiation ended my professional singing career."

"But you didn't stay in the business at all. You walked away from it completely." Erika was still dumbfounded by Dess's complete rejection of her fame and her career, of the solid and successful reputation she'd built. She could have continued in so many ways—as a model or spokesperson for cancer survivors, as a music producer or even manager. Something, anything.

"Yes, I walked away because I was utterly devastated. Like a nuclear bomb had gone off in my life. It felt like there was nothing left. Even my girlfriend…"

Ah, the other half of Dess's pain, it occurred to Erika. "Don't tell me your girlfriend left you? When you were sick?"

Dess nodded, her face a picture of anguish.

"But how could someone do that?" Outrage burst inside Erika. What kind of monster was this woman?

Dess shrugged, but there was no apathy in her voice, in her face. Her pain was stark, raw, unhealed by time. "She did. She was my manager. We'd been together for five years. She told me she couldn't handle my illness, but I really think what she couldn't handle were the paychecks that dried up, the phone not ringing anymore. So you see, I lost everything."

"Oh God, I'm so sorry, Dess." She let go of Dess's hand and pulled her into a deep hug.

"There was too much loss, too much devastation," Dess mumbled into her shoulder. "I didn't have the confidence or the joy to go back into the business. I couldn't face the pity, the questions, the reality that I couldn't sing anymore. I guess I wasn't brave enough. Christ, I wouldn't even have known where to start."

Erika released Dess but held her face in her hands, looking deeply in her eyes. "You are brave, Dess. You can do anything you want. You're a survivor."

"No," Dess said, shaking her head. "I almost didn't survive."

"What do you mean? The cancer?"

"No, not just the cancer. I thought of ending it, even once I knew I could beat the cancer." Dess's face collapsed. Her breath came in hitches. "I had the pills to do it. And I almost used them."

Erika pulled Dess into her again and let her cry, rocking her gently, rubbing her back in light circles as Dess emptied her pain. She knew exactly those feelings of utter desolation. Knew what it was like to have lost hope, to look out on a future that seemed to hold nothing but the promise of more pain.

After Dess cried herself out, Erika planted a tender kiss on her forehead. "I'm so glad you're here. With me. And that you found your way again. It would have been a terrible loss for so many people if you hadn't persevered."

"Thank you," Dess said, her voice strengthening. "I think I'm still finding my way."

What Erika hoped for at that moment, with a feeling more powerful than she'd ever had in her life, was that Dess would keep finding her way. Not alone, but with *her*.

* * *

Breakfast of fresh fruit and yogurt made the need for conversation temporarily nonexistent. Dess was glad for the silence. She felt awkward about her little breakdown last night and her emotional confession. Erika had been gracious, completely understanding, selflessly tender in comforting her. They understood each other better now, but Dess still felt exposed and vulnerable, having confessed things only Sloane and Carol knew about her. She wasn't used to revealing such raw weakness, of shedding light on the darkest corners of her soul. She was accustomed to having it all together, to commanding others—whether it was her backup band or her management team—and to slipping on a mask and functioning at an extremely high level no matter what problems or distractions pestered her. It was frightening to dredge up again that period of her life where she almost gave up, where she'd had such little control over what was happening to her.

She was saved from her self-pity when Erika suddenly cleared her throat and rested quivering hands on the table.

"There was something I neglected to share last night. And I should have. Especially after the things you confided in me."

Dess was about to say it wasn't necessary but stopped at the despair in Erika's face.

"Thank you, by the way, for trusting me," Erika said.

"I do trust you. And I meant what I said about wanting us to get to know each other better. Even when it's difficult."

"Good. Then I need to tell you…" Erika drew in a deep, shuddering breath, but her hands had stilled and her voice was firm. "When I told you about the bullying, about how kids treated me like I was a weirdo, and how my parents—they were so hard on me. So narrow minded and fixated on me being a successful pianist."

"Yes?"

Tears sprang to Erika's eyes. "God, they used to make me practice until my fingers were so sore, I couldn't move them. They didn't give me any time to play and have friends, even if the other kids had liked me. And girls…I knew by the time I was fourteen that I liked girls, but my parents would have thrown me out if they'd known. Being who I was inside was not an option."

"Oh, Erika, I'm so sorry."

"Wait. There's more. I tried to kill myself, Dess. Not very seriously. Nothing that amounted to more than a few gouges on my wrist, but it was an attempt."

"When?" Dess said, absorbing the pain behind Erika's confession until it fused with her own. She couldn't imagine the world having lost such a talent as Erika Alvarez. Thank God her attempt hadn't been successful.

"My last year of high school. I didn't try it again. I knew somehow if I could just hang on until I could escape to college, it would get better. And it did."

"I'm so glad you did hang on." Dess reached across the table and threaded Erika's fingers through her own. "And I'm glad I did too. Let's make a pact, right now."

Erika's eyebrows shot up in surprise, but she gave no opposition.

"Let's agree that if either of us is ever feeling despondent again or feeling that things are too overwhelming, no matter what it's about, no matter where we are or what time of the day it is, that we'll talk about it. Together. Okay?"

Erika broke into a grin, and it was like storm clouds parting for the sun. "That sounds like a deal to me."

Dess smiled. A weight had been lifted from her heart. "Who knew neither of us was perfect?"

* * *

They spent the afternoon working on their ballad, and suddenly the parts that had been difficult before seemed to have shifted to something much easier, Erika realized. The second and third verses had been their stumbling block, along with the little bridge on piano, but now, she felt sure, they'd nailed it.

Before Erika thought about what she was saying, she blurted out, "Why don't you try singing it with me, Dess?"

The look of horror on Dess's face made Erika realize the huge tactical mistake she'd made. Yet again. And just when they were beginning to build a true friendship. *Shit.* "I mean, a little bit of background harmony or something?"

"Erika, I—"

"I know you don't sing anymore. I'm sorry. I didn't mean to make you feel bad. But it's just us. You don't have to be afraid of how you sound."

Tears welled in Dess's eyes, and Erika scooted over beside her. They'd spread out on the floor of her apartment's living room, sheet music scattered around them like fallen leaves. Erika put her arms around Dess and held her as she cried softly. Her shoulders were shaking as though she were standing in a cold rain, and Erika pictured her doing exactly that. Standing on a street corner, maybe downtown Chicago, in a cold gray rain, an umbrella doing little to ward off the showers and the chill. People passed her, ignoring her, and she looked so sad and lonely in Erika's mind.

"Let me be your shelter," Erika whispered, wanting it to be so.

Dess snuggled in closer. After a few moments, she raised her face to Erika, and Erika, with the soft pad of her thumb, brushed away the tears. Then she kissed the wet trails the tears had taken on their journey downward. Dess smiled, her face transforming into a look of peacefulness and capitulation.

"Let me love you," Erika said as she gazed into Dess's eyes. It was the purest, most heartfelt statement she'd ever made to anyone. She could love this woman to the ends of the earth. Could make love to her until every single feeling, everything that had ever mattered in her life, compressed into that single moment of shared orgasm.

"Yes. I'd like that."

Erika didn't wait for Dess to say more. Or to change her mind. She kissed the corners of her lips, her mouth, with every ounce of tenderness she felt for Dess. Desire exploded inside her, surging up her spine and through her chest. But it was much, much more than simple lust. Dess had unlocked something inside her that had wanted to spring out for so long, but didn't know how. It was love, she knew. She'd been waiting for exactly the right woman who would understand her, who would love her back for who she was. She had so much love inside her, and she wanted to give it all to this gorgeous, smart, talented woman who was kissing her back with a passion equal to her own.

Sheets of paper crunched and crumpled under their weight as Erika eased Dess to the floor, her lips never leaving her mouth. She could kiss that mouth forever, those lips. Screw food and drink. Dess's lips were all she needed for sustenance. She wanted to kiss her for hours, naked or clothed, it didn't matter. Lying down, sitting down, standing up. She wanted to kiss Dess every which way. And not only on her beautiful mouth, but everywhere.

Dess moaned softly as Erika's mouth slid over her throat. She kissed the sinewy muscles there. Kissed the faint scar from her cancer surgery. She kissed her way down that gorgeous, silky neck, felt Dess's chest rise and fall faster as her kisses trailed further down her body. God, that body felt so wonderful beneath her—strong and supple at the same time. Warm and thrumming with desire.

Erika's hand crept under Dess's ribbed tank top and onto the flat of her stomach, where it lingered with soft, circular strokes. She loved the tiny flinch Dess's stomach muscles made in response to each touch. *So responsive!* Dess was going to be so delicious, so sensuous, so perfect to make love to. Erika could almost taste it, could already feel the magic of it in her body.

Higher her hand traveled until it cupped a breast, and Erika suddenly knew without a doubt what heaven must be like. She felt herself grow wet as her thumb caressed Dess's nipple through the lacy fabric of her bra. The nipple hardened immediately, and Dess invitingly arched her back, a clear signal she wanted Erika's mouth on her. Her eyes were pinched shut and from her mouth came tiny, hungry moans. Oh, how Erika wanted to fill that hunger, wanted to give Dess everything she had to give until she cried out. She inched the tank top higher to expose the pink Victoria's Secret bra. Through the expensive fabric, Dess's nipples strained for release.

"Wait," Dess squeezed out between breaths. Her hand gently came to rest on Erika's forehead just as she was about to place her mouth against the lace covering her nipple.

"Anything, darling. Tell me what you want."

"I—" Her breath came hard and fast. "I want you, Erika. I want to make love with you. But I'm afraid to go too fast. I—"

"Shh, it's okay." Erika tried to keep the disappointment from her voice. She wanted to make love to Dess. Urgently. So urgently, in fact, that she was within a breath of ripping that bra right off, shorts and underwear too, and having her way with her no matter how much Dess protested. But it was important that Dess set the pace, that her wishes be respected. If Dess didn't want to rush things, then they wouldn't rush things. "We'll slow down, okay?" *Oh, God, what am I agreeing to?*

Dess smiled up at her. "Why don't we cool down with some dinner?"

It took all her willpower, but Erika crawled off Dess. She remained beside her, however. Lovingly, she stroked the side of her face. "I know a great Thai restaurant. And hey, why don't we celebrate by going to a gay club later?"

"What are we celebrating?" Dess flashed her a coy look.

"Um, our newfound…intimacy?" *The fact that we're going to be making love before the week is out?* The thought sent a fresh wave of excitement through Erika that threatened to annihilate her willpower. She was wet and throbbing, and it was almost too much to bear when her eyes made the mistake of drifting down to Dess's lacy pink bra, which was still exposed. She could see the outline of Dess's nipples, still hard, and it was all she could do not to drop her mouth onto them and suck them until Dess cried out for release.

Dess grinned at her, her eyes sparkling with a happiness that Erika had only seen before when she played the guitar. "I like the idea of the restaurant. But not the nightclub."

Erika's eyebrows posed the question why.

"I don't want to wear that damned disguise I've been using for the concerts. Which means people might recognize me. I don't want to risk that."

"All right. I understand." Erika kissed Dess's cheek. "I just wanted to dance with you, that's all."

"I'd like that. A lot." Dess grinned, and it was like an arrow pleasurably piercing Erika's heart. "Why don't we finish our date back here with your iPod? You must have some songs on that thing we can dance to."

Erika smiled back at the woman she couldn't get enough of. "Now you're talking."

"Just let me change first and we can go."

"Need any help with that part?" Erika called after Dess. Her answer was the click of the door closing.

CHAPTER THIRTEEN

They parked Erika's aging compact car—rust was forming around the wheel wells like sloppy wallpaper borders—and walked the three remaining blocks to the Thai restaurant. Dess nearly reached out to hold Erika's hand, but stopped herself. They weren't a couple, and holding hands would be getting ahead of themselves, she told herself, even as she fought the overwhelming urge. *It's just that her hands are so beautiful, so soft and strong at the same time, and so nimble the way they play piano, so skilled the way they stroke my breasts... Oh God, get a grip, Dess, or you're never going to make it through dinner!*

"I know it's a cliché, but a penny for your thoughts," Erika said, surprising Dess with her uncanny ability to read her.

Oh, Jesus, I cannot tell her I was thinking about her touching my breasts! "Who said I'm thinking about anything?"

"I can tell by the way that little line forms between your eyes and how your jaw gets a little tighter."

Dess looked at Erika as she held the door to the restaurant open for her. A woman who noticed the smallest things about her was impressive. And something she definitely wasn't used to.

Dayna had never been able to read her. *Oh please, don't let me think of that bitch tonight. Or ever again, for that matter.*

They were shown to a corner table that afforded them privacy and were left with menus that were plain in design but full of enticing selections. Dess had learned a long time ago, from eating at countless restaurants, that the ones that tried to make their menus look the fanciest didn't often serve the best food.

Dess decided to start with *som tam*—a spicy papaya salad—while Erika ordered *tom kha* soup. They also ordered a pitcher of homemade ginger lemonade with fresh mint sprigs.

"I have a feeling the food here is going to be amazing," Dess said.

"It is. Only the best for you, sweetheart."

"I bet you say that to all your dates." Something in Dess made her want clarify that this was only a date, nothing more promising than that. Erika was the kind of woman you could fall head over heels in love with, she warned herself. And she wanted—needed—to take things slow.

"It's been so long since I've been on an actual date that I don't remember what my lines are supposed to be." Erika's suggestive smile hinted that she was thinking of their make-out session. But her eyes were the antithesis of playful. "Are you having second thoughts about being on a date with me?"

"No. Definitely not."

"Good." Erika appeared to relax but only a little.

Their appetizers arrived, the coconut smell of the *tom kha* soup nearly making Dess regret her salad choice, but as she delivered a forkful to her mouth and tasted the sweet and sour of the shredded papaya, she knew she'd made the right decision.

Watching Erika eat made Dess tingle all over. Her lips, her mouth, were so sexy every time she delicately lifted the spoon to her mouth. And the way she closed her eyes in pleasure with each mouthful nearly made Dess moan, because that blissful look reminded her of the endless, passionate kisses they'd shared. And of how they'd nearly made love. The thought quickened her pulse, excitement and fear battling for supremacy. Making love was definitely a new and deeper level of commitment, an implied promise of some kind of a future together. At least for Dess it was. And while she wanted Erika with a ferocity that surprised and thrilled her, she feared she wasn't ready for a relationship. Her head spun with how fast everything was happening, especially for someone who hadn't dated anyone in years and wasn't looking for a relationship.

It seemed like it was just last week she'd only met Erika and that it was just yesterday she'd first become aware of the growing attraction between them. And now…now they were at the stage of kissing and making out and looking at each other like they couldn't wait to get out of here and rip each other's clothes off. When did all this happen?

"Earlier…" Erika said, appraising Dess again with those penetrating eyes. She leaned closer and lowered her voice, sending another tingling current through Dess. "When we were making out, you said you were scared to go too fast. Will you tell me what you mean? What you're scared of?"

She did not, as she gazed into those deep, dark pools, want to be scared of anything with Erika. *I want to trust you*, she thought. *I want to be safe with you.* She'd been burned so badly before, she didn't know if she could let someone fully inside anymore. She took a deep breath, knowing Erika would not allow her question to be dismissed.

"I guess," Dess replied, setting down her sweating glass of ginger lemonade, "I'm afraid of getting serious too soon. We still have three months ahead of us on this tour, and—"

"Are you worried we'll have a falling out and won't be able to work together?"

"Partly, of course. Or that it will somehow change the dynamics between us and interfere with our work."

"Do you trust that we're both professionals? That we can keep the two areas separate?"

Dess thought about that and knew Erika was right. "Yes, I do trust that we can handle working together no matter what's going on in our personal life."

"All right, we've got that out of the way." Erika smiled softly. "Is it the age thing?"

Unable to help herself, Dess laughed. "Have you ever used a dial telephone? Or a typewriter?"

Erika smiled a little sheepishly, then laughed. "No, but if it will make you feel better I'll visit the nearest antique shop so I can say yes."

Still smiling, Dess said, "No, I'm only kidding. Getting to know the woman you are has definitely removed the age thing from the equation." *Except—oh God, she'll be relentless in bed, absolutely voracious. How the hell am I going to keep up?* Then Dess was struck with the thought that if she couldn't keep up, that was more than okay. *I'll just lie back and enjoy!*

"You're blushing."

Dess raised a hand to her cheek. Yup, it was warm. "You caught me. I was thinking about…certain things." She felt her blush deepen as Erika's eyes shone with pleasure.

"I definitely want to hear more about those thoughts," Erika whispered as their large bowl of shared *pad thai* was set in front of them.

Watching Erika eat again, Dess was overcome by the urge to kiss her. To taste the lime and ginger on her lips. To explore that luscious, warm mouth with her tongue. She wanted to be dizzy with desire again, to ache from want. More than anyone she'd met in the last six years, Erika could make her forget all those reasons that had held her back from relationships before. *Reasons? Hell, what reasons?* she wondered, now unable to think of a single good one.

Erika's voice snapped her out of her lightheadedness. "So what are you really scared of, Dess? With me."

Dess took another bite, stalling for time. She knew Erika deserved a truthful explanation, but it was going to dredge up a lot of memories she'd hoped were buried for good. "Can we wait until later, when we're alone?"

"Sure. So in the meantime, how about you tell me what you were thinking of when you were blushing?"

Dess felt heat infusing her cheeks again. She couldn't think of Erika now and *not* think about kissing her while they were rolling around on the floor. And how turned on she was as Erika had cupped her breast and stroked her through her bra. Days ago she'd begun wearing nice underwear with the secret hope that things might soon escalate between them. She had to cross her legs now to stem the rush of desire flooding through her. How, she wondered, could she have gone from entrenched celibacy to *this* in such a short time?

"If I tell you," Dess finally said, "they'll need to call the fire department to hose me down."

Erika growled playfully. "If you're wanting to get wet, I can think of a few ways."

Dess nearly choked on her noodles. *Christ, I'm already wet. Don't you know that?*

"Sorry," Erika said, clearly not sorry at all.

The waiter asked them if they wanted coffee, but Dess and Erika only needed to look at each other in a tacit agreement that they had to get the hell out of here.

* * *

While Dess was out on a short stroll with Maggie, Erika poured them each a glass of white wine, then lit the half-dozen candles she'd hurriedly placed around the living room. Her iPod was ready to go with a romantic playlist she'd put together last night after Dess had gone to bed, wanting to be prepared for anything. She smoothed her hands over her jeans, released another button on her white cotton blouse to reveal yet more cleavage. She wanted Dess to look at her again the way she'd looked at her over dinner. Like she wanted to eat her. *Oh please*, she thought hopefully, *eat me up as though I'm the last thing there is between you and starvation!*

But as much as she wanted to make love with Dess, she wanted so much more. She wanted all of Dess. Wanted her secrets, her joys, her tears, her laughter, her fears—all of it. She wanted them to have a future together, but she was realistic enough to know that wasn't going to happen until Dess fully trusted her. There were still things, she felt, that Dess wasn't telling her.

Dess and Maggie bounded through the door, Maggie immediately marching up to her as if to tell her all about their walk.

"Did you have fun on your walk?" Erika said to the dog, patting its smooth head.

"Wow," Dess said, looking around appreciatively. "Candles and wine. I'm impressed."

Erika hit the play switch on her iPod docking station, then handed Dess a glass of wine. Tracy Chapman began singing about a fast car. "If I'm not mistaken, you promised me a dance."

Dess set down her glass of wine. There was a hint of a question in her eyes, but there was no hesitation in the beckoning gesture she made with her hand. Erika wanted to run into her arms, where she knew she would feel sheltered, as though her heart had found its home. Instead, she walked up to Dess, placed a hand gently on her left hip, and held up her other hand, which Dess quickly clasped. They began to sway together in time to the music, their bodies keeping a respectable distance apart, as though they were strangers.

Ha, that's a laugh, Erika thought. Only a few hours ago they'd been making out like a couple of teenagers, fitting together on the floor like the pieces of a puzzle slotting into place. They'd gotten to first base, she supposed. Or was feeling up Dess second base? Na, she thought, probably just first base. Second base definitely would have entailed a little bit of nudity. The thought made her gasp out loud.

"You okay?"

"I'm good. More than good. Except I really need to hold you closer."

Dess stepped closer. "You only needed to ask, you know."

"Hmm, that simple, is it?" Erika purred. If that were true, she had plenty of things she wanted to ask Dess. Like asking her to get down on her knees, for one. Taking off all her clothes for another. *Oh God, stop it! She wants to go slow, remember?*

"You're burning up," Dess whispered. "Are you sure you're okay?"

"A little overheated, that's all. Okay, more like a little overexcited."

"Then maybe we should take a little break." She led Erika by the hand to the sofa, where they collected their glasses of wine.

Taking a break was the last thing Erika wanted, but it was probably the wise thing to do. Any minute now, she was going to explode.

"Can we talk?" Dess asked, her eyes hard to read in the low light.

"Of course. I'd love to talk." *And as soon as I make love to you about fifteen times, we can talk all you want.*

"Earlier," Dess said, the seriousness in her voice immediately sobering Erika, "you asked me the real reason why I was scared to get serious about you. About us."

"Yes?" Erika's heart pounded like steel against an anvil. A part of her was afraid to know the answer.

"I…" Dess took a slow sip of her wine first. "I need to be sure this isn't just a fling for you. Because I don't want this to be only about sex."

"Oh, sweetheart." Erika took Dess's hands in hers. "Of course it's not a fling. I don't do flings. And even if I did, I would never waste a fling on you."

Dess's eyebrows rose adorably. "You wouldn't?"

"Of course I would. I mean…no, that's not right. I wouldn't. Waste it, I mean. Because I'd love to…you know, but not in a way that…oh shit, I'm making this worse, aren't I?"

Dess threw her head back and laughed. *Oh, that neck*, Erika thought with a fresh wave of desire. *So soft, so smooth, and the sexy way it curves. I want to kiss that. Now!*

Instead, she quickly gathered herself. "What I really mean to say is that sex with you would be like the cherry on an ice cream sundae. And what I want is the whole sundae."

Dess swallowed visibly, all traces of laughter gone. "I've never had a good relationship. I don't even know if I know how. Honestly? Relationships scare the shit out of me."

"They scare me too. I'm no expert at them, but I'm not afraid to fail."

"I think I am," Dess whispered. "But I don't want to be."

Erika took her into her arms and rocked her gently, and for a long time they didn't speak, just listened to the quiet guitar picking of Jesse Cook on the iPod. Erika kissed Dess's forehead, ran her fingers through the soft stands of her hair, wanting to promise a litany of things. She'd promise her the world right now. But Dess didn't need her promises. Dess needed time to see that her actions meant more than words.

"You know that I was hurt before," Dess finally continued. "And I don't know if it's fair to blame everything on Dayna, but I don't want to start something with someone who might leave me again when the chips are down. That's what I truly fear."

"Dess—"

"No, let me finish, please. I'm cancer-free now, but there are no guarantees."

"Of course there aren't. There never are. With anything."

"Erika—"

"No, Dess. Wait." She tilted Dess's chin up so they could look into each other's eyes. "I'm not a quitter. I would *never* do that to you. I play for keeps, okay?"

A tear trickled down Dess's cheek. Tenderly, Erika wiped it away. Then she pressed her lips to Dess's because she needed that connection between them. Trust was going to take time, she reminded herself. But a kiss was a damned good start.

She was about to pull away when Dess surprised her by throwing her arms around her neck and pulling her closer. She pressed her body into Erika's, pressed her mouth harder into hers and instantly deepened their kiss until they were both gasping for air.

"If you keep kissing me like that," Erika said hoarsely, "I can't be responsible for my actions."

She could feel Dess smiling against her cheek. "Feeling a little animalistic?"

"Oh, if you only knew," Erika said, silently acknowledging to herself that she would remain in a tangle of pleasure-pain for as long as she was around Dess. There was no release from this. Even if Dess were to make her come six times right now, she'd never get her out of her blood, never be liberated from her insatiable desire for her.

"Then maybe we should settle things down with another dance." Dess held out her hand. "I love this Uncle Kracker song."

Erika smiled. The song was exactly the way she felt about Dess, and she knew in that moment that she was in love. *You make me smile*, Erika began to sing along, and they laughed as they moved into each other's arms.

CHAPTER FOURTEEN

Dess and Erika danced to another three or four songs, never stopping their rhythm even as they fell into a romantic kiss every verse or so. Dess had pondered many times the question of whether there was a heaven after death. And while she was no closer to an answer, she knew that if there was, she wanted it to feel exactly this way.

"Penny for your thoughts," Erika whispered against her.

"Hell, I'm holding out for at least a dollar."

Erika squeezed her. "You drive a hard bargain, lady. Especially since you're the one with all the money."

Dess feigned surprised horror. "Oh no. You're not a gold digger, are you? My mother warned me about those."

Erika's laughter made Dess smile. "Tell me you didn't spot my shovel and hard hat in the closet?"

"Come to think of it—"

Erika swatted her ass lightly. "Keep it up and I'm going to spank you for real. And with your pants pulled down."

A tingle swept up Dess's thighs. Imagining Erika sliding her pants down her legs, caressing her way back up... It was almost too much, and Dess stumbled a little.

"Whoa, I've got you, baby."

They tightened their hold on each other, and Erika bent her head to kiss Dess. *Oh*, Dess thought, *I could kiss these lips for hours*. It was like a guilty pleasure, except there was nothing to feel guilty about. Dess happily let the kiss go on and on, losing herself in the thrill of it until all sense of time and place vanished. The kiss only stopped when Erika pulled back to look deeply in her eyes.

"Do you feel safe with me, Dess?"

There was nothing to think about. She did feel safe with Erika, and that was no small thing. She felt strong with Erika too. "Yes. I do. More than you know."

Erika stroked her cheek, her jaw, her eyes never leaving Dess's. "Then come to bed with me."

Dess gasped. A low thrum at the base of her spine, in her belly, had commenced at Erika's bold suggestion. "This," she answered in a trembling voice, "is going to change everything."

"I know. But with you, I want everything to change."

Dess placed her hand in Erika's and let herself be guided to the bed. Giving up control had never felt so easy, so right. For once, she didn't question her next move, didn't analyze the crap out of it. Whatever happened now was going to be exactly the right thing.

Erika sat on the edge of the bed, her eyes roaming ravenously over Dess as she stood, legs apart, before her.

In a voice thick with lust, Erika said, "Take your clothes off."

Dess shed her blouse first, slowly sliding it from her shoulders, letting it billow to the floor like a parachute. Her eyes never left Erika's face, and she smiled at the slight tremble in Erika's jaw. And at the rapid rise and fall of Erika's chest. Knowing she was turning Erika on only heightened her own desire. She wanted Erika to touch her. Anywhere. Everywhere. She needed Erika to touch her. But only Erika's eyes caressed her as she unclasped her bra and let it too fall to the floor.

"Oh, my," Erika muttered on an exhalation.

"More?" Dess teased.

"Oh God," Erika moaned. "I might not survive it, but yes. Please."

Dess released the button on her capri pants, then the zipper. She'd never felt so desired, so appreciated, as she caught a flash of Erika's tongue escaping her mouth, as if it were impatient to get to work. *Oh, yes,* Dess thought. *I want that tongue, those lips all over me. I want her mouth to suck me, to lick me, to make me come.* Her legs trembling, she slipped the cotton pants down her hips and to the floor, where she kicked them away. Only her panties remained.

"Goddamn, you're beautiful," Erika breathed, her eyes again sliding over Dess like a blanket. "But, um, sweetheart?"

"Yes?"

"You forgot something."

Dess laughed and said in a teasing voice, "If you want my underwear off me, you're going to have to do it yourself."

Erika leapt from the side of the bed and knelt before Dess, her face inches from Dess's belly as nimble hands reached out and carefully slid the underwear down her hips and thighs. Dess held her breath, ready to burst as she waited for Erika to touch her.

"You're so, so beautiful," Erika whispered in a voice full of awe.

Then touch me.

Erika reached for her ass, cupping each cheek firmly, as her mouth kissed each hip, each thigh, and Dess wanted to collapse into a heap. She was so wet, her desire a thundering pulse between her legs. All she wanted now was to experience the joy she knew Erika would give her, followed by its sweet, mind-blowing, violent release.

The first touch of Erika's tongue sent a laser beam up and down her spine. She clutched two fistfuls of Erika's hair, pulled gently on the silky waves as confirmation resonated that this was really happening, that this gorgeous young woman was actually kneeling before her, pleasuring her with her mouth. Her legs shook, and they threatened to collapse under Erika's oral ministrations.

"My...legs," Dess sputtered, pleasure rocketing up into her belly.

Erika guided her to the bed, the momentary absence of her mouth nearly making Dess beg for its return. Erika settled her on the edge of the bed, and, still on her knees, kissed and nipped her inner thighs.

"Oh," Dess breathed. "Please, baby." *Okay, I'm begging now, but I don't care.* "I need you. I need...your...mouth...on me."

It was pure liquid pleasure as Erika's tongue circled her clit, then delivered the quick hard strokes that Dess craved, tossing her like a little boat in a thrashing sea. Every nerve ending ignited, every sense was thrown into overdrive. And when Erika plunged two fingers inside her, Dess was a goner. Synchronized perfectly, the strokes launched a wave of ecstasy that began in her curled toes and rumbled its way up her legs, like a massive tsunami overpowering everything in its path. *Oh, yes*, Dess thought, *I am going to be selfish, dammit. I am going to come over and over again. I don't want this to stop. Ever.*

She reached down and pulled Erika's mouth harder against her, pushed her hips higher to accept Erika's fingers more deeply. "Oh God," she cried out. "I'm coming, baby. Oh, I'm coming so hard." The shudders roared through her body with a crushing force. She rode the sweet, powerful, undulating waves like a surfer. And Erika, God love her, didn't stop for a single second. Her tongue kept flicking, kept stroking, kept pushing her back to the precipice to start the delicious sequence all over again.

"Oh, Erika," Dess rasped. "Honey, you're going to kill me with kindness."

"Good," Erika muttered against her thigh. "That's my plan. And just so you know, I'm not stopping until you come at least three more times."

Her mouth resumed its glorious pursuit, and Dess welcomed the gathering of another volcanic orgasm. She was melting from the inside out. She would be a puddle on the floor before this was all over. But God, she couldn't stop. She was giving her body completely over to this woman as pleasure consumed her like an out-of-control wildfire. She let herself be possessed by Erika and her spectacularly talented mouth and fingers. God, she loved the way this woman made her feel. That was the truth, even if her voice refused to give life to the words.

Erika's fingers remained inside Dess, even as she let Dess pull her up so they could kiss.

"You're wonderful at this," Dess purred, the glow of orgasms and happy exertion leaving her sleepy and spent. She pelted Erika's face with more kisses. "Do you know how wonderful you are?"

"Only with you, sweetheart. Only with you."

Erika's fingers began moving inside her again, and instantly Dess grew hard and wet. She was ravenous with Erika—a horny, libido-driven teenager who couldn't get enough sex, who couldn't say no. And it set her free. For the first time in decades, she was untethered from her fears, her cares, her worries. What it all meant for her, for them, for their summer tour, for after their summer tour, she would think about later. Much later. Right now she wanted to come again, and she moaned her acquiescence. Yes, her moan said, fuck me good.

And Erika did. Her fingers plunged hard inside Dess and her mouth devoured her breasts, her nipples. Dess was quick this time, rocking against Erika as the violence of her orgasm pulverized her. She opened her eyes to a self-satisfied grin.

"You're...pretty pleased with yourself," Dess said, smiling through her breathlessness.

"No, sweetheart. I'm pleased with *you*. You're a tiger in bed."

Dess squirmed, embarrassed. "I'm not normally...I mean, I didn't...I haven't..."

"Stop trying to apologize. Or justify. I love it. And I love you." Devotion and conviction rose in Erika's eyes. She wasn't lying.

Dess swallowed hard against the tide of emotion. She cared for Erika too, but it wasn't that simple. Love was much more than the dopamine-saturated high she got whenever she was around Erika. And it was certainly much more than the great sex they were sharing. And *great* was an understatement!

Dess rolled herself on top of Erika and kissed her neck, her luscious throat that sang directly to the heavens. She wanted to do all the things to Erika that Erika had done to her. And more. Slowly she worked her way down, feeling Erika tense in anticipation. Her skin quivered wherever Dess touched her.

Erika moaned. "I want you so badly, Dess."

"And I want you, darling."

"I'm not a patient woman, just so you know."

Dess smiled against her stomach. "I'll remember that."

"No. Really. I mean it."

Erika gently pushed her down, down, down, until Dess was nestled between her thighs. Her center rose up to meet Dess's mouth, not waiting, and her need shot fresh arousal through Dess. With her mouth and her tongue, she worked the velvety moist flesh as though it were the most delectable, sweetest fruit she'd ever tasted. Erika pushed into her, and Dess devoured her with a fervor and boldness she'd not shown before in making love to anyone. She nearly came herself when Erika bucked against her and screamed her name. "Oh, yes, baby, I've got you," Dess answered soothingly and slid her way up Erika's body. They moved against each other, whispering dirty things to each other, nipping each other's flesh, leaving little bruises. Heat and friction and tension fused them together in a possessive dance that said yes, they belonged together. They rocked harder and harder together, increasing the friction until they both exploded in a shattering orgasm.

Exhausted, sweat-slicked, Dess moved off Erika and lay beside her. They both panted as if they'd completed a marathon.

"Oh my God," Erika said. "That was incredible."

Dess giggled wearily. "I don't know what we're going to do for an encore, but I think it's going to have to wait."

In seconds they were asleep, limp noodles curled in each other's arms.

* * *

It was after five in the morning when Erika slid her hand over Dess's naked thigh, wanting to wake her but not wanting to be obvious about it. She wanted Dess over and over again. Even her dreams during their scant hours of sleep had been about making love to Dess.

She'd been thrilled and surprised by Dess's eagerness in bed. Each time they'd made love, they'd only grown hungrier for each other. And Erika knew exactly why. It was because they were in love, because only love made sex this good. Even if Dess couldn't say the words, it was okay. Erika wouldn't rush her. She would be patient with Dess, because she loved her. And because Dess was worth it.

Dess shifted against her, awakening with Erika's bold caresses that had moved to the soft skin inside her thigh. Erika felt Dess's breathing increase and moved her hand higher to cup Dess between her legs. She was greeted by velvety moistness.

"Oh," Dess gasped. "Oh, yes."

"Yes, what?" Erika teased, knowing she was being evil.

"Make love to me. Please."

Erika kissed her on the mouth, flicking her tongue against her lips, enjoying the feel of her body coming alive beneath her fingers. Dess was wet and quivering, moving against her hand. Erika palmed her in a circular motion, muffling her moans with more hot kisses. Fingers pushed inside, and she met the slick softness there with rapid strokes until Dess shuddered and quaked and groaned her name. God, how she loved the sound of her name on Dess's lips as she spent herself.

"One of these days," Dess said, "we're going to have to get out of this bed."

"Hmm, I suppose you're right. Unless we can teach Maggie to bring us food."

"Ha. You're asking a Lab to bring food?"

"Oh, right. What am I thinking? Besides, I don't need food. I'll just eat you instead."

Dess laughed, her eyes gleaming with mischief in the light of dawn. "Come here, you."

Erika let Dess climb on top of her, let her playfully restrain her hands by the wrists.

"Now I've got you where I want you," Dess breathed.

"Fine. I give up. Have your way with me." *I'm yours, Dess Hampton. All yours.* In a flash, she knew she would do anything Dess asked her. Go anywhere, say anything, be anything. *As long as she keeps loving me.*

Her thoughts quickly dissolved in the tumult that Dess's fingers were causing. She squeezed her eyes shut and surrendered to the orgasm bearing down on her like a freight train.

CHAPTER FIFTEEN

It took no small effort to get out of bed, shower and eat, then feed and walk Maggie. Afterwards, Erika laughingly serenaded Dess with "Afternoon Delight," and they made love again.

"You're unstoppable," Dess said, but she wasn't complaining. She loved that Erika couldn't stop wanting her. Her desire, carnal but full of love and tenderness too, was a gift that made Dess feel more alive and vibrant than she'd ever felt. Even singing to tens of thousands of hysterical fans couldn't come close, because that stuff wasn't real. This sure was.

Erika stroked her cheek tenderly. "And you're incredible. And lovely. And so sexy."

"Hmm, does that mean we're having a stay-at-home date again tonight? That may or may not involve us getting out of bed?"

"Well," Erika said, nuzzling her neck and planting tiny kisses. "I'd always vote for that kind of date with you. But actually, do you know what I really want to do with you tonight?"

Dess could only imagine, and she grew wet at the visions that began rampaging through her mind. "Tell me," she said throatily.

Erika cupped Dess's breast and laughingly said, "Okay, I want to do all those things you're imagining too. Especially before Sloane returns tomorrow."

"But?" Dess's heart began to sink a little.

"But nothing, sweetheart. Except that I want to go onstage with you tonight. Just the two of us. And only for fifteen minutes or so."

"What? Where?"

"My friend Laurie owns a coffee house in the gay district. It's open mic night tonight."

"But wouldn't you rather stay here and…you know?" Dess grinned, her hand creeping down to Erika's stomach. Then lower. But Erika's eyes were dancing at the prospect of performing as a duo, and Dess knew she would be hard to dissuade.

"Of course I would. But I want to share you with the world. I want to be on a stage with the woman I want to be with more than anyone else in the world." Erika captured her hand to still it. "I want to look at you as I sing, knowing the words are only for you. I want to celebrate the way we feel about each other doing what I love doing the most." Erika kissed her on the mouth. "Well, besides pleasuring you."

The love sparkling in Erika's eyes stalled Dess's heart. *Oh God, she's so in love with me. And I can't say no to her.* "Okay, let's do it. But just two or three songs, all right?"

Erika wrapped her leg around Dess's middle. "You have plans for me afterwards?"

"You could say that," Dess teased, cupping her. Erika nipped her finger, then drew it into her mouth and began slowly sucking it. Dess gasped at the sight of her lover fellating her finger, and it charged her desire all over again. "Keep that up and we'll never get out of here."

"I wouldn't be tempted if you weren't so damned hot. But if we're going to perform tonight, I guess we better figure out which songs to do."

"Can we do some dirty ones?"

Erika kissed her on the chin. "We can do anything you want. Anytime."

"I plan to take you up on that."

"I'd be very disappointed if you didn't."

* * *

Laurie Skilling had been a mentor to Erika in her early singing years, when she was struggling to be heard as a singer at night and taking college courses during the day. Laurie was more than a mentor; she was a mother figure who'd offered Erika and other college students like her a place of safety and encouragement. She was, as she described herself, a big ol' butch, who, if she'd had a daughter, would have wanted it to be Erika. She always gave her an open mic at the café and helped her find paying gigs. Erika remembered the first time she'd walked in, her battered guitar slung over her shoulder, her confidence about the size of a pea. Laurie didn't even ask if she could sing before she signed her up for a time slot, gave her a hug, then told the crowd that if anybody gave the kid a hard time, they'd have to deal with *her*.

Their hug was long and meaningful, then Laurie moved to hug Dess...well, Dora...just as intensely.

"You look familiar, honey." Laurie's eyes traveled over Dess like she was studying an exotic creature. "Your eyes. Something about your eyes. Where have I seen you before?"

Dess patted her wig in a self-conscious fashion, and Erika instinctively stepped in front of her. "All right. You found us out. She's really Kelly Clarkson in disguise, wanting to slum it at your café."

Laurie frowned, then broke into a laugh so deep it was a roar that jiggled her over-sized belly. "You got me there, kid. Kelly, welcome to my dump. Now get your asses up there and knock the shit out of the crowd like I know you're going to."

"Whew, that was close," Dess whispered, unpacking her guitar from its case backstage.

"It's okay. Laurie's one of the good ones. Even if you told her who you were, she wouldn't tell anybody." Erika captured Dess's eyes with her own. "But it's for you to tell, not me."

"Thank you for that." Dess leaned in and kissed her on the mouth, and Erika wanted to scoop her up and find the nearest dark corner.

"You keep kissing me like that," Erika whispered, "and we'll never get on stage."

Dess shrugged, pitched a smile at her. "Okay by me."

"Nice try, but you're not getting out of this so easily. Next to being in bed, the stage is where I love spending time with you."

Something deep stirred inside Erika whenever she and Dess performed on a stage together. It was like a switch turning on. A switch that turned her world from black and white to full color. There was magic present, and it was because of Dess. Dess possessed such a quiet, calm charisma. A confidence that an earthquake couldn't dislodge. Her playing was smooth as butter too, and just knowing she was there, this woman who'd performed in front of crowds a hundred times this size, filled Erika with a fearlessness she felt she could ride to the very top.

"Ready for 'Smile'?" Erika said, and Dess nodded.

They stepped onto the stage, which felt not much bigger than a postage stamp. Dess plugged her guitar into an amp. Erika stepped behind the keyboards, and they waited for Laurie to take the microphone and introduce them. The crowd, Erika was happy to see, was large for the small venue. Every table was filled and a few people stood as well, but few were paying them any attention.

"Listen up, folks," Laurie announced in her no-nonsense way. "You're in for a real special treat tonight! And you're gonna want to remember this night and this woman's name, trust me. Put your hands together for my good friend Erika Alvarez and her accompanist, Dora Hessler!"

The reception was polite but tepid, and that was okay with Erika. She was here, with Dess—the woman she loved—doing the thing she loved doing most with Dess. Well, okay, the second best thing she loved doing with Dess.

"Thanks, everyone," Erika said into the mic perched on the keyboard. "Thanks very much. It's a real pleasure to be here and to spend some time with y'all." She gave them a playful wink. "We're going to start things off with a little 'Smile.'"

She played the opening notes, keeping the beat jaunty. Dess came in with the acoustic guitar after the intro, and Erika's heart soared. Dess did make her smile like the sun, made her feel all the crazy things the song talked about. She hoped with all her being that Dess felt the same way about her. She was pretty certain in the way Dess touched her that she did, but she ached for her to say the words. She smiled at Dess, was rewarded with a grin. She scanned the audience. Heads began turning in their direction. Conversations stopped. The crowd was right where she wanted them—attentive, curious, on the edge of delightful discovery. It was intoxicating playing to an audience that had never heard them before and seeing folks swing from indifference to exuberant appreciation. Eclipsing their expectations provided a high like little else.

The song ended, and the crowd cheered loudly, almost endlessly. A few wolf whistles pierced the air.

"Well, thank you very much," Erika said into the microphone. She never took the applause and appreciation for granted. "Something tells me you liked that one, hmm?"

"Yeah, baby!" a woman yelled. "Give us more!"

Erika laughed. "All right. How about I give you something a little sweet?"

She started into "How Sweet It Is," but not the fast tempo Motown version. This one she slowed down to a sultry, sexy, bluesy pace. She sang the words to Dess, watching her deftly move her fingers along the fretboard and sway her body to the beat. *Oh, that body*, Erika thought, remembering the feel of her soft skin beneath her fingers, the taut muscles, the curves. Already she was beginning to memorize everything about Dess's body, about what Dess liked, what made her crazy with desire, what she begged for.

Dess returned her gaze, smiled at her, and Erika's heart lifted to the ceiling. It was incredible, unfathomable, that one woman's smile could make her feel as though the tumultuous seas of her life had calmed, as though all her roads converged in one direction. It was as though all the love and affection her parents had withheld from her throughout her life now coalesced in a fierce desire to shower Dess with all her love. The knowledge that she possessed so much love—a revelation, really—empowered her to share it.

"And now," she announced after a consenting nod from Dess, "a very special song that we've never performed before. It's called 'The Song in My Heart.'"

Dess played the slow, opening riff. Erika sang and stroked the keys to begin the verse, closing her eyes and singing with every ounce of love, desire, companionship and happiness she felt with

Dess. It was perfection—her voice, the guitar and keyboards, the lyrics, the joyful melody—the way it all came together. And the audience knew it too. After a moment of stunned silence, they clapped and hooted and demanded more.

"Sorry," Erika told them. "Laurie was very firm with us that three songs was it, and you all know how she can be."

There was a collective groan, but it was the kind that said they were disappointed but accepting. There were other acts lined up behind the stage, ready to perform. And besides, Erika couldn't wait to get Dess back to her apartment again, fantasies of stand-up sex in the shower giving her fresh motivation to get moving.

"*That* is a surefire hit," Laurie told them near the back door.

Erika kissed her on the cheek. "I sure hope you're right, Laur." *Hit or not*, she thought, *it's our song. Mine and Dess's. And it's perfect.*

"I am right." Laurie leaned closer. "Am I also right in thinking you got a little somethin' goin' on with Miss Hessler?"

Erika winked. "Yeah, you'd be right about that. And it's more than a little something."

"Good for you. And you owe me a longer visit. Come by when you can stay, and we'll catch up."

"Thanks for tonight. And I will, I promise."

"Yeah, yeah." Laurie was shaking her head, unconvinced. "That's what they all say on their way to fame and fortune."

After stuffing Dess's guitar case into the back seat, Erika grabbed Dess's wrist and spun her around.

Dess grinned slyly. "What?"

"Have I told you lately how sexy you are?"

"No, it's been a couple of hours. I was wondering when you were going to get around to it again."

"Well, you…are…one…*hell* of a sexy woman." Erika breathed in her scent, let it fill her lungs. Then her heart.

"Not as sexy as you, my dear. Not even close. Come here." Dess kissed her, flinging her arms around her neck, and Erika waited for the words she knew weren't coming.

That's okay, Dess, she thought. *I have you. And that's enough.*

CHAPTER SIXTEEN

Sloane had a penchant for making an entrance. She flung the apartment door open and thrust out two fistfuls of flowers—daisies in one hand, roses in the other. "For my two lovely ladies!"

"And to what do we owe this?" Dess asked, kissing her best friend on the cheek and accepting the flowers.

"For so graciously lending me out to Melissa." Skinny as a fence post and shaggy haired, Sloane was looking every bit the part of rocker chick. "She says hi, by the way, asked how you were doing."

Dess entered Erika's tiny kitchen in search of two flower vases, Sloane behind her. She settled for a couple of chipped coffee mugs and filled them with water. "I hope you didn't tell her about Dora Hessler."

"Nope. But I did tell her about Erika. Where is she, anyway?"

"Taking Maggie for an epic walk. Want some coffee? I was just going to make some."

"Sure. You look right at home in Erika's kitchen."

Dess filled the kettle and plugged it in, then spooned some ground coffee into the French press.

"Holy shit," Sloane proclaimed, dropping loudly into a chair at the tiny table for two.

"What?" Dess pulled out two more coffee mugs.

"You're sleeping with her."

Dess refused to answer what hadn't been a question.

A slow smile spread across Sloane's face, one that said, "You can't fool me, sister."

"It's more than that, isn't it?" Sloane suggested.

"What?"

"The sex! I can see all over your face that you're having the time of your life in bed with her. But you're falling for her too, just like I thought."

"Okay, wait. You're jumping to conclusions."

"What? You're saying I'm wrong that it's not the best sex you've ever had?"

Dess's face burned, and she got up to pour the boiling water into the coffee press. Yes, it was the best sex she'd ever had. Hands down. But as for the rest...

"C'mon, spill the deets, Dessy!"

The heat in her face, in her chest, intensified. "I will not!"

Sloane sighed, feigning disappointment. "Fine. But at least admit Erika's a hottie in bed."

Hands defiantly on her hips, Dess tried to glower at her friend, but it was useless against the smile that refused to be smothered. "All right, yes," she whispered, as though Erika were lurking outside the kitchen.

"Ha, I knew it."

Dess filled their mugs and brought them to the table.

"And the other?" Sloane prompted.

Dess sat down, stirred cream and sugar into her mug. "What other?"

"That you're happy as hell and in love with each other."

Dess frowned. Erika was in love with her, that part was true. But she wasn't sure yet how she felt about Erika. Other than happy. And insanely satisfied in bed. "I'm not so sure yet I would describe it that way."

"What do you mean you aren't sure? You look happy, Dess. Happier than I've ever seen you. And I know you love Erika."

"It's not that simple."

Sloane shook her head, her blue eyes stormy. "It could be that simple if you'd let it. Can't you let yourself be happy for once without fearing the bottom's going to fall out?"

"Oh, Sloane."

"Don't 'oh, Sloane' me. I'm serious. Why won't you let yourself be happy?"

It was a good question, but her answers were good too. She thought of trying to evade the question, but Sloane was a pit bull. "I told you a long time ago I was never going to get into a relationship with anybody in the music business again, and I meant it."

"Oh, come on, Dayna's a snake. There's lots of people in this business who are nothing like Dayna. And on the flip side, there are a lot of snakes out there who *aren't* in the business."

"True, but there's so much pressure in this business, so many distractions. It's a completely unconventional and difficult way of trying to maintain a relationship. It's almost impossible. And Erika is on the way up, you know that. You knew that before I did. She's going places, and I'm not. The only place I want to go when this little tour is done is home."

Sloane sipped her black coffee before she spoke again. "I'm hearing a lot of reasons you've rationalized in your head. A lot of after-the-fact reasons."

Their conversations were often like this, Sloane throwing out little barbs that required Dess to dig deeper. "What do you mean 'after-the-fact reasons'?"

"See, here's how I see it."

Oh Lord, Dess thought.

"You started caring for Erika a while back. Started feeling attracted to her too. Any dummy could have seen that. You two were like two freight trains on the same track, headed straight for each other."

Dess silently laughed at the metaphor. Sloane wasn't book smart, wasn't sophisticated, but she was one of the sharpest, wisest people Dess knew.

"You had great sex," Sloane continued. "Hot, I'm-ruined-for-anybody-else sex. The kind of sex that—"

"All right, all right. I get the picture."

Sloane grinned. She loved sex and thought everybody should be getting hot sex. As much as humanly possible. "But a funny thing happened on the way to all that great sex."

She knew Sloane wouldn't continue until she asked, "What's that?"

"You fell in love, Dess. L-O-V-E. That's the part that scares the shit out of you. And that's when you started rationalizing why it could never work between you two. It's your little shield, so you won't get hurt."

Heat rose to her cheeks again, but for a different reason this time. Sloane was wrong. She wasn't rationalizing as some kind of defense mechanism. All of her reasons were true, and she had to be careful. Not just with her heart, but with her money too. There were tons of people out there who would be quick to use her. Not Erika, but others for sure. She was being prudent. Yes, that was it.

"I'm being prudent," she said, jutting her chin out defiantly. "I'm taking my time with this, that's all."

Sloane stood up, drained her cup and set it on the counter. "You're right. Careful is good. And even though that girl is madly in love with you, you should keep using her for all that great booty for as long as you can. Hell, that's what I'd do. Get laid as much as possible. Three, four times a day, matter of fact. And when the tour's done, you can go back to Chicago and to your guitars and your books and your dog. That sounds like a spectacular plan."

Sloane marched out, and Dess wanted to chase her down and beat her.

* * *

"Are you sure Sloane's not going to walk into the apartment any minute and hear us *in flagrante delicto*?" Part of Erika hoped Sloane would do exactly that. She wanted the world to know that she loved Dess, that they were in a relationship and that they shared a fantastic time in bed. If she could shout it from the rooftops, she would.

Dess stripped off the last of her clothes and crawled into bed next to Erika. "She said not to expect her back tonight, that she has plans to get lucky at that gay dance club you tried to take me to the other night."

Erika slid a hand up and down Dess's thigh. "I can't help it if I want to dance dirty with you. And for wanting everybody to see me dirty dance with the hottest woman around."

Dess frowned. "You mean hot for a washed-up, forty-one-year-old cancer survivor?"

"No." Erika kissed her neck, the hard points of her collarbone. "I mean the hottest woman in the city. In the state. In the whole wide world." She kissed the tender flesh of Dess's throat. "And you're not washed up. Far from it. You're the woman I love, and I'd want you whether you're a cancer survivor or just a plain old survivor like the rest of us." *We all have battle scars*, Erika thought, *and we're all survivors of something or other*.

"Fine. But I'm still a cougar, dating you."

Erika grinned, loving the idea of being with an older woman. The difference in their ages didn't bother her in the least. If anything, it was a turn-on. There was an inner and outer beauty about Dess that came with life's experiences, and she had the kind of poise and wisdom seldom possessed by women under thirty. As for the sex, Dess simply couldn't be matched in her sensuality. She was a woman who, once she trusted and let herself go, knew exactly what she wanted in bed. And knew how to give as good as she got.

"Sweetheart, I love that you're older than me. In fact, I'd even love you if you were seventy."

Dess giggled. "Now that's a bit extreme. You're very funny."

"Not funny at all." Erika held her with her eyes. "I mean every word." *God, I would give you the world, Dess. All you'd have to do is ask.*

Dess quickly closed up, shutting down as usual once the conversation turned serious. She was good at changing the subject, at dialing things back between them when talk turned to love or a future. Well, Erika had at least one surefire way to make Dess open up and let her in.

She kissed Dess on the mouth, her tongue parting Dess's lips and slipping inside even as her hand dove between Dess's legs. Dess moaned as Erika palmed her, dancing her fingers around her slick opening, teasing, circling, rubbing, pushing inside a fraction of an inch before retreating again. It drove Dess nuts. She groaned and moved her hips in a hungry demand for Erika to enter her, but Erika resisted. "I want to fuck you," she told Dess. "I want to fuck you with my mouth. I want to suck your clit, I want my tongue inside you. Would you like that, baby? Would you like me to fuck you with my mouth?"

"Oh my God," Dess groaned, her breath coming short and hard. "Oh yes, yes, please."

"Please what?" Erika moved her hand harder, faster.

"Please...fuck me...with...your mouth."

Erika sucked the soft skin of Dess's throat on her way down, stopping briefly at her breasts, her stomach, to suck the quivering flesh. With abandon, she took Dess's clit into her mouth and sucked it, thrusting her fingers inside her, possessing her. She tongued Dess's clit frenetically, her fingers matching the rhythm. Harder, she mashed her face and fingers into Dess until Dess screamed her name, her body bucking in a wild orgasm that seemed to go on for several minutes. Erika held her tightly, wanting nothing more than to go at it again. She couldn't get enough of pleasuring Dess, of enjoying her body.

Dess had stilled beside her. She was staring up at the dark ceiling.

"Sweetie, what's wrong?" Erika whispered. She hated when Dess blanked out on her emotionally.

"What makes you think anything's wrong?"

"I know you, Dess. And I can tell when something's on your mind."

Dess smiled benignly. "There's almost always something on my mind, don't you know that? Especially after you've made me come like that."

Erika studied her. She knew the unspoken things that roiled in Dess's mind. "Well," she finally said in a voice she hoped was full of understanding. "Those things that are on your mind, that give you pause? It's okay, you know. I know you have good reasons to...pause. And I'm not worried. And I want you to take as much time as you need to explore your feelings, and I want you to not be afraid to ask anything of me that you might need. Okay?"

"You're the most special woman I've ever known," Dess said, staring at her with eyes that to Erika were maddeningly full of love, love that she couldn't bring herself to acknowledge. To believe.

Erika snuggled closer. "Thank you for saying that. But I'd really rather you showed me."

"Oh, I'll show you, all right." Dess rolled on top of her, pushing a thigh between her legs. "I'm going to show you right now."

CHAPTER SEVENTEEN

It was time to get back to work, something Dess viewed as a godsend. She even welcomed the mundane ride along the interstate towing their "home" behind them as they made their way to another festival. This time it was Madison, Wisconsin—a day's drive from Minneapolis.

Getting back to work meant getting back to predictable footing for Dess. It meant less time to question her every action, her every thought, where Erika was concerned. She was tired of the inordinate amount of introspection of the last few days. Was exhausted from asking herself exactly how much she cared for Erika, if she needed her as much as she feared, if the little skips her heart made meant she was in love with her.

There were so many good reasons why being in love with Erika was not a good idea, Dess thought, even as she reminded herself that love transcended reason and logical deduction. That was the thing about love, she thought with frustration. The good part was that it made you lose your mind. But that was also the bad part.

With schedules, practice sessions and performances lined up for almost every waking moment while they were in Madison, there would be new distance between them—a solid obstacle to their cocoon of intimacy. They'd even agreed, for Sloane's sake, not to share the double bed in the trailer and to keep the sleeping arrangements as they had been. Erika was displeased, but to Dess, the space was another chance to give her some perspective on Erika and on where their relationship was heading.

The word "relationship" burned at the back of her throat. It was such a foreign concept to her. She lazily wrapped an arm around Maggie, with whom she was sharing the back seat of the truck while Sloane and Erika sat up front singing along to a pop song on the radio. Dess had sworn after Dayna and after her horrifying battle with cancer that she wouldn't get involved with anyone again. It wasn't worth the possibility of waking up one day and discovering that your partner had lied when she said she loved you. Had lied when she said she was in it for the long haul. Dess would never allow herself to be that vulnerable, that trusting, again. She could rely on herself, on family, on Sloane and even on Maggie. But that was it.

Oh God, Dess thought helplessly. *I don't want to hurt you, Erika, but I don't know what to do.* She was afraid of her feelings for Erika, of how deep they ran. She didn't want to be in love with a woman so much younger, who still had her whole career in front of her and who stood on the verge of greatness. Most of all, she didn't want to be in love with a woman who was going to leave her one day. Oh, Erika could swear up and down that she would never do that to Dess. But someone with all that talent and all that drive—well, there was no denying she was on the move. She eventually would want to spread her wings and fly. Dess couldn't blame her. And she sure as hell didn't want to stop her. She couldn't, even if she tried.

She caught Erika looking questioningly at her through the mirror on the back of the visor, and Dess winked to give her a small measure of reassurance. Erika was a real gem, a real keeper under any other circumstances. It was clear that Erika was in love with her, was devoted to her. And Erika could certainly turn her on like no one else. With their raging passion, it was so hard to keep their relationship—or whatever it was—from running away on them. When they were alone together, Dess couldn't restrain herself from ravaging—and being ravaged by—Erika. She closed her eyes for the rest of the journey and envisioned them making love outside, in a field beneath a tree. She loved Erika's breasts, the way they felt beneath her fingertips, the fullness of them in her hands. Firm and soft at the same time, lusciously round and supple. So incredibly responsive. Smiling, she fell asleep for the rest of the journey.

Setting up camp took an hour. After that, they puttered with lighting the fussy little charcoal barbecue Erika had picked up in Minneapolis because, she told them, she was sick of fast food. The grilled chicken breasts and salad were a definite improvement, and Dess gave Erika two thumbs up. After cleaning the dishes and feeding Maggie, Erika insisted on joining her and Maggie for a walk around the camp while Sloane set off to chat with the festival's organizers.

"Am I right," Erika said, "that you seem to be enjoying the stage again?"

"You mean I don't look like I'm going to crap my pants anymore?"

"You never looked like that." Erika reached for her hand, and Dess gave it to her, intertwining their fingers. "But you look more relaxed lately on stage. Happy to be there."

"I am. Playing to these smaller crowds is way more gratifying in most ways than playing to packed stadiums. I'd forgotten what it's like to be able to pick out individual faces, how you can feel each person's energy and enjoyment. And how you know right away if they like—or don't like—something. The connection is more intimate, more immediate." She smiled. "It's a lot more fun than I expected. Or remembered."

They waited for Maggie to sniff near a tree, then to chew on a couple of shoots of grass. "But what about you?" Dess asked. "Is the tour better than you thought? Different?"

"Oh, it's *much* better. And way different than I expected." Erika slipped her a wink, launching an immediate tingle in Dess's center. At the smallest gesture or tiniest hint of their bedroom life, a cascade of pleasurable memories zoomed through Dess's mind, setting her nerve endings on fire.

She took a steadying breath. "Seriously. I mean, is there anything you think we could improve upon or change?" She laughed lightly. "On stage, I mean."

"No. I don't want anything to change. I want it to stay exactly the way it is."

"Ah, but it will change. Which is exactly why I hope you enjoy every minute you're singing to these intimate crowds." She could see that Erika believed her, could sense she was happy hanging on so tightly to these outdoor, intimate performances. But Dess knew the end was drawing nearer for Erika. The press had cottoned onto them, crowds were showing up for their performances in greater numbers, calls and emails were steadily coming in, requesting appearances. They were on a train and it was rapidly picking up speed. And when that kind of momentum started, Dess knew from experience that it couldn't be stopped until it had run its course.

"What if I don't want it to change?" Erika said, a note of desperation in her voice.

They stopped walking and faced each other. "But getting discovered is what you want."

"But that was before…"

She didn't need to finish the sentence. "No. Dreams don't die because someone new comes into your life. You have to go for what you want, because if you don't, you'll be haunted by the what-ifs, by regrets. You have too much talent to settle for anything less than going for it, Erika."

"But you yourself walked away from it so easily. Maybe it's not worth it."

Squeezing Erika's shoulders for effect, she said, "I was ready to walk away. I *needed* to walk away to save myself. But that was me. You can't give up before you've even really tried."

"What if the price is too great?"

"No," Dess answered, refusing to let Erika give in to her doubts. "There is no place for fear if you're going to do this. You have to be all in. It won't work otherwise."

If only I could take my own advice, Dess thought cheerlessly. She wasn't all in with Erika, not with her heart, and that alone doomed their future.

Erika turned from her, immersed in her own private thoughts, while Dess silently dwelled on her own pain. There was always a price to pay for the things you want most.

* * *

Erika glanced nervously at the darkening sky, wishing their set was over and they could get the hell off the stage before the storm struck. They were sitting ducks among all the scaffolding, lights and speakers that were the size of compact cars. The wind had picked up considerably, but the organizers were pushing forward, saying that if they didn't get a couple more sets in, they'd have to refund people's tickets. Refunds equaled financial disaster, Erika knew, and like everyone else, she wanted to be paid.

Dess and Sloane were totally fixated on tuning their instruments. Erika wished she had even a tenth of their confidence and concentration right now. She glanced again at the threatening sky, back at her watch, then at the duo on the stage ahead of them.

"Stop worrying," Sloane shouted over the music and the wind. "We'll be on in a few minutes, do our five songs and get out."

"We could give up our spot," Erika said. "Let the group behind us take it."

"Absolutely not," Sloane said, pointing a finger for emphasis. "You do that, and pretty soon people won't sign you to play these things. We're professionals with a job to do. We don't let people down."

"Well, they should damn well be shutting this whole thing down." A thunderclap in the distance underscored Erika's point.

Sloane shook her head. "Nothing gets in the way of business, darlin'. You should know that by now."

All right, fine, Erika thought helplessly, but she was going to hate every minute of their five songs and question why she was going against her gut feeling every second she was out there. She could be holed up somewhere with Dess, safely braving the storm over a bottle of wine together, and the thought gave her a modicum of hope. *As soon as we're out of here, that's exactly what we'll do.*

Their turn onstage came as wave after wave of low-lying black clouds rolled by so close it seemed they could almost be touched if you reached up high enough. The stage manager gave them the thumbs up. The thought burned in Erika that it wasn't going to be his ass up there getting struck by lightning.

The crowd—what was left of them—recklessly urged them on. Perhaps they were too drunk to care, Erika thought. Or just young, stupid and disillusioned about their mortality. Erika gritted her teeth and smiled through the opening chords of "I Put a Spell on You"—her own angry, edgy, rock-fueled rendition. At the last minute they'd decided to drop the two ballads they'd planned, including her and Dess's song, because there was no way they would be heard over the booming thunder and the cracks of lightning now cutting through the air like sniper fire.

One down, four to go, Erika thought, as they launched into an acoustic version of Linkin Park's "What I've Done." She wasn't feeling the music. She had to shout the lyrics to be heard, which was turning her voice to crap. She glanced at Dess, who'd moved to the far corner of the stage to get closer to a trio of enthusiastic fans who reached up as though they were trying to pluck fruit from a tree. It struck Erika how much Dess was enjoying the moment, rocking out with the fans, staying just beyond their reach but teasing them with her guitar, letting their fingers brush its glossy coat at one point, the guitar a connecting point between them. Her smile was bigger than Erika ever remembered seeing on stage, and it was a beautiful sight that sent her heart soaring. It sparked a glimmer of hope that Dess would continue to perform with her even if she was lucky enough to get bigger venues. Or that she would play alongside her should she get a record deal one day. Why couldn't they continue performing together?

Erika heard it before she saw it. The wind sounded like a truck engine bearing down on them, gathering speed and intensity with each second. She turned in time to see a web of metal scaffolding buckle, then topple in slow motion like a child's Meccano set. A speaker crashed onto its side. Lights dangling from the scaffolding suddenly let go of their hold, shattering on the stage below.

"Dess!" Erika yelled, her heart in her throat. But even as she yelled and tossed the mic away and began to run toward her, she knew she was too late. Metal, wood and plastic had tumbled down on top of Dess in a twisted, sickening heap, swallowing her instantly.

Oh, God, Erika thought as the screech of metal and the roaring wind suddenly came to an eerie silence. "Dess!" *Oh please, please don't let her be hurt. Please, God, anything but that!* Others had dashed onto the stage. Arms began frantically pulling at the debris, and people shouted for a doctor, for someone to call 911. Sloane was there pitching in, unhurt and trying hard to get to Dess. "She's under there," Erika shouted tremblingly, shock and fear paralyzing her. "Get her out of there. Hurry!"

Slowly, a hand emerged from the rubble. It was Dess's right hand, with the instantly recognizable emerald and gold ring on her third finger. Her fingers wiggled. "Oh, thank God," Erika cried, her heart beating again, and she fell to her knees. "Dess, are you okay?" *Shit, I'm supposed to be calling her Dora,* she remembered too late. *Oh, fuck it.* "Please, baby, are you okay?"

Sloane's face was the color of chalk. She was closer to Dess and carefully bent her head into a small gap in the debris to get a better look. She gave Erika a tentative thumbs up.

It was going to be okay, Erika decided. Because it simply had to be.

CHAPTER EIGHTEEN

Dess's groan came out muffled, the pressure on her chest squeezing it like a vise. She tried to take mental stock of her body, but it was impossible under the heap of material on her—some of it sharp and cutting into her, some of it heavy, like rocks. Her arm hurt like a bitch—she knew that much—and it hurt to breathe.

Sloane was yelling at her, saying they were going to get her out of there. She thought she heard Erika's voice too, but her mind was swathed in gauze. Everything had happened so fast. She remembered a storm approaching. They'd just finished playing a song when all hell broke loose. She heard the crack of lights and scaffolding dislodging from above, but there'd been no time to escape, only time to throw an arm up to try to protect her head. It seemed to be still pinned above her. Pain lanced through her again and again, stealing what little breath remained in her lungs.

Sirens, faint in the distance, and voices that were loud and persistent, gave her some measure of reassurance. The noise also kept her from giving in to the dizziness, the pain and the blinding fatigue. She wanted to sleep, to disappear. But she also feared never waking up again.

Strong hands pushed away the last of the debris, but someone shouted that they shouldn't move her until the paramedics arrived. The pain from her arm was a hot poker right up into her shoulder, and she groaned again. Louder now. *Oh fuck*, she thought. *This isn't good. My arm's broken.*

Erika's face appeared above her, hovering, and for a moment Dess wondered if it was her imagination or a dream. Then Erika tenderly stroked her cheek, and Dess cried tears of gratefulness.

"Sweetheart, it's going to be okay now. Help is coming. How do you feel? Where does it hurt?"

She tried to speak, but the words refused to form. "Arm," she managed to say through the pain and fog.

"It's going to be okay," Erika said again. Her voice was hoarse, as though she were choking on her concern, and it tore at Dess's heart. She wanted to turn the tables and reassure Erika, but she couldn't move and could barely speak.

"You," Dess said, pushing out the words. "Okay? Sloane too?"

Sloane's face swam in her field of vision. Her eyes looked worried, but she was smiling. "We're good. And you're going to be good too." She leaned closer to whisper. "The kid here is pretty worried about you, so don't let her down, okay?"

Dess tried to smile. "I'm tough."

"Oh, you don't have to tell me that. Takes more than a little old storm to knock the stuffing out of you, pal."

She closed her eyes as the sirens drew closer, wanting so badly to sleep. More than that, she wanted Erika cradling her, rocking her to sleep, whispering comforting words to her. Yes, it was exactly what she wanted.

* * *

Erika paced in the emergency department's waiting room, trying desperately to keep from boiling over. She'd save it for the concert's organizers, who'd refused to shut things down as the storm approached. She'd sue their asses off, and so would Dess. And as soon as she was sure Dess was okay, she was going to track them down and tear them new assholes.

Sloane returned and handed her a cup of coffee. "You look like you want to kill somebody."

"I do want to kill somebody. One guess who that might be."

Sloane slumped in the plastic seat. "We're lucky it wasn't worse. But don't go getting yourself sued or blacklisted. It's up to Dess what she wants to do about this later, and the cops will investigate too. If there were safety violations, it'll be dealt with, okay?"

"Dess had better be okay, or else—"

"She will be. Now sit."

Erika grudgingly took a seat. She didn't want to sit here like a useless lump; she wanted to be with Dess. Her mind raced with questions that couldn't immediately be answered. Like how Dess's injuries might affect her in the long run. Whether she was going to be fit enough to play the rest of the tour. And more important, if Dess had to leave the tour, whether Erika even wanted to continue with it. She couldn't imagine not seeing Dess every day, not having her right there onstage with her, not kissing her, not being able to hold her hand, not being able to make love to her every day. Her absence was something Erika couldn't fathom right now.

"This is all my fault," she muttered, close to tears.

Sloane sighed impatiently. "Don't even start. We were all in it together, wanting to get through the set. And if this is anyone's fault, it's mine."

"What do you mean?"

"I'm the one who convinced her to join our tour, remember?"

It was Erika's turn to offer solace. "Right. Okay then. Let's make a deal to stop blaming ourselves. It's not like it's going to help Dess, is it?"

Sloane leveled scrutinizing eyes at her. "I can see why she loves you."

Erika's heart somersaulted. "She loves me?" she asked weakly, hoping like hell Sloane wasn't toying with her.

Sloane waved a dismissive hand. "Of course she does. She just doesn't entirely know it yet. Or maybe she knows it, but she doesn't want to admit it. In any case, she does and she will."

"She will?"

"Stop repeating everything I say." Sloane laughed, and Erika did too. Laughing made her feel instantly better.

A doctor—tall, thin, silver haired—strode purposely toward them. Her authority cloaked her like a suit of armor. "I'm Dr. Metcalf," she said tersely. "You are the family of my patient?"

Sloane answered for them. "Best friends. Her mother and sister are coming up from Chicago in the morning. How is she doing?"

The doctor hesitated, her eyes suspicious. "My patient is noted as having some celebrity status. I can only give updates to family members."

"Please," Erika implored. She was desperate and wasn't beyond shaking the information out of this doctor.

"We came in with Dess," Sloane added. "We're her bandmates, her best friends. Hell, I've been best friends with her for almost twenty years." She pulled out her wallet, the leather so cracked it was curling, and flipped to a picture of the two of them. She flashed it at the doctor like it was a badge.

"All right." The doctor relented, and Erika's tensed shoulders collapsed in relief. "She has a badly broken arm and will require surgery in the morning. She also has a mild concussion and bruised ribs. We'll need to keep her for a few days. She's lucky. It could have been much worse."

"Thank you," Sloane said. "And thank you for protecting Dess's privacy. Can we see her?"

"I'm afraid not. It's late and she's on morphine anyway, so she's not very aware of her surroundings at the moment. She needs her rest tonight."

Tears welled again in Erika's eyes, as they'd done many times over the last couple of hours. She needed to see for herself that Dess was all right, but Sloane was steering her away from the doctor and toward the door.

"Come on. We need to get back to Maggie anyway. We'll see Dess first thing in the morning, okay?"

Erika glanced back one last time toward the hallway. Somewhere in that maze, her lover, her *love*, lay seriously injured and alone. It tore Erika's heart to leave her.

"Seriously," Sloane urged, tugging her along. "They'll take good care of her, and besides, she would want us to look after Maggie for her."

Outside, as they waited for a taxi, a couple of reporters, a photographer and a television cameraman rushed up to them.

"Hey," a reporter said, pushing his way to the front of the pack. "You two are in the band, right? The one that was on the stage tonight when the storm hit?"

Erika and Sloane traded a glance, one that implied Sloane would take the lead on this. *Thank God for Sloane.* "Yes, we were onstage, and we're fine, thanks for asking."

Undeterred, the reporter pressed on. "What about the third member of your group? The guitar player named Dora Hessler? Is she okay? We heard she was hurt."

"Yes. She's going to be fine."

A young woman stepped forward, the magazine reporter who had interviewed Erika and Sloane in Des Moines a couple of weeks ago. She shoved a tape recorder into Sloane's face. "How badly was she hurt?"

"Look," Sloane said tonelessly. "You're going to have to direct any other questions to the event organizers or to hospital officials. We have nothing else to say about it."

A cab driver with impeccable timing pulled up, and Sloane pushed Erika toward the car. *Great*, Erika thought. *My first brush with the paparazzi.* It wasn't nearly as fun as she'd imagined it would be.

CHAPTER NINETEEN

The pain in Dess's arm was numb rather than acute. The drugs were doing their thing, letting her tread water, making her feel slightly apart from herself. The light from her hospital room window told her it was late afternoon. Her mother and her sister Carol were in the room, sitting quietly in chairs they'd pulled up to her bedside.

"Sorry," she mumbled. "I must have fallen asleep again."

"Don't you worry about it, sweetie," her mother said, patting her hand—the one without the IV in it. "We just want you to get better."

"Dess, I'm so sorry this happened," Carol said in a defeated voice. "I'd never have urged you to do this if I thought—"

"No one could have known," Dess said. "Besides, I'm going to be just fine. Right? Or is there something you two aren't telling me?" The thought made her stomach bottom out, sending her back to that awful moment when she was told she had throat cancer and that surgery and radiation were no guarantees. Nothing could be that bad again, she decided, and she commanded herself to calm down. It was only a broken arm, and her mother and sister had always been honest with her.

"Of course not, dear," her mother replied evenly. "And yes, you're going to be fine. The surgeon said your arm will be as good as new in a few months. It was a clean break."

"No nerve damage?" Dess asked, somewhat disbelieving of her mother's simple prognosis. Victoria (never Vicki) Hampton had somehow maintained her eternal optimism and youthful looks, in spite of outliving three husbands and seeing a daughter through cancer.

"No," Carol interjected. "No complications are expected. You'll be able to play the guitar again. Just not for the rest of this tour with Sloane and Erika."

Oh shit, Dess thought. *Erika.* She'd been hazily aware of Erika's presence earlier today, of Erika kissing her forehead, touching her cheek. What would happen to their relationship if Dess had to leave the tour? Or should she tag along like a groupie? The thought both appalled and tantalized her. Groupie sex with Erika created a whole new collection of titillating fantasies, and she chuckled out loud before she could catch herself.

"Boy, those drugs must be good," Carol said. "I hope they're manufactured by my company."

Her mother squeezed her hand while shooting Carol an admonishing look. "Come and stay on the island with me for the summer while you recover. Maggie and I will take good care of you."

"Sloane and Erika are looking after her, right?"

"Yes," Carol said. "They're taking good care of her. In fact, you might never get her back. I hear she's become quite the dependable little roadie."

Dess was so used to having Maggie by her side that the dog's absence felt like a limb had been amputated. Maggie had been a gift to her from her family after the cancer had struck. And to combat her loneliness after Dayna's departure. Maggie had been more loyal and much more of a comfort than Dayna had ever been, no question.

"I hear Sloane and Erika are going to try to sneak Maggie in tonight to see you," Carol said with a conspiratorial smile. "They said they'd do it even if they had to pretend one of them was blind and Maggie was their guide dog."

Dess laughed as much as her bruised ribs would allow.

"Well?" her mother asked impatiently. "Are you going to accompany me back to the island after they let you out of this place in a few days?"

Carol rolled her eyes. "Oh Mother, don't pressure her. You know she and Erika are a couple now, and besides, being around music is good for Dess. Right, Dess?"

"Whoa," Dess said, her face burning. "How do you know I'm involved with Erika?" Had Erika or Sloane told them this morning while she was sleeping?

"Duh," Carol said, her eyes bright. "I can tell from the tone of your emails to me the last few weeks. And I can tell she makes you happy. Even now, while you're lying here all banged up, you're happy."

Dess thought of protesting or at least explaining that things weren't necessarily serious with Erika. But the drug-induced fog was rolling in and dulling her thoughts once more. *I'll just close my eyes for a minute.*

* * *

Erika kissed Dess on the forehead and waited for her eyelids to flutter open. When they did, Maggie squirmed at her side and Erika reached down with a soft pat to quiet her.

"Hi, sweetheart."

Dess smiled lazily. "Hi. I'm so glad you're here."

"Me too. And someone else is really glad to be here too."

Maggie lifted her head high enough for Dess to reach her.

"Oh, my little angel." Dess's smile swallowed her face. "I missed you, Maggie Waggie. Are you okay, honey?" She stroked Maggie's brown head and snout, and Maggie nuzzled her back. It was clear that being separated had made them both terribly unhappy.

"She missed you," Erika said around the lump in her throat. "And she's not the only one."

"Oh, darling, I'm so sorry." Tears sprang to Dess's eyes, and Erika quickly kissed her to snuff out her sadness.

"We've been so worried about you," Erika said softly. "I'm sure Sloane will only be too happy to tell you what a miserable bundle of nerves I've been since last night."

"Speaking of the devil, where is she?"

"Making some calls. She'll be here in a minute."

"No doubt she's calling in every favor she can think of to find you a replacement for me. God, Erika, I'm so sorry." Dess's eyes were swimming again, and it was almost enough to make Erika want to cry. That and the fact that the Chicago Blues Festival next week would be her biggest and most prestigious festival yet. If Sloane failed to find a guitarist, their performance was in serious jeopardy.

"Honey, it's not your fault," Erika soothed. "All that matters is that you're going to be okay. Anything else is just a bonus."

"If I have to play one-handed, I—"

"You're not playing one-handed. But I can think of some other things you can do one-handed that would give me great pleasure."

Dess smiled, her eyes smoky, and Erika shuddered pleasurably. "Come here and give me another kiss."

Their kiss was more tenderness than flirtation, more relief and gratefulness than mischief and desire. For Erika, kissing Dess gave her an immediate sense of coming home, no matter their surroundings. If she could kiss Dess for hours, she would gladly do so.

"Where's Carol and my mom?" Dess asked, breaking their kiss.

"Having dinner. They'll be back later, though Carol told me they'll probably head back to Chicago tomorrow morning, now that they know you're on the road to recovery."

"Ah, so you've met Carol and know that she believes in telling it like it is."

"Yes, and she's great. So is your mom."

"You might not think so when I tell you she's pressuring me to join her on Mackinac Island for the rest of the summer."

Erika reeled for a moment. She couldn't imagine being separated from Dess for the rest of the summer. She battled against the urge to selfishly beg her to stay. "Probably a wise suggestion," she lied.

"Maybe, but I don't want to leave the tour, unless you're kicking me off the bus."

Erika's heart lifted like a jet plane soaring above the clouds. "Are you kidding me?" She lowered her voice. "But there is one thing concerning me about you staying on the tour."

"You mean besides the fact that I'm of no use to you onstage anymore?"

"Well, there is that, but no. If you're going to stay on the tour, I can't have us sleeping separately again. You're going to need close medical supervision, after all, and I'm the only woman for the job."

Dess laughed, then winced sharply. "Ow, jeez, don't make me laugh. And you're right. Separate beds is out of the question. As soon as they spring me from this joint, we're all staying at my condo for this blues festival."

"I was hoping you'd give us a reprieve from being trailer trash."

"Hear that, Maggie old girl? We get to go home for a while."

Maggie bounced lightly on her front paws, and Dess scratched her under her chin until the dog's lips curled back in a smile.

"Your mom will be disappointed about your decision."

"She's had me with her on that island for the last six summers. She'll get over it."

Sloane pushed through the door, her mouth twisting into a scowl.

"And a fine how-do-you-do to you too," Dess said.

"Sorry," she said with a smile that didn't come close to reaching her eyes. "I'm very happy to see you've rejoined the land of the living."

"Yes, well, looks like I'm still burning through my nine lives. But if you're so happy about it, why do you look so miserable?"

Sloane exchanged a glance with Erika that said something was terribly wrong.

"Oh, no," Erika said. "Tell me you were able to find a guitar player for at least the blues festival next week." Panic throbbed in her gut like a second heartbeat. Pulling out of this festival would represent a catastrophic setback to her career—and just when she was starting to get noticed. Record label reps would be in the audience, other concert promoters, journalists, songwriters, you name it. She didn't want to sound like she cared more about the concert than Dess's well-being, but dammit, this one was the pinnacle of the entire summer!

"I got you a guitarist. Greg Reddicker. Red. He's great, one of the best in the business, right, Dess?"

"Without question. Erika, he's a real master. Much better than me."

Erika began to protest that there was no one better than Dess, but Dess waved a hand at her. "That's great news, Sloane, but why do you still look so upset?"

Sloane bit her bottom lip, paced a few steps, before turning to face them both. "Dess, I'm sorry to have to tell you this. Really sorry, and you're going to hate me."

"If I was going to hate you, it would have happened a long time ago. Tell me what's going on."

"The press has found out your real identity."

Dess's face immediately colored, but she managed to keep her voice schooled. "How?"

"I don't know, but I think someone who works here at the hospital probably leaked it. Some radio station reported it about an hour ago, and now the phone lines are lighting up. A whole pile of reporters are camped out in front of the hospital now. I've told Carol and your mom to hightail it back to Chicago immediately."

Tears trickled down Dess's cheek.

"I'm so fucking sorry, Dess," Sloane said, slumping down on the side of the bed. "I got you into this thing and now—"

"I don't understand," Erika interjected. "I mean, there was a chance your identify would be found out eventually anyway. This doesn't change anything, right? You weren't going back on the stage for the rest of the summer anyway."

"No," Dess said in a quavering voice. "This changes everything. *Everything*."

CHAPTER TWENTY

Even with the numbing benefits of the pain pills and Sloane's obsessive efforts to drive carefully, the six-hour drive to Chicago was unpleasant for Dess. The slightest bump triggered a flash of pain along her arm and through her bruised chest. She closed her eyes for most of the drive, pretending to sleep while thinking about how she was going to break the news to Erika that she could no longer tour with them. Now that her identify had been so crudely revealed, she, Sloane and Erika would be hounded for weeks and possibly months by reporters, bloodsuckers from the music business and other curiosity seekers. The unwanted attention would take the focus squarely off Erika and her music and place it onto Dess, and that was not something Dess would allow to happen.

She'd stayed away from the Internet in the days since the accident had happened. In the back of her mind, she'd known there was a good chance that eventually she'd be found out on the tour. It was a risk the three of them had been well aware of, and Dess had willingly accepted it. Maybe, she thought now, she'd simply wanted to do the tour badly enough that she didn't give enough consideration to having her identity blown. Or maybe, she thought with fresh horror, just maybe she'd wanted to be found out. Maybe, subconsciously, being forced out of her self-imposed exile from the music business, from the whole world in some ways, was something she had secretly desired.

She hadn't wanted it like this, though, dammit. She'd gotten enough snatches of information from Erika, Sloane, Carol and her mom about the news reports. It was gotcha journalism—the kind that took sick pleasure in gossip and scandal and in revealing secrets. Like forcing a celebrity out of the closet or revealing someone's long-lost love child. The coverage of her accident made it sound like she had been intentionally trying to dupe people. There were fuzzy pictures of her onstage in her Dora disguise, headlines that read: "Reclusive Ex-Singer Turns Up on Backwater Tour"; "Dess Hampton Crawls Back to Music Business as Nobody Guitarist"; "Afraid of the Spotlight, Hampton Slums It at Summer Music Fests." Journalists and bloggers were making her sound pathetic and frightened, which, she supposed, wasn't entirely wrong.

Sloane dropped Dess, Erika and Maggie at the condo, insisting on staying with one of her many fuck buddies—Sloane's words—for the week, so that Dess and Erika could have some alone time. The minute they walked in the door, Erika began babying her. She helped her to bed, fluffed her pillows, fetched her water, gave her a foot rub, insisted on running out for food and a few groceries.

After takeout Chinese for dinner, she ran Dess a bubble bath. Carefully and meticulously, Erika helped ease her into the tub, softly scrubbed her body all over, tenderly dried her off, then helped her back to bed.

"I won't break, you know," Dess muttered, not intending to sound ungrateful, but she wasn't used to all this singular attention.

"I know that." Erika's smile turned lusty; her eyes were dark smoke. "But it gives me a chance to touch you all over."

Dess laughed low in her throat, the absence of sex for nearly a week making her dry kindling to Erika's torch. "All you had to do was ask."

Erika lay down on the bed beside her, stroking her good arm. "In that case, I'm asking. But only if you're up to it. And I'll be super careful."

Minutes later, Erika was between her thighs, her hands cupping Dess's ass, her mouth devouring her. All pretense of being gentle had been subordinated to a sexual hunger that consumed them both, driving their pleasure to dizzying heights. It was a delicious absence of time and space for Dess, a vanquishing of all worry, all brooding, all deliberating, all physical pain. They needed to talk, but—*oh, God!*—not now. Now was for the sweet joy and pleasure that wracked her body in ambrosial spasms, threatening to shatter every bone in her body. It was so easy to give herself over to Erika, so easy to surrender to her physically. *Why can I not give her my heart as easily?* Dess wondered with sad resignation. There was an invisible wall in her heart that she had no idea how to demolish, even with a beautiful, sweet, caring, adoring woman like Erika on the other side of it.

Erika gently cradled her in her arms, kissing and caressing her lovingly. Dess could at least give her lover physical love and affection—of that there was no shortage on her part.

"Let me love you back," Dess whispered.

"Sweetheart, no. I don't want you to hurt yourself."

"There has to be a way I can pleasure you. Please."

After only a moment's hesitation, Erika stripped off her clothes, promise and mischief dancing in her eyes. "Here, prop your head up against the pillow. And don't move anything but your mouth."

Dess gladly followed the command and watched with anticipation as Erika climbed on top, scooted toward the headboard, which she grabbed onto, and lowered her herself onto Dess's waiting mouth. She took the beautiful offering with her tongue, her lips. Felt Erika use her strong legs to power herself up and down, back and forth, to create friction. Dess suckled the soft, wet folds of skin, savored the feel of Erika against her lips and on her tongue. Erika was both hard and wet, and Dess stroked her slow, then fast. Faster than she'd ever stroked her before. They matched each other in rhythm and intensity, moan for moan, heat for heat, until Erika went rigid, then shuddered and rocked herself against Dess's slickened face.

Erika carefully climbed down, still breathless from her orgasm, and stretched out beside Dess. "Are you okay, sweetheart? I didn't hurt you, did I?"

Dess smiled as she gingerly nestled against Erika. "Hurt me, are you kidding? You just made my entire week. God, that was so hot!"

Erika laughed softly and held her closely. "It was pretty hot, wasn't it?"

"You're a genius."

"I prefer 'love guru.'"

Dess smiled, tried to stifle a yawn. "Okay, my little love guru. I think you wiped me out."

"Good. Sleep now, my love. I'll be right here."

Her cheek contentedly resting against Erika's breasts, Dess allowed sleep to swallow her.

* * *

The sun sliced through the bedroom blinds in sharp, bright slashes as Erika brought a tray of coffee, juice, toast and a poached egg to Dess's bedside. She'd wanted Dess to sleep as long as possible, but she had a rehearsal with Sloane and the new guitar player in an hour, and she wanted to make sure Dess ate something before she left.

"I hope you're hungry," Erika announced brightly.

Dess pushed herself up to a sitting position against the headboard. "I do remember working up an appetite last night."

Erika beamed at the memory of their lovemaking. She'd been so worried about Dess's fragility, yet both of them had so easily become caught up in the passion of enjoying each other's bodies. "Good, because I hear sex has some amazing healing properties."

"In that case, how about another round tonight?"

"I don't even want to wait that long, except I'm rehearsing all afternoon with Sloane and Red. Your sister's going to come and stay with you while I'm gone."

"I don't need a babysitter, you know. Or a nurse."

"True, but I told her I nearly killed you with sex last night and that you might be a little weak today."

An adorable blush flooded Dess's face. "You didn't."

"No, I didn't, but I'm sure she's figured out that we're sleeping together."

"I'm sure she has, but my sister does not need to know the juicy details."

Erika set the tray on the side table and lay down next to Dess. "*I* need some details. To get me through the rest of the day."

"What kind of details?"

Erika lowered her voice to that sexy octave she knew made Dess melt inside. "The details of what you're going to do with me tonight."

"Ooh, dirty talk. I love it! But I wouldn't want to get you all excited and not be able to rehearse properly."

Erika sighed for effect. "Oh, all right. You're always the practical one, aren't you?"

"Speaking of practical..." Dess's expression hardened. "We need to talk."

Erika had known this was coming, ever since Dess had proclaimed from her hospital bed that with her identify blown, everything would change. A sickening feeling gathered in her stomach. Was this exactly the excuse Dess needed to wiggle out of their relationship? Would it throw Dess back into living as a recluse? Their relationship aside, it would be tragic to see Dess retreat into herself again, to live as if she were only existing. She had so much to give, so much to live for.

"All right," Erika said tentatively, stalling for time. She jumped up from the bed and set the tray on Dess's lap. "But not until you eat."

"Okay, okay. I'll eat." Dess picked up a fork and knife and plunged into the egg. "Thank you for cooking for me."

"I love cooking for you," Erika said. "And doing anything else you need." She knew Dess resisted being taken care of, but Erika loved it. It was what people did when they loved someone, she wanted to say, but didn't. Dess knew damned well by now how she felt about her.

They talked about Erika's set list for the upcoming blues festival while Dess finished her breakfast. When Dess spoke again, it was like a bolt of lightning splitting a clear sky.

"I can't ever be Dora Hessler again, Erika. And that means I can't stay on the tour."

"No." Erika couldn't accept this. "Dora Hessler was my lead guitar player. But Dess Hampton is my..." her voice broke, and she had to hold herself back from expressing the full depth of her feelings "...is my lover. And I want you to stay. So much."

"Oh, sweetie."

Dess squeezed her hand, but it wasn't enough. Erika wanted to curl up in Dess's arms, cry like a baby. She needed to find a way to hold on as tight as she could, even as Dess was slipping further through her fingers.

"There's no way I can do that, honey. I'll be hounded by the press, stalked by the paparazzi. Possibly for months. As it is I'm going to have to hire a public relations firm to try to deal with this mess."

"But we could work through this together."

"No. You have no idea what an onslaught this is going to be. And I can't put you through this. Or Sloane."

"But I don't mind being put through it. I want to be put through it, as long as we're together."

Dess's sigh was sharp, impatient. "It would be too much of a distraction. For you, for the fans, for the festival organizers. And for me. We'd be like animals in the zoo. And right now, you need to focus on you. And on your music."

Erika couldn't stop herself from sounding like an entreating child. "But maybe the attention would actually help my career. Help me get discovered. This could be a good thing, couldn't it?"

Dess eyed her challengingly. "Is that really how you want to make it? By being a footnote in stories about me? By riding my coattails?"

"No," Erika conceded. Dess was right. She wanted— needed—to make it on her own terms. "But I don't want to lose you. I *can't* lose you."

"You won't lose me." Dess kissed her softly on the lips.

"Seriously? Because I think that would destroy me." Erika knew she should feel happy, grateful, that Dess wasn't dumping her. But she couldn't shake the feeling that her earlier proclamation about everything changing had been an understatement. This felt much more ominous, like a total clearing of the decks. As much as she wanted to believe—desperately—that she wouldn't lose Dess over all this, she feared it was exactly what was going to happen.

"Oh, Erika. Don't you know how much I care about you?"

No, Erika thought, *I don't know. Why don't you tell me exactly how much?* God, how she wanted Dess to say the words. Just once. To say them and mean them. If she spoke them now, she'd dissolve into tears.

"You're going to be late if you don't get going," Dess said. She couldn't wait to change the subject, Erika realized, couldn't wait to get her out of the house.

She fought the urge to call Sloane to say she wasn't coming. Not only that, but that she was pulling out of this damned tour so she could stay behind and fight for Dess.

Wordlessly, she rose from the bed, stumbling, her vision blurred by tears.

CHAPTER TWENTY-ONE

Another day of rehearsals, another day in which Dess sequestered in her condo like a criminal. This self-imposed imprisonment harked back to the black days following her cancer diagnosis, when facing the public and the press was a chore that she simply couldn't manage. Carol lectured her just yesterday that she was going to have to go out eventually and face the public curiosity and the endless personal questions and that hiding out wasn't the answer. To Dess, however, it was the only answer she could see for now. She didn't want to add to the distractions already looming over Erika and Sloane. As soon as their Chicago appearance was finished and they had safely moved onto the next venue—Ann Arbor, Michigan—Dess would try to figure out how to get the media off her back.

The intercom buzzed. It was the doorman's voice, raspy as though he'd spent a lifetime smoking cigarettes and sipping whiskey. Her manager was on the way up, he told her.

Dess opened mouth, about to tell him she didn't have a manager, when a knock sounded at her door. "Fine," she told him, not at all sure it was fine. What if it was a reporter in disguise? Or some nutcase? She'd raise hell about the security breach later.

"Who is it?" she called out through the thick door, relieved that Maggie had moved alongside her, her body rigid and alert.

"Dayna" came the muffled reply through the thick door.

Uselessly, she contemplated how many women she knew by that name, but there was only one—her one-time manager and ex-girlfriend, Dayna Williams. Dess's voice came out as cold and stiff as a good January Chicago breeze. "I have nothing to say to you, Dayna."

"Let me in and at least listen to me."

"There is *nothing* I want to talk to you about."

Their parting words, that night more than six years ago, when Dayna coldly announced she was leaving her, had been brutal. Epithets and accusations had spiraled into an ugly stream, turning downright malicious. Dess was finally rendered speechless when Dayna said the most honest thing she'd said in years: "If you can't sing anymore, then there is nothing left for me to love."

"It's better that you talk to me," Dayna said now, tauntingly, "than my lawyer."

"Oh, give me a break," Dess ground out. Dayna had used the lawyer threat one too many times over the years to have any effect on her now.

"Actually," Dayna clarified, "it's not so much *you* my lawyer will be talking to, but to Erika Alvarez."

Dess's heart stopped for a full five seconds. She pulled the door open so hard the effort strained her good arm. *Dammit!*

Maggie let out a protective growl, but Dayna ignored the warning, marching past Dess and her dog as though she owned the place.

"Your dog has more bite than you, and that's not saying much."

"Shut up." *Bitch*, Dess thought. "What the hell do you want?"

"Can we at least be civil towards each other?"

"No. Any other questions?"

Presumptuous as always, Dayna sat down on the leather sofa, looking cool and flawless in all her meticulous artificiality. She wore clothes made of the finest fabrics and shoes that were hand tooled and without a single scuff. A neat, outer package, but Dayna Williams was the devil in disguise, as far as Dess was concerned.

She had no choice but to follow and sit too, but she'd be damned if she'd offer Dayna anything to drink.

"Just say what you came here to say, Dayna. Then you can climb back on your broom and get the hell out of my life again." If Carol, Erika or Sloane discovered Dayna here, they'd tear her apart, limb from limb. The thought made Dess insanely happy.

"Ah, the pain medication for your broken arm must be making you cranky."

"No, *you* are making me cranky. And you've got five seconds to tell me what the hell you want or I'm calling security."

Dayna's smile had that disingenuous, syrupy quality that was entirely nauseating. Her hair was bleached to a blond that was almost white, and her makeup was thick, yet it failed to hide a maze of wrinkles much more pronounced than Dess could ever remember seeing. The window dressing was a typical byproduct of Dayna's insecurity. Her nails were also fake, and so were her boobs these days, by the look of their unnatural perkiness. With a churning stomach, she wondered how she had ever been attracted to Dayna.

"I'm here about your *girlfriend*." Dayna's tone was accusatory, as though Dess had been unfaithful or had done something wrong. What a joke that was. Dayna was the one who could never be trusted. There were rumors of at least two affairs in the years they were together—the last one when Dess was sick.

"I should have thrown your ass out long before you left me," Dess said in a tone full of venom that was understated, but precisely meant to injure.

"Please. You want to rehash all that ancient history?"

"No." Dayna was right. She'd moved on, and, until this stupid goddamned storm had happened, she'd been in the best place in her life in years. Decades, perhaps. She was enjoying music again. And she was in love. A small gasp escaped her lips at the realization.

"So it's like this." Dayna's smile hinted at some secret and valuable possession, and Dess wanted to smack it right off her face. "Erika Alvarez is quite the young talent."

Dayna was about the last person on earth with whom Dess wanted to talk about Erika. "Get on with it."

"I snuck into her rehearsal yesterday for a few minutes. Long enough to see for myself her incredible potential. With her looks, her voice, her stage presence..." Dayna let out a long, rapturous sigh that unnerved Dess. "The sky is really the limit."

"Spare me the report card on Erika. She's an A-plus, and that's obvious to anyone with half a brain. Now tell me why you give a shit."

"That's easy. When the press outed you after your accident last week, I got curious. I thought, who could possibly manage to drag Dess Hampton out of her self-imposed exile from the music business? I figured it'd have to be somebody pretty spectacular. And my, my, Erika Alvarez certainly is that."

Dess didn't like the sexual undertones in Dayna's words. Didn't even like her saying Erika's name. Inside, she was coiling up like a snake, ready to strike if Dayna said one more goddamned word about Erika.

"Is she as good in the bedroom as she is onstage?"

"You fucking bitch!" Dess exploded. If she'd had two good arms, she'd pummel Dayna into a miserable little lump.

Dayna simply smiled at the outburst. "Sorry, that wasn't very polite of me, was it? I just figured, a tiger on the stage has to be a tiger in the bedroom too. Although, sadly, I could never say that about you."

It took a moment before Dess was calm enough to speak. If she couldn't smack Dayna, she could at least verbally bruise her before she kicked her ass out of here. "She's a fuck of a lot better in the bedroom than you ever were. And maybe you would have gotten more out of me in bed if you'd been worth the effort."

Laughter bubbled from Dayna's collagened lips. "Touché. Nice to know I can still get a rise out of you."

Dess hated her lack of self-restraint around Dayna. The bitch knew how to push her buttons, and Dess always fell into the trap. Well, enough of that. "You wanted to see who I was fucking and who I was collaborating with musically. Fine. Show's over. You can crawl back into your cave now, Dayna."

"Ah, that's where you're wrong, my dear." Dayna unzipped the sleek leather portfolio from beside her feet, carefully sliding out a thin sheaf of papers. "This is the last contract you had with me."

Dess waved away Dayna's offer to examine the papers. "Our contract was terminated when I quit the business. You said so yourself at the time when you...left."

"That was mostly true. But our business arrangement wasn't exactly terminated. It went into a period of dormancy."

"What the hell is that supposed to mean?"

"It means that as long as you stayed away from either performing or recording for a minimum of ten years following our dissolution, your management contract with me would become invalid. The minute you resumed those actions—performing in this case—within that ten-year frame, the contract became active again."

Dess couldn't believe this sorry attempt at blackmail. Could Dayna really be so desperate? So vengeful? "Look, I've made peanuts from this tour. Less than four thousand dollars so far. If you're so poor that you need a few grand, then fine. You can have it. I don't care."

"I'd forgotten how naïve you can be sometimes, Dess. It's almost charming." Dayna's smile oozed contempt and ridicule. If Dess never had to look at her face again, it would be too soon. "My dear, it's not your earnings from this little two-bit tour I'm interested in. I'm interested in something much bigger than that."

"Look, the tour was fun while it lasted, but I'm done. I can't play guitar again for months. I still can't sing. By the end of this summer, Erika will have outgrown my meager talents anyway. There's nothing for you to try to horn in on, okay?"

Ignoring her, Dayna flipped through the contract after extracting pink-framed reading glasses from a pocket of the portfolio case. "Oh, it's not you and your cheesy guitar playing I'm interested in," she said, peering over her glasses. "It's your young protégé, Erika Alvarez."

Well, you can't have her, Dess shouted inside her own head. What she said to Dayna was, "Erika won't go near you with a ten-foot pole, so you can forget trying to sign her."

"Now that's where you're wrong. The escape clause in your contract stipulates that if you collaborate with another musical artist in any way and if that artist is unsigned during that collaboration, the right to manage said artist falls to me."

Dess felt her blood go cold. "What? Are you fucking kidding me?"

"It's right here, in black and white. And that's your signature at the bottom of it." Dayna triumphantly held up the contract. "Sounded like a pretty innocuous little paragraph at the time, didn't it? Especially when you had no intention of ever re-igniting your career again."

"Jesus Christ, Dayna. You can't be serious about this. I signed that thing to rid you from my life once and for all. I was still sick, still in chemo."

"Oh no, don't you try to act like you didn't know what you were signing. That you were too distraught or too physically and emotionally unwell. You would have signed away the rights to your firstborn if you'd thought it would keep me out of your life."

"I wasn't well, goddammit, and you took advantage of me!"

"No court would support you on that now. Not after all this time."

Dess's arm throbbed, and she craved a pain pill to help dull the burning rage consuming her. "So you're going to sue me? Is that what this is all about?"

"Oh, I don't want to sue you. Not unless I have to." Dayna tucked her glasses away and leaned forward. "What I want is a piece of Erika. She's got the goods, and I want to manage her. You're going to make that happen. And if you don't? Then yes, I will sue your ass off. And Erika's, too."

"Get out!" Dess shouted. "Get the fuck out of my house and don't come back."

Dayna retreated hastily to the door, but not before sliding her business card onto the table in the hallway. "I expect to hear from you or your lawyer in the next couple of days. And you *will* let me know once you've set up a meeting between you and Erika and me. And it needs to happen before she leaves Chicago."

Dess slammed the door so hard behind Dayna that it caused Maggie to bark in surprise. Sliding down the door to the floor, Dess began shaking uncontrollably.

* * *

It was Sloane's idea to rent a twenty-one-foot powerboat and take the three of them out on Lake Michigan for a lazy afternoon. Sloane had grown up around boats, and Erika agreed that it would be the perfect way to escape the paparazzi and to relax before tomorrow night's big concert. The performance was going to be the biggest of her life so far—the Chicago audience would be sizable, and there were sure to be record label scouts and potential management representatives in attendance. The media would be out in droves, especially since word had gotten out about Dess's connection to the band. The pressure would be intense, but weighing more on Erika's mind was Dess's somber mood. Last night she hadn't even come to bed, preferring to curl up on the sofa instead. She'd barely spoken over breakfast and couldn't seem to look Erika in the eye. A lesser woman, Erika supposed, would give up on Dess or blame herself for the growing chasm between them. But Erika knew that if she waited long enough, Dess would come around.

Erika glanced helplessly at Sloane, who also seemed to understand that something beyond last weekend's accident and the pesky reporters was bringing Dess down.

The waves on Lake Michigan were small rollers—under a foot high—and provided just enough motion to rock the boat rhythmically once Sloane silenced the motor and lowered the anchor. The sun sparkled on the water, as though a thousand large diamonds had been sprinkled around them. In the distance, the tall shadows of skyscrapers drizzled dark along the water's blue edge.

"It's so peaceful out here," Dess said, her face to the sun. "Calming."

Sloane swiveled the captain's chair to face Dess, who had sprawled next to Erika on a wide bench seat in the stern. "Is it?"

"Absolutely," Dess said right away, but her voice lacked any enthusiasm.

Sloane reached into the cooler beside her and cracked open a Budweiser. "You going to tell us what's wrong?"

Leave it to Sloane, Erika thought with a mix of concern and relief, to get right to the point.

Dess pushed her sunglasses to the top of her head. Her stormy gray eyes were red-rimmed, sleep-deprived. "Ah, so that's why you got me out here on this boat. Confess or be dumped over the side, is that it?"

Sloane's smile was shark-like. "If it works, why not?"

Dess pointed at the cooler. "I think I need one of those."

"Aren't you still on your pain pills?" Sloane asked cautiously.

"Like I said, I need one of those."

Sloane tossed her a can.

"Easy, honey," Erika whispered.

"If I was going to become an alcoholic or a drug addict, believe me, it would have happened long before now." Dess popped the tab and took a swig. Her feet were in Erika's lap, and Erika massaged her toes gently. She closed her eyes at her touch, but the muscles in her legs remained tighter than Sloane's drumheads.

Quietly, Dess said, "Most of this pertains to Erika. I think it's better if—"

"No," Erika said. If Dess was in the mood for a heart-to-heart, she wasn't about to let the moment slip away. "Whatever it is, Sloane's going to know about it sooner or later anyway." Erika had already told her that Dess had changed her mind about remaining on tour with them, thanks to the brewing media storm.

"Fine," Dess replied. "But I want you both to promise me you won't do anything rash once I tell you."

"Fuck that," Sloane said. "I'm forty years old, which means I've earned the right to do all the rash things I want."

Dess's laughter immediately dissolved the tension. "You were doing rash things well before you were forty, my friend. But I get your point."

"Well, I can at least guarantee you I won't murder anyone. How's that?"

"That," Dess said with a sad smile, "I'll take."

Sloane tossed her crumpled beer can into an empty bucket. "So who am I going to have to restrain myself from wanting to kill?"

Dess looked from Sloane to Erika, resignation in her eyes. She looked decidedly unhappy. Miserable, actually. *Maybe I will kill whoever's done this to Dess,* Erika thought with fresh resolve.

"Dayna Williams," Dess answered quietly and without emotion.

Sloane flew up from her seat, the sudden movement rocking the boat.

"Jesus," Dess said, removing her feet from Erika's lap to steady herself. "Don't frickin' drown us!"

"Sorry. It's just...I hate that bitch. Don't tell me she's come crawling out of the woodwork?"

"Yes. She has."

Fuck, Erika thought. By extension, she too hated Dayna, but by the look on the faces of Sloane and Dess, Dayna's reemergence was very bad news.

Sloane sat back down with a heavy sigh. "Fuck it. I *am* going to kill her."

"No, you're not."

"What the fuck does she want? Money?"

"Not exactly." Dess leveled apologetic eyes at Erika. "She wants you, babe."

Dread gathered like a hard knot in the pit of Erika's stomach as Dess explained what Dayna wanted. And her ruthless terms.

"I don't want anything to do with her," Erika said, anger pulsing through her. "After the way she treated you? How could she even have the nerve?"

"Easy," Sloane answered. "She has balls and no morals. Which is exactly why she's one of the best in the business."

"I don't care," Erika said, raising her voice, "if she's the second coming of Colonel Tom Parker. I will never agree to let her represent me." She squeezed Dess's hand with a confidence she didn't feel. Things were quickly slipping away from her—first Dess, now control over her own career. *Is this how it is in the music business? With every rung you climb, you lose more and more control?*

"Honey, I know how badly you want to succeed in the music business. And Sloane's right. Dayna is one of the best. She took me to the top, after all."

Erika shook her head. "I won't do it if the price I have to pay is associating with her."

Dess studied her for a long moment, nodded once. "All right then. I'll call my lawyer as soon as we get back onshore."

Sloane chewed on her fingernails, looking uncharacteristically worried.

"What?" Erika prompted her.

When Sloane finally spoke, her voice cracked like a tree limb splitting from its trunk. "That bitch stops at nothing until she gets what she wants. If she doesn't want to let you go, Erika, she won't."

CHAPTER TWENTY-TWO

"There's good news and bad news."

Dess expelled an uneasy breath, squeezed the hand of Erika beside her and nodded at her lawyer, Jennifer Parker, to continue.

Jennifer whipped off her reading glasses, tossed them onto her desktop and pushed her thick, wavy red hair behind her ears. "I'm afraid Dayna Williams does indeed have you both over a barrel. She's right that she has first dibs on representing Erika."

"What if I choose not to hire a manager?" Erika suggested, her voice hopeful.

Jennifer shook her head, her massive mane of hair once again unruly. "First of all, you'd be eaten alive in this business without representation. Secondly, if you don't hire Dayna, she's within her rights to have a court order you to surrender a certain percentage of your future earnings to her. That's whether you manage yourself or hire someone else to manage you. Dayna will own a piece of you either way. And if it were me?"

Dess and Erika moved to the edges of their seats.

"Better," Jennifer continued, "to have the devil close at hand, if you know what I mean."

Erika sat back, closed her eyes in a look of defeat. Her jaw was clamped tightly in anger.

"This is all my fault," Dess said disconsolately. "I should never have signed off on that exit clause." To Erika, she whispered, "I'm so sorry, honey."

Erika's eyes flew open. To Dess, she said, "Don't ever say that, sweetheart. You have nothing to be sorry for. You could never have known that you would be making music with me or anyone else. Or that—that *bitch*—would come after us. Besides, you did what you had to do to get her out of your life." Erika turned to Jennifer, calmer now. "So you're saying I don't have a choice in this?"

"Not if you want to accomplish anything with your musical talent, no. Quite frankly, with a litigious Dayna Williams hanging over your head, no one else will want to touch you anyway."

Traffic noises from eighteen floors below faintly penetrated the thick windows of Jennifer's office, as the three women sat in contemplative silence. Dess wasn't surprised her ex was trying to glom onto Erika, because anyone with even the tiniest shred of instinct or knowledge about the music business understood inherently that Erika had the goods to go far. But she couldn't help thinking that it was personal, a way for Dayna to get back at her for cutting off her source of income, diminishing her power and influence in the business, when she chose to end her career.

"You said there was some good news too," Dess remembered.

Jennifer's expression remained grim, and her blunt honesty was one of the qualities Dess admired most about her. It also helped that she was probably the best entertainment lawyer in the Midwest, even though it would be hard to guess that from her simple, modest office.

Jennifer steepled her hands on the desk. "The contract requires that Erika only need sign a fair, industry-standard contract with Dayna. Now…" She looked pointedly at Erika. "Dayna will undoubtedly try to convince you to sign for much more than that, but as it stands, you only need to sign with her for one year and twenty-five percent. That's a reasonable industry standard."

Erika perked up. "So after that I can dump her?"

"Absolutely."

Dess watched a cascade of emotions march across Erika's face. Relief, hopefulness, puzzlement, resignation, futility, anger.

"I don't know what to do." Erika's eyes darted anxiously between Jennifer and Dess.

"I think this is something the two of you need to discuss," Jennifer suggested, rising from her chair. "Take as long as you need."

Alone together, Erika swiped an errant tear from her cheek. "Baby, I can't do this to you. I cannot collaborate with someone who abandoned you during the most difficult time in your life. I could never respect someone like that. What she did to you…" Erika balled a fist in her lap. "It makes my blood boil."

There was no point in listing Dayna's flaws. They were many, and they were inarguable. "You don't have to respect her, Erika. And don't forget. The very things that make her a nasty person make her a very successful business manager. I just didn't have the good sense to keep those two things separate."

"Can I ask you something?"

Dess's heart broke a little. "Of course. You can ask me anything, you know that."

"What did you ever see in her? As a girlfriend, I mean."

Erika didn't have to say the words, but what Dess was sure she meant was, how could you have loved her but you won't commit to me?

"Trust me," Dess said. "I've kicked myself many times in the ass, asking myself the same question. I think what I was attracted to was her ability to take care of things, to take control, to *handle* everything so that I didn't have to. She was competent, capable, the take-charge type. And that allowed me to concentrate on my music, which was what I loved most. I chose to ignore her faults, and by the time I began to realize I wasn't in love with her, I was becoming ill."

Erika's eyes widened. "So you weren't sorry she left you?"

"I was sorry about the timing. I needed all the love and support I could get when I was sick. But no, I wasn't sorry the relationship ended. It took me dozens of sessions with my therapist and a couple of years of being well before I realized that her leaving me was for the best." *Even though seeing her face still makes me want to kill her*, Dess thought. She could never be friends with Dayna, nor could she ever completely forgive her for her heartlessness. *And if she ever does anything to hurt Erika…*

"I won't do this if you don't want me to," Erika said. "Even if it means never earning a single penny from singing again."

The honesty in Erika's face, the scale of what she was offering, brought tears to Dess's eyes. "You would do that for me, wouldn't you?" Dess's voice broke.

"I would do anything for you, Dess."

With her good arm, Dess pulled Erika closer and stared hard into her eyes. "Then you will sign for one year with Dayna Williams."

Erika gasped. A maelstrom of conflicting thoughts and emotions were going through Dess too.

"If you don't," Dess continued, trying to tamp down the tremble in her voice, "you will never get this out of your system. You will never know what you might be, and I can't live with that. And besides, if you don't do this, Dayna wins. We'll both be her prisoners."

Jennifer rapped softly on the door, announcing her return, and Dess collapsed back in her seat.

She might, she realized, have just made the biggest mistake of her life.

* * *

Erika took a deep breath, cast a final look at Sloane for strength, and somehow managed to stride onto the stage like she hadn't a care in the world. How she made it look so easy came from the practiced battleground of her childhood—that scarred place where she had to pretend she desired the same goals as her single-minded parents, pretend her home life was a happy one, pretend the kids at school didn't bully her. Oh yes. With her dazzling smile, straightened shoulders, her cocky strut across the stage, she could pretend with the best of them.

"Hello, Chicago!" she shouted into the mic, bowing deeply to show off her cleavage. And her ass. Sell the assets, she thought, because voice alone doesn't make you a star these days. "How you all doing tonight?"

The crowd responded with a passion that continued to amaze her, even though her popularity had steadily grown with each concert and festival. The wolf whistles, the shouts were well past simple politeness. Maybe two thousand people—her largest crowd yet—were on their feet with a thrum of anticipation that buzzed like an electrical current. It was, she supposed, largely because of Dess's accident and their connection to each other. People wanted to see who the famous Dess Hampton had come out of retirement to play guitar for. There were rumors—false, of course—that Dess might appear. There had also been conjecture in the press that Erika and Dess were romantically involved, though nothing had been substantiated. Still, people wanted to feel that connection to Dess's greatness, no matter how remote.

Dess. God, how she wished Dess were onstage with her. Her absence was like having a tooth freshly extracted and the tongue insistently finding and worrying about the gap. It was almost painful to have her gone. The fact that Dess wasn't even in the audience—it was too risky with the press out in full force—simply drove home the fact that she might as well exist on a different planet right now.

Don't, Erika told herself. *Don't go to that dark place. This is joyous, this is music!*

Sloane and Red launched into the opening of an old Hendrix blues song, "Hear My Train a Comin'." The electric guitar work was dynamic and rousing, the drumbeats charged. Erika rolled out her voice slowly, tantalizingly, like a distant train gathering speed as it approached. With every phrase that was sung, her voice intensified in timbre and her body loosened and moved in the same groove as the guitar licks. It was as though the guitar notes were shooting straight through her veins and out her skin; she wouldn't have been surprised to see sparks. She became so immersed in the music that for long stretches she forgot everything—where she was, who she was, everything that had come before, everything that was expected henceforth. It was a sliver of time that existed in its own dimension, right here on the stage.

When it was time to slow things down with "I Put a Spell on You," Erika found her eyes involuntarily searching for Dess in the crowd. Her heart ached at her inability to capture Dess the way Dess had captured her, so deeply and irrevocably and right to her soul. She sang from the depths of her walled-off frustration, from the gut-wrenching pain felt only by someone who has loved completely but can never truly be in possession of that love.

If only I could put a spell on you, baby, Erika thought, *I'd do it in a flash. And you'd be mine.*

The crowd went nuts, and Erika was left to wonder in amazement how a girl from rural Texas managed to affect people to such a degree. Dayna Williams, she knew, would want to figure out the magic formula, so they could bottle and sell it like widgets off an assembly line. She'd told Erika as much in their meeting an hour before the concert began. We're going to sell you, she'd promised, and people won't be able to get enough of you. Erika didn't know if she could believe the woman or even wanted to. As soon as she had signed on the dotted line, the agent had bolted to O'Hare to catch a flight back to California so she could get started right away on making Erika a star, she'd promised her.

It turned her stomach to have to sign with Dayna—the woman who'd treated Dess like crap. But Dess, Sloane, that lawyer woman Jennifer, had all insisted that it was her only viable option. And it was only for a year. *One year.* She could put up with almost anything for a year, she reminded herself. In fact, it would pale in comparison to the years of misery she'd survived as a child.

But if the price resulted in the loss of Dess, well, *that* she wasn't yet sure she could survive.

Moving to the keyboards, her voice thick with emotion, Erika announced, "This next song I want to dedicate to a very special woman. A woman who is 'The Song in My Heart.'"

* * *

Dess drew in a breath; it stalled painfully in her chest as Erika began singing their song. The song—Erika's voice—was so beautiful, so passionate, so fervent, that if she were not already in love with Erika, she would be by the song's conclusion.

"You okay?" Carol whispered beside her.

They'd snuck into the concert, Dess swaddled in an oversized ball cap and wraparound sunglasses, her trussed-up arm hidden inside the open flap of her baggy denim jacket. It had been impossible for her to stay away, so she'd dragged her unwilling sister along for support.

"Yeah," she finally answered. "I'm fine."

Carol mumbled something that Dess, completely mesmerized by Erika singing the words they'd written together, couldn't distinguish. She didn't need to be told that she had to be some kind of fool to let Erika go off into the crazy world of the music business. And not only without her, but with the despicable Dayna Williams at her side, guiding her. Carol was probably scolding her—she'd voiced her opposition to the plan when Dess explained it to her on the way to the concert. But Carol didn't know Erika the way she did. She didn't fully appreciate Erika's potential, her gifts, her drive and ambition. She couldn't possibly understand that there was no other way, that anything short of Erika reaching for the stars would be a slow suicide. And besides, it was the reconciling of a debt Dess felt she owed the universe. She'd never be free of her shame if she didn't push Erika to climb to the heights she so richly deserved.

"Shit!" Carol exclaimed, loud enough to be heard this time. She clutched Dess's good side, began sharply steering her away.

"What?"

"Don't look, don't look."

"What the hell is going on?"

"A photographer. He's spotted you."

There was a stirring in the crowd not far from her. She ducked her head, instinctively pulled her ball cap lower over her ears, but it was too late. She glimpsed a long-lensed camera pointed at her as Carol began roughly pulling her away. Whispers escalated, people around her began calling out her name, pointing. A movement of bodies shifted, like water currents, in their direction. Panic rising in her throat, Dess broke into a run. Her arm smacked into something, and pain shot through her like a lightning bolt. *Fuck!* Did they have no mercy, chasing her down like this when she was hurt and clearly in pain? It was just the way it had been six years ago, when, sick with cancer and radiation that had permanently ruined her singing voice, she'd begged for privacy, yet still, they refused to leave her alone.

"C'mon," Carol yelled, tugging her faster. "Just a little farther."

Dess fought the urge to cry. She'd just wanted to see Erika sing one last time, before things turned irrevocably complicated for them. But already, nothing was simple and never would be again, and the bitterness of that realization crushed her hard, made her stumble on the uneven earth of the park. Carol pulled her along again, and her tears gushed from her like a waterfall.

CHAPTER TWENTY-THREE

Even knowing it was the last evening she'd spend with Dess for a few weeks couldn't diminish the high tonight's concert had given Erika. Her voice had been as near perfect as she could ever hope, she and the band had performed flawlessly, and the crowd— *man!*—the crowd had loved her. They didn't let her go until she sang two encores, and she happily rode the wave of their energy and their rabid appreciation. She was vibrating by the time she sang her last note, bowed and strode regretfully from the stage.

Over a glass of wine at Dess's condo, she recounted every detail of the concert. Sitting next to her, their thighs touching, Dess smiled, toasted Erika with her glass.

"I knew you'd be wonderful, darling. I'm so proud of you. You deserve every last ounce of love from that crowd."

"Thank you, sweetheart." Erika's heart swelled. Dess's words were far more satisfying than the cheers of thousands or the gratification of some ridiculously generous contract. "I really wish you could have been there. I swear it was my best performance yet."

"Actually…" Dess shifted sideways to face Erika. "I was there. Carol took me."

"You were?" *Maybe that was why things had felt so right onstage,* Erika thought. Why everything had fit together so perfectly. *Because Dess had been there all along. A loving, bolstering presence, even as an anonymous member of the crowd.*

"Only for a couple of songs," Dess clarified. "Then a photographer spotted me, and Carol and I had to run out of there like a couple of cats being chased by a pack of dogs."

"Oh, shit. I'm so sorry. Are you okay?" Dess had been right about the paparazzi. They weren't going to leave her alone anytime soon.

"I'm okay, especially now that we're here. Alone."

Dess's eyes shone in the flickering candlelight. Her mouth broke into a slow, sultry smile, and it was all the invitation Erika needed. She lay against Dess's chest, content to snuggle there and enjoy the instant tranquility of being in Dess's arms.

"Oh, honey," Erika said, her voice cracking at the thought of the many nights ahead she would spend alone. "Do you know how good this feels? How this is the only thing I ever really want to do for the rest of my life?"

A chuckle of amusement vibrated from Dess's chest against Erika's cheek. "Actually, I can think of one other thing that beats this, hands down."

It wasn't the first time Erika had noticed that when talk turned serious and heartfelt between them, when their affectionate murmurings edged closer to proclamations of love, Dess often steered them toward sex. Not that Erika was complaining. Sex with Dess was simply fantastic. No, sensational. Phenomenal. But it wasn't a replacement for what she needed to hear Dess say.

"Dess…"

Kisses quickly snuffed out further conversation. Gentle, tender kisses that quickly veered to ravenous and demanding, until finally Dess uttered breathlessly that she didn't want it slow and soft tonight. Hard and fast, she said, her voice ending on a moan as Erika pulled her shirt apart, buttons flying like raindrops. At first touch, Dess's nipples were rock hard, and she thrust herself into Erika's willing mouth. There would be bruises, Erika was sure, as her mouth showed no mercy to Dess's breasts.

"Oh God," Dess moaned, her body beginning to tremble beneath Erika. "I need you to make me come, Erika. I want to come so hard for you."

Her voice low in her throat, Erika said, "I want you to come for me, sweetheart. I want you to come for me like you've never come before."

"Oh, yes, yes, yes."

Dess's shorts were easy to remove. Better yet was the surprise beneath them—Dess wore no underwear.

"Perfect," Erika rasped, breathing her lover in, burying her face against her hard wetness. She consumed Dess with a fervor she hadn't shown before, stroking every ridge and valley with a lightning quickness that brought Dess to the edge—and over—in mere minutes. Dess shuddered and screamed Erika's name, clutching her hair by the fistfuls, digging her nails into her shoulders as violent shudders wracked her body.

Erika remained where she was, between Dess's legs. "Sorry, not leaving. Not leaving here until you come at least twice more."

Dess laughed and stroked Erika's head. "I love a woman with perseverance."

"And dedication."

"Yes, that too. And stamina."

"Mmm. Tenacity too."

"And unrelenting. God, you're wonderful."

Erika nipped the inside of Dess's thigh. "I want to hear you say that right as you're coming."

"Hmm, I think I can...oh God!" Erika had pushed herself inside Dess, lingering inside the warm wetness before setting a rhythm. "I don't think...I...can talk...anymore."

"That's okay. Moans will do just fine." Erika flicked her tongue briskly against Dess's clit, and felt the satisfaction of her lover growing rigid with the onslaught of yet another orgasm.

* * *

Dess barely slept all night. Held gently in Erika's arms, she couldn't quell the racing thoughts, the hopeless churning in her mind that left her more and more bereft with each hour that ticked by on her bedside clock. She wanted to be with Erika more than she'd ever wanted to be with anyone. She did love this woman. Was in love with her. *But that isn't enough*, she tried to convince herself over and over. There was no such thing as love conquering all, she thought with growing desolation. Love couldn't bridge their diverging paths. Couldn't sustain them through what she was sure would be a rocket ride to the top for Erika. No. Erika needed to spread her wings, see where she could go without the drag of a lover who had eschewed everything to do with fame and superstardom and the music business. Erika needed to be free. Free of her, no matter how much pain it would cause them.

Erika stirred. "Baby, you're crying." Delicately, she thumbed the tears from Dess's cheeks.

The morning light filtered lazily through the blinds, bathing the room in a dusky glow. It was going to be a cloudy day, which suited Dess's mood perfectly.

"Are you okay?" Erika asked with urgency.

Dess rolled onto her back. She didn't want to hide the way she was feeling, because there was no way to soften the blow. And no more time to delay the inevitable.

"No," she said simply. "Not really."

"Is it because I'm leaving today?"

"Yes." Dess's breath caught painfully in her chest at the thought of being alone again. She'd spent every waking moment with Erika—and Sloane—for almost three months. Not only had she become used to their company, she enjoyed it. Talking about music, fooling around on guitar and piano, writing songs with Erika, bantering with Sloane, playing for appreciative but small crowds—all of it had become a lifesaver for Dess. It had given her life meaning again, gave her a reason to get up in the morning, made her feel more alive than she'd felt in years. "I'm going to miss you," she said, her voice cracking with emotion. "So much."

Erika caressed her face lightly. "Are you sure you won't change your mind about joining us for the rest of the tour? I wish you would."

"No. We've been over this. I can't have the paparazzi all over us, hounding us every minute." Her hands balled into fists beneath the sheets. "And I can't be around *her*." Meaning Dayna, of course.

"Then fly in and meet me every couple of weeks. Or I'll fly here. We can spend a couple of days together before—"

"No, honey. We can't."

Anguish swept across Erika's face. Her voice was barely above a whisper. The look on her face said she knew exactly what Dess was about to propose. "Dess, no. Please."

There was no denying that what she was about to say was going to crush Erika and, by extension, herself. But there was no other way. Erika was going to have to embark on her musical journey without her. At least for the foreseeable future. It was the fair thing, the sensible thing, to do. Dess had had her career, had attained her dreams and goals and then some. Erika, on the other hand, had barely begun.

It took great effort to find her voice, to sound strong. "Erika, what you need to do right now, you need to do on your own. Without me."

"No, no. Please don't say that, Dess. I can't do any of this without you." Tears sprang from Erika's eyes.

Dess let Erika cry, even though each tear pierced her heart. She rocked her, kissed the top of her head, held her in a way she'd probably never been held before in her life, it occurred to her. "You know," she whispered after a while, "that I would only hold you back. And I can't allow that to happen. Not until you've shown the world your gifts."

"No," Erika said, her voice unyielding. "It won't mean anything without you."

"That's not true. It will mean everything. I've been there, remember? And if you don't do this, Erika, you're cheating yourself. And you're cheating the world of something you were meant to do and meant to share." She cupped Erika's chin and tilted her face up until they were looking into each other's eyes. "You were *born* to do this."

The sting still present in her voice, Erika said, "Why were you so quick to help me if you were only going to let it all go?"

"Because," Dess said. She could no longer delay explaining the shameful side of her motivation. "I needed to make amends, in part."

"Make amends for what? To whom?"

"Make amends to myself, the universe. Years ago, when I was reaching the very peak of my career, I irreparably harmed a young singer's career. Intentionally. And I've been ashamed about it ever since."

"I can't imagine you would ever—"

"I did." She'd never admitted to anyone what she'd done, other than Dayna, who approved wholeheartedly, snake that she was. But Dayna hadn't made her do it. There was no one else to blame but herself.

"What did you do?"

"There was a young woman, a singer, about a decade younger than me. Her voice was very much like mine, her style, her choice of music. She'd obviously been very influenced by me. She even looked a little bit like me. I was convinced she was better than me. A better singer, better looking, more talented. And even though it was during the most successful part of my career, there was never a moment when I wasn't very afraid of it all collapsing. You see, that's the irony about success. You want it so badly, and then once you get it, you can think of nothing else but losing it. You'll do anything to keep it." The public, the music company executives, concert promoters, even your own agent, Dess knew, only cared about what you could do next for them. Nobody cared about what you'd done a month ago, much less a year ago.

"I hadn't thought of it like that before. It sounds…unpleasant."

"If you're not careful, you can become something—someone—you don't even recognize," Dess continued. "And this girl. Eva was her name. My record company wanted to sign her, wanted her to open my concert tour for me. But I vetoed it. And I did it in a way I'm not proud of. I made things up. Told them she was uncooperative, unprofessional, and that it was a mistake to sign someone who was a virtual, although younger, carbon copy of me. I was given a lot of latitude in those days, and she was cut loose."

"That hardly qualifies as sabotaging her career, Dess."

"No, but it gets worse. Dayna took it from there, spread the word, or I should I say lies, about her far and wide. Added a few more embellishments too, like how she was a coke head. Nobody would touch her after that, and she drifted into obscurity."

"Okay, so you did a mean thing. But if she was talented enough, she would have made it anyway, with or without your interference."

Another thing Erika was naïve about, and Dess's heart began to pound in frustration. "No, Erika, you're wrong about that. I know you don't realize it yet, but talent does not equal success. Far from it. Without a lot of luck or the murky scruples of someone like Dayna or the timely kindness of influential people, you're screwed in this business. And I screwed that girl when I could have helped her."

"So that's it then," Erika said, her voice building to an angry crescendo. "You've made your penance now by helping me. You can feel good about yourself again. Well, good for you, Dess, glad I could be of help!"

"Erika, wait, it's not like that and you know it. You asked me what made me want to help you. I was honest just now, that's all. But I would never have helped you if I didn't believe in you."

They lay in silence together until the room's shadows disappeared. Then Erika swung her legs over the bed and threw on her robe. Turning to Dess, her gaze fixed and uncompromising, she said in a steely voice, "We're not done yet, Dess. This... between us...is a hell of a long way from being done." She turned and over her shoulder added, "Just so you're clear."

Watching her depart, Dess sank back into her pillow and smiled faintly into it. Erika was one of the most determined, confident women she knew. There was comfort in the knowledge that she would not give up on them, and maybe, just maybe, she thought with the first strand of hope she'd felt in days, they'd find a way somehow. Someday.

CHAPTER TWENTY-FOUR

The weeks following the Chicago Blues Festival were frenetic ones for Erika. The rumors were true—Dayna Williams was absolutely relentless in pushing both Erika and herself. At her behest, Erika accepted a growing number of performance offers, agreed to a string of newspaper, radio and magazine interviews, and even signed an endorsement with Taylor Guitars in California that required a racy photo shoot to capitalize, Dayna insisted, on a body that was made to instantly raise hard-ons everywhere. An exaggeration if there ever was one, Erika figured, but she understood the need for ramping up her exposure. She had come to accept that her musical talents alone weren't enough to set herself apart from all the other amazingly talented artists plying their trade. But it was damned exhausting work. Work that she hoped paid off and soon, because she was all-in with everything she damned well had, including her shredded heart.

She was in the midst of a string of West Coast performances. Three days ago it was Portland, Oregon, for an evening featuring the country's best young blues performers. Last night it was

Seattle. Now it was Vancouver, British Columbia, where Erika would open in twenty-four hours for the popular Canadian rock group Nickelback. It would be her first stadium concert, with an expected audience of about thirty-five thousand people. If she thought too far ahead, her nerves would rattle her too much, so she kept her mind occupied with thoughts of anything and everything unrelated to music. She had even taken a long walk through the city's beautiful Stanley Park to keep herself distracted and, hopefully, worn out enough to get a good night's sleep tonight.

Back in her room at the posh Pan Pacific Hotel, Erika anxiously showered and changed into jeans and a lavender tuxedo blouse. She was meeting Sloane for dinner downstairs in the hotel dining room. She was thrilled to be seeing her friend again. She hadn't seen her in over a month, although they'd traded a few texts. After the Chicago Blues Festival, Dayna had announced that as her new manager, she was pulling Erika out of the rest of the summer's Midwest festival tour because it was "beneath" her. She'd said it in the most insulting way possible, of course, as if Erika might catch leprosy or something equally despicable if she continued with the circuit. Sloane was cut loose, which wasn't exactly a tragedy for the drummer, since she couldn't stand to be within a mile of Dayna Williams and anyway had no shortage of other offers. Their paths were serendipitously crossing in Vancouver because Sloane was filling in for Nickelback's absent drummer.

The butterflies in Erika's stomach were not because Sloane was downstairs, but because Sloane was her only remaining connection to Dess. She wanted so badly to hear about Dess—any detail, no matter how infinitesimal. She missed Dess terribly, as though a vital organ had been cleaved from her body. Most days it was like being underwater, seeing the world through a blurry film. She felt slightly disengaged from every emotion. Anything joyful was not truly uplifting, and that which was painful had lost its sharp edges.

Sloane hugged her hard beside the table for two with a view of the ocean. "God, it's good to see you, woman."

"It's good to see you too, Sloane. I've missed you."

"I missed you too, kid. Let me look at you." Sloane's brown eyes flicked over her, clinical in nature, like a big sister appraising her. "You've lost weight," she said. "Wicked Witch of the West not feeding you?"

They sat down, Erika chuckling at Sloane's reference to Dayna. "I'm eating, don't worry. Just crazy busy."

"Well, don't let her treat you badly, because she'll treat you like a dog if you let her."

"Don't worry, I won't." Erika tried to smile but couldn't. Dayna Williams wasn't even a blip on the radar of what was making her feel like shit.

A waiter, his dark hair slicked back like that of a television mafioso, stopped to take their drink order.

"A bottle of Dom," Sloane said indulgently. "We should celebrate how well you're doing."

Erika began to protest, but Sloane wasn't listening. She'd never tasted champagne that expensive before, though, so what the hell. Maybe getting a little drunk was exactly what she needed. Because as glad as she was for their little reunion, it was also a painful reminder of what she'd lost.

"How are you doing?" Sloane asked, her voice low. "I mean, really?"

"Really?" Erika took a deep, sharp breath that bit her insides like a cold gust of wind. "I miss her, Sloane. Without her, it feels like...like..."

"Like what?"

"Like I'm just going through the motions. Like I don't even give a shit if—"

"Don't say that." Sloane's voice was like a slap. "Don't ever say that. This is a sacrifice for her too, you know. If you give up, Dess is going to kick your ass and so am I."

Erika had a vision of Dess doing exactly that. "Did she say that?"

"Yes. A few days ago, matter of fact."

Erika's heart skipped a beat. "You saw her?"

"Sure. I had a few days off and caught a plane to the island to stay with her and her mom."

"How is her arm healing?" It was only one of many questions Erika wanted to ask about Dess, and the least agonizing.

"Beautifully. She's even back to some light guitar playing now."

The waiter delivered their bottle, popping the cork with maximum drama and pouring with a flourish. Erika silently prayed for him to hurry up, but he took his time, asking them next if they were ready to order. Erika hadn't even glanced at the menu yet. Food was well down her priority list these days.

"Just get us a couple of medium steaks, baked potato and something salad-y," Sloane told him, glancing at Erika for approval.

"Make mine salmon instead of the steak," Erika said to the waiter, then turned back to Sloane. There was no use delaying the inevitable any longer. "How is she, Sloane?"

Sloane raised her glass and clinked it against Erika's, the tiny bubbles shooting rapidly to the foamy top. "To you, my friend, and your success. I'm so happy for you."

"Thank you." Erika raised her glass to her lips, her impatience matching the ascending bubbles. She forced herself to savor the crisp tingle in her mouth before swallowing. Damn, that stuff was good.

"Honestly?" Sloane said. "She's dying inside. Like you."

Erika's gaze slid past Sloane and out to the ocean, layered in orange by the setting sun, darkened in spots by the low range mountains rising beyond. It was impossible to believe that Dess could be hurting as much as she was. She loved Dess. She ached for Dess. She wanted to spend the rest of her life with Dess. But Dess couldn't say the same, and that hurt a hundred times worse than any absence or banishment or breakup.

"She doesn't love me," Erika said, her voice shaking. "Not the way I love her."

"Oh, please." Sloane rolled her eyes. "Of course she does. More than she's loved anyone before. She's in love with you."

"Bullshit." Anger exploded through Erika like a match igniting white gas. "She's never said it, Sloane. Not once has she said those words to me. Do you have any idea how much that hurts? Do you have any idea how much that makes me question what the fuck we were doing together? Besides having a mind-blowing time in the sack?"

Sloane sipped her champagne and regarded Erika carefully. "I've known Dess for a long, long time. Since you were barely out of diapers. I know what's going on in her head, and I know she's questioning every day whether she did the right thing in letting you go, okay? Trust me, she loves you. But she's been burned before. And she's one of the most practical people I know. Dess likes to be cautious. She likes to take her time with things, make sure they're right."

"She's a control freak, more like. Or maybe cautious is just another word for coward?"

Sloane's expression darkened. "She's doing what she thinks is best right now. For both of you. And I know that's hard to accept."

Bile crept up Erika's throat, and her voice came out high and pitched. "Don't you dare lecture me, Sloane. I am not some fucking kid, and I'm tired of you and Dess acting like my goddamned mothers, professing to know what's best for me! *She's* what's best for me. Period."

Throwing her napkin on the table like a gauntlet, Erika nearly toppled her chair in her haste to get to the washroom. Locked in a stall, she clawed at the toilet paper roll as tears poured from her eyes, sobs racking her, doubling her over. It wasn't fair. Dess wasn't giving her an equal say in anything. Wasn't giving her—them—even the tiniest chance to try to make it work. Dess hadn't put a damned thing on the line for them. She held onto all the control, doled out her emotions as she saw fit, made all the decisions. Plain and simply, Dess didn't trust her. And without trust, they had nothing.

Fine, Erika decided, as her emotions coalesced into a hard knot. If this was what Dess wanted, then to hell with it. No more crying over the past. No more agonizing over something that wasn't going to change. As of right now, she vowed to herself, she was moving forward with her life—something with which she was well acquainted. She knew how to shed the past like a layer of unwanted skin. She could do this, she reassured herself, wiping away her last tear and flushing the toilet.

Sloane stood as she returned to the table.

"You okay?"

"Fine," Erika said, clenching her jaw tightly. "I'm fine."

"Look, about Dess. What I meant—"

"No." Erika held up a hand for emphasis. "I don't want to talk about Dess anymore tonight, okay? She wants me to move on, and that's exactly what I'm going to do." She replaced the napkin neatly in her lap, took another sip of her champagne. "Good, here comes our food."

* * *

"She really rocked it last night, Dess. As in, she kicked major ass!"

Dess smiled into the phone. All morning she'd been dying to call Sloane for every last detail about Erika, but she'd chickened out. Sloane, bless her soul, must have read her mind.

"Even Chad Kroeger told me afterwards it might have been a mistake having her open for them. He said it was like when the Stones had to go onstage after James Brown opened for them back in the sixties. It was like she'd sucked all the air out of the room."

That's my girl, Dess thought, doing a fist pump in the porch's shadows at her island home. She had to swallow back tears of pride. "That's a huge step for her. Bet she didn't show an ounce of nerves, either."

"Nope, not one. She's solid, Dess. A real pro. And I know your influence had a lot to do with that."

Dess had watched a YouTube clip of Erika's performance first thing this morning, and while she shouldn't have been surprised, Erika still managed to astound her with how fearlessly and commandingly she moved around the stage. She was sexier than ever, if that was possible—her thighs looking rock hard in their tight jeans, her tight leather vest hugging her fabulous breasts. Her face was as classically beautiful as ever—the generous mouth and luscious red lips, eyes the color of night that could swallow you whole. Dess had trembled at the sight of her.

"She was going places with or without any influence from me," Dess finally said. "God, her voice sounds better than ever, doesn't it?"

"I don't even think she's hit her stride yet with her voice." Sloane whistled. "Imagine what the world's in for when she matures into it? Oh, and she's hitting the recording studio next week to get a couple of singles out."

Dess smiled into the receiver. Hearing about Erika this way and seeing the clip of her latest performance gave her a dizzying sense of satisfaction. She'd been right to push Erika to pursue her career, no matter how painful the sacrifice.

"How is she doing otherwise, Sloane?" Dess was almost afraid of the answer.

Sloane hesitated. "She misses you. She's hurting. But…"

An intake of breath stalled in Dess's chest. "Tell me."

"I think she finally understands that she has no choice but to keep moving forward, professionally…and personally."

Dess leaned against the porch railing for support, closed her eyes against the fresh wave of pain.

"Good. That's good." She trembled, and it took every ounce of her strength to keep her voice from failing her. She didn't want Sloane to hear how much she was hurting, even as her heart tumbled into her stomach.

Tonight, she thought, she'd look at the stars and hope that, wherever Erika was, she was doing the same.

CHAPTER TWENTY-FIVE

Hitting the recording studio was not nearly as much fun as Erika had anticipated. It sucked, actually. At least, compared to performing in front of a live audience. Recording was pure drudgery, she had quickly learned. It was tedious and repetitive and required long hours of standing around, waiting for others to do their part. It took three days to learn and record the song, called "Down Where You Belong," which had been penned by a blues band from Tennessee that Dayna knew. A half-hearted attempt to convince Dayna to let her record one of her own songs was quickly dismissed. According to Dayna, Erika was nowhere near ready to record anything she'd written herself. She had a solid, proven formula, Dayna told her, and by God they were going to stick to it.

The latest tactic in Dayna's so-called rock-solid plan was for Erika to attend *MTV*'s annual music video awards later this week in Inglewood, California. She wasn't nominated for anything, hadn't been selected to perform or to present. Hell, few people at this echelon of the industry even knew she existed. Next year by this time, they'll be stepping on top of one another to get to you, Dayna had promised her. But for now, it was important to network, to be seen as though she belonged there with the likes of Beyoncé, Katy Perry, Imagine Dragons, OneRepublic.

Erika was skeptical. She would be an interloper, practically a nobody. "And exactly how am I supposed to make an impression?"

Dayna triumphantly retrieved a magazine from her briefcase. It was a copy of *Us Weekly*, featuring a photo and article of a twenty-six-year-old-up-and-coming actress who'd just filmed her second feature film—a romantic thriller with Bradley Cooper.

Erika crossed her arms over her chest at Dayna's shit-eating grin. The woman had more tricks up her sleeve than a magician. "Okay, I'll bite. What does Bethany Dunlop have to do with anything?"

"Lots, I hope," Dayna said. "You're going to be her date at the *MTV* awards."

"Get serious." Bethany Dunlop had been called one of the world's top ten beautiful people, and last month she'd been crowned by *People* magazine as the country's most eligible bachelorette. She was a lesbian, and she was out. But what the hell would she want with an unknown singer when she could be on the arm of someone in the same celebrity stratosphere? Someone who, like her, was a household name?

"I couldn't be more serious," Dayna said, growing animated. "Her manager owed me a favor. And after Bethany watched a YouTube clip of you, she happily agreed. Said you were incredibly hot and that she wanted to get to know you better."

"Christ, Dayna. Anyone else you want to prostitute me out to? Do I have to fuck her too at the end of the night?"

Dayna leaned back in her chair and unceremoniously hoisted her Prada-sheathed feet onto her desk. Her laughter filled the large, pretentious office. "That's rather a personal decision. But if it were me…" Dayna stared dreamily at the ceiling. "I'd fuck her like a cowboy."

Erika rolled her eyes. *Whatever the fuck* that *means*. It occurred to her that Dayna had a second agenda with this little ploy. Parading her around on the arm of a hot young starlet would further sabotage any chance she might have of getting back with

Dess. Not that that seemed like even a remote possibility. She hadn't seen or heard from Dess in three months now, and she doubted she ever would again. Dess had made it abundantly clear that Erika was on her own, that chasing her dreams meant there was no chance for them.

"Fine," she finally relented. "Whatever." There would be more of this phony crap, she fully expected. Staged alliances with people who could supposedly boost her career, pretend friendships with celebrities, appearances that would maximize her exposure. The blind date with Bethany would hardly register as a blip on the bullshit meter six months from now, she supposed.

A limo picked her up promptly at seven. Though she accepted it as part of doing business, she was still annoyed by the whole maneuver. How dare Dayna pass her off like a piece of meat! And who was to say this Bethany wasn't going to be a stuck-up bitch? Or a head case? It was going to be a night from hell, no matter how it was sliced, she decided. Would she be expected to bow in Bethany's presence? Walk three paces behind her? Would Bethany act like she was doing her a huge favor, letting her tag along as her *date*?

She'll probably ditch me the minute we get there, Erika thought, then decided that might not be such a bad thing. Let the photographers get their red carpet shots, then sayonara, baby.

The limo stopped before a one-story, Spanish-style bungalow in Brentwood. Moments later, Bethany Dunlop emerged. Along with a man. A very flamboyant, slender man in a Popsicle orange tux who minced his way to the car. *Perfect*, Erica thought. *I'll be a third wheel, and they won't even miss me when I slip away.*

"Hi," Bethany said, extending her hand to Erika as she climbed into the back seat beside her. "I'm Bethany. How do you do?"

She was pretty. God, she was pretty. Gorgeous. Her blond hair was up off bared shoulders that were as creamy as satin. Her eyes were emerald green, matching her very expensive-looking earrings and necklace. Her lips were done in a pale pink shade of lipstick so as not to draw attention away from her eyes and her ridiculously snow-white teeth. She was a Barbie doll. A perfect specimen. And completely out of Erika's league.

"I'm well, thank you," Erika managed to squeeze from an impossibly dry throat. With a moist palm, she shook Bethany's tiny, smooth hand. "I'm Erika Alvarez."

"And I'm Raymond," said the orange-suited man who climbed into the seat across from them. His dark, thinning hair stuck up in about three different directions. He held out a hand as limp as last week's bouquet of flowers. "I'm Bethany's assistant. And her best friend."

And you're higher than a kite, Erika thought, shaking his hand.

He leaned forward, giggling. "Don't worry, girls, I won't intrude on your privacy tonight. I know how to disappear." He winked and laughed in a soprano voice. "Poof! Just like that, Raymond disappears. You watch."

Erika stole a glance at Bethany, who gave her a benign smile. Her eyes, however, said she wanted to do Erika right here in the back of the limo, as soon as they could ditch Raymond.

Oh, shit, Erika thought, her palms really sweating now.

* * *

Dess sat at her computer, a glass of wine in her hand. She'd taken to drinking a glass or two a night lately—something she'd not been in the habit of doing for years. Back then, it was because of the stress and exhaustion from her performance and travel schedules. Now it was the aching hole in her heart that only alcohol seemed to soothe. She couldn't shake Erika from her mind, her heart. Maybe if she, like Erika, had something to move forward with, her emptiness would not be so crushing. She shook her head, thinking how naïve she'd been to think she could go back to her predictable, staid, safe life.

Through Sloane, Dess had heard that Erika would be attending the *MTV* awards tonight, and like a love-struck teenager—or maybe a loser who had to resort to stalking—Dess clicked on the live stream of the ceremony on her computer. The event wouldn't air on television until tomorrow night, and she couldn't wait for that. Pathetically, she wanted—needed—to see Erika, no matter how brief a glimpse.

Dess squinted at the grainy footage of couples strolling the red carpet, looking resplendent as they stopped briefly to pose for photos or for a quick word with a fan or a journalist. Jay-Z and Beyoncé, Carrie Underwood and her hockey player husband, Rihanna and her date (not Chris Brown!), Taylor Swift—a steady stream of the beautiful and the powerful. For a moment, Dess was transported back to what seemed like just yesterday when she was strolling down red carpets with Dayna on her arm. Of course, Dayna had lapped up all the attention like the glamor slut she was, while Dess had treated it as an obligation to be endured. It was like running a gauntlet of blinding camera flashes, microphones, arms jutting out for autographs—all for the sake of being seen as someone who mattered in the entertainment industry. *God, I'm so glad that stuff is behind me,* Dess thought, taking another sip of wine.

It seemed that dozens of couples had strolled past the camera before, finally, Erika appeared. A flutter, so sweet and familiar, began in Dess's stomach as Erika's sheer beauty stole her breath. Her hair, black and shiny and wavy, hung loosely over her ears and past the collar of her white blouse, which was deliciously unbuttoned halfway down her chest. Her jacket and pants, custom fitted to perfection, were the color of Dess's glass of cabernet. But her eyes had no more time to appreciate her former lover before she stopped and waited for a tall, slender young woman in a long, tight gown to catch up and latch possessively onto her arm. Dess recognized her immediately—Bethany Dunlop. A hotshot young film actress who'd been nominated for an Oscar for her very first film. It was either great luck or she had one hell of a future before her. She was an out lesbian too, a rarity, although not as rare as when Dess came out at the height of her career more than a dozen years ago.

And now she's dating Erika! The thought stirred something dark and granite-like deep within her that she couldn't immediately identify. Another glass of wine, she decided, might help her figure out why she felt like throwing something against the wall.

* * *

Unfortunately, Popsicle guy had melted away from Bethany's side by the time the ceremony ended, leaving the two women alone. There were more photo ops, more introductions and pretend interest from people whose fleeting glances gave away the fact that if Erika's name didn't immediately register, she was a waste of their time. *Screw them*, Erika thought. If Dayna was right, these same people would one day be eating out of her hand. She thought about how that would feel as she watched Bethany laugh about something out of earshot with one of the stars from the television show *House of Cards*. Would joining their inner circle make her as phony and pretentious and superficial as most of them? Would she have to check her brain and her scruples at the door? Dess wasn't like that, and she'd been one of the most famous musical performers on the planet for a while, Erika reminded herself. But Dess was special. Dess was one of the most grounded, genuine people she'd ever known. Even Dess's confession about railroading another singer's career had not changed Erika's respect and admiration for her. She'd had a weak moment, had, for a time, become someone different. But Dess was not that person now, and Erika longed for one more moment with her, one more conversation, one more touch.

Thinking of Dess this way was always followed by a sick, weary feeling that turned Erika's legs to rubber, made her head swim. It was followed, always, by a twist of panic in her gut. Which was then chased by the mountain of self-doubt that hovered over her like a shadow. Would any of this ever be worth the price she was paying? It had to be, she thought, because it was the only thing that kept her going.

"Sweetheart, are you ready to ditch this place?" Bethany purred in her ear.

Erika bristled. She wasn't anyone's sweetheart. Not anymore. "Sorry. I don't think I'm in the mood for one of the after parties."

"Oh, that's perfect." A predatory smile played on Bethany's lips. The tip of her tongue played between her teeth. "Let's go back to my place."

Every shred of common sense told Erika not to do it, but at this moment, she was sick of trying to live up to self-imposed standards that, quite frankly, hadn't been working so hot for her lately. She didn't want sex with this woman—or any woman who wasn't Dess—but the thought of another night alone held zero appeal. Tonight she needed the company of someone who had absolutely no connection to Dess. Someone the polar opposite of Dess and who wouldn't in the least remind her of Dess. And yes, even if it was with this hollow shell of a woman. *At least there's no danger of me falling in love with her*, Erika thought with some consolation. That part of her was reserved only for Dess.

"Joint?" Bethany held out a gold-plated cigarette case to Erika in the back of the limo.

"No thanks."

"God, you're boring." Bethany threw her head back and laughed. "Honestly, it's okay. As long as you're not boring in..." big green eyes danced in Erika's direction "...other areas of your life."

A hand crept onto Erika's thigh, lightly massaging. Bethany snuggled closer, laying her head on Erika's shoulder, moving her hand higher, feathering it down to the inside of Erika's thigh, leaving no doubt of the possibilities that lay ahead. Erika flinched as the contact came within an inch of her crotch, but she didn't push Bethany's hand away. *I'm not that much of an angel. Not tonight.*

Dayna's advice flooded back to her. Get a few dates out of Bethany, she'd said in a tone that implied it was not merely a suggestion. Those dates will get you more press than eight months of trying to get it on your own, Dayna said. The idea of using Bethany—or anyone—made Erika's skin crawl. But as Bethany's long thigh slid against her own, it occurred to her that maybe everyone in this business ended up using each other one way or another. Perhaps, she thought, as her breathing intensified with every new stroke that neared her center, using people is simply an unavoidable part of playing the game. *And you want to be a player in this game*, she reminded herself. *You are a player in this game. This is not about you, the person; this is about Erika Alvarez, the future star.*

Bethany's slender fingers skittered across her clitoris, circling it like a shark zeroing in on its prey. Her breath lodging in her throat, Erika tried to back up against the seat, but there was nowhere to go. Bethany began kissing her neck, her throat, as her hand pressed harder, faster, cupping and stroking Erika now for all she was worth. *Oh, Christ* Erika thought, squeezing her eyes shut, wishing for once that her goddamned body wasn't so responsive to the touch of another woman. *I'm going to come, and it's going to be the most useless, unsatisfying orgasm of my life.*

"I want to see how hot you really are," Bethany whispered, nipping at her earlobe, her hand urgently unzipping the fly of Erika's pants and slipping inside to continue her explorations. She palmed her clit in a back and forth motion.

"Aw fuck." Erika groaned at the orgasm that had a mind of its own. She came against Bethany's hand, thinking all the while how stupid this was, how weak she was being.

"Oh, yes, that's what I like, baby. I like making you hot. And making you come." Bethany's hand retreated from inside Erika's pants, reached for Erika's closest hand, and thrust it up her dress, between her own moist thighs. She wasn't wearing underwear. "My turn."

Erika didn't need to be told twice.

CHAPTER TWENTY-SIX

When Dess returned to her condo with Maggie, both of them wet from a soaking November rain that pelted them with icy needles from the sky, her sister Carol was waiting inside for her.

"Hey, you," Dess said, shaking off her raincoat and hanging up Maggie's leash in the front hall closet. "This is a nice surprise."

"I took the liberty of starting a pot of coffee. Hi, Maggie, how's my sweet girl?" Carol scratched Maggie's chin—the only dry spot on her. The dog lapped up the attention until her wet wiggling became too much, and Carol gently shooed her away.

"To what do I owe this surprise visit?" Dess poured them both a cup of coffee.

"To invite you to my place for Thanksgiving. Mom's coming too, of course. And Sloane."

Dess glanced at the wall calendar. Thanksgiving was just sixteen days away, and she wondered how she'd forgotten it was so close. But she did know why. It was because the days, weeks, were rolling into each other with little to differentiate them.

Playing her guitar, reading, cooking, walking Maggie had, once again, become the landmarks in her life by which she marked time's passing.

"Great, I'll be there." Dess carried the two steaming mugs to the breakfast bar and set them on the granite counter.

"Perfect." Carol dumped cream and sugar into her cup, then lazily opened the *Guitar Aficionado* magazine Dess had left there. She stopped the flurry of page turning suddenly and Dess knew precisely why. "Holy shit." A low whistle was her exclamation point.

Dess watched her sister study the Taylor Guitars full-page ad with a look of surprise, then appreciation. The ad featured a profile shot of Erika sitting in a straight, plain wooden chair, her head thrust back to expose her long, smooth neck, her denimed legs stretched out fully in front of her. A guitar had been strategically placed between her legs. Her boots were snakeskin. She wore her trademark black-leather vest with nothing beneath it, and it cradled her breasts like a pair of adoring hands. The months had done nothing to dim the memory for Dess of touching those breasts, of kissing them, of sucking those dark nipples until they became rigid. In fact, the months had not dimmed anything about Erika in Dess's lonely mind that, these days, spent more time casting looks backward than looking forward. Or even dwelling on the present. The good things in her life always seemed past tense—a pattern she'd fallen into again like sliding into a comfortable pair of shoes.

"So you've been torturing yourself with this?" Carol asked, her tone suggesting she already guessed that Dess had been obsessing over it.

"No," Dess lied. Of course she had been torturing herself with the magazine image, with the memories of Erika in her arms, in her bed, on the stage with her. She missed Erika every bit as much—maybe more—as the day she'd left. But admitting as much to Carol would solve nothing.

Carol continued to casually flip the pages as though she were browsing the shop windows along the Mag Mile. "Her blues song is doing pretty well. I hear it on the radio all the time. She sounds great, don't you think?"

"Yes. She does."

"And how about her and that actress, Bethany Dunlop. I didn't see that coming, did you?" More page flipping, more pretend casualness.

Dess sipped her coffee. "No, I didn't."

"They look pretty impressive together, but I can't imagine they have much in common. And they must never see each other, both with such busy careers and all. I'm sure it's nothing."

Dess hoped that was true, but she had no idea, and she did not want to spend time and energy worrying about something she had no control over.

"Do you think, you know, that they're just doing it for publicity, or..." Carol looked up from the magazine. "Or do you think it's something more?"

"I wouldn't know." Dess tried to keep her voice neutral, but it was like holding down the lid on a boiling pot.

"Erika doesn't seem the type who would date someone just for the attention. She's not that calculating, right?"

Dess slammed the counter with a closed fist. To hell with pretending not to give a shit. "Goddammit, Carol! I know you're trying to get a reaction out of me. Well, fine, you've succeeded."

Carol's eyes softened with sympathy. "I'm not spoiling for a fight. But yes, I'm trying to get you to talk about Erika, because you're terribly unhappy without her." Carol reached for her hand and gave it a squeeze. "Dess, honey. Please talk about it. I know it's killing you."

"There's nothing to say," Dess answered sharply. "Erika is doing what she needs to do. She's moving forward with her life. She's with somebody else, and I can't do a fucking thing about it. It's done. It is what it is."

"No, don't say that. You can still change things. You can still change your life."

Dess wanted to cocoon herself, to disappear into her habitual solitude. "We've been over this before. You know I can't go back to that lifestyle. Small festivals are one thing, but where Erika's at now, it's too...painful for me."

"All right, fine." Carol had that take-no-prisoners look in her eyes—the one she'd perfected long ago in looking out for her younger sister. "Yes, it's painful for you to be around concert halls, airports, grip-and-grins, media interviews, people like Dayna. But it's goddamned painful the way you're living too. You ever think about that?"

"Of course I think about it." Dess's chest constricted. She and pain were conjoined twins and had been for years. "I live it, for God's sake. You know that."

"Oh, honey, you're right. I'm so sorry." Carol placed her arm around Dess's shoulder and squeezed her tightly. "I want you to be happy, that's all. I hate seeing you sad."

"I know you do. I'm sorry I bit your head off."

"It's okay. I sort of asked for it. But listen, nobody says you have to go back to the music business, to that lifestyle. But you do need to deal with your fears. You've never had closure from losing your voice, from leaving your career, the music you loved so much, your fans. You never said goodbye, you never explained. You just…disappeared."

Dess pulled out of her sister's embrace and looked her in the eye. For almost seven years she'd eschewed everything to do with the music business, had coldly avoided anyone or anything connected to her life in show business. Setting a toe back onto the stage as Dora Hessler had been as risky, as brave, as she'd ever dared. But that little experiment hadn't come close to reconciling everything she'd lost. It had done nothing more for her healing process than if she'd dressed up in a costume and played make believe. "What are you suggesting?"

* * *

From behind the stage curtain, Erika peeked at the audience. They were growing restless waiting for her, but what—for once—intrigued her far more than the people was the facility. It was the iconic Ryman Auditorium in Nashville, so much like a church both inside and out, and now, as she prepared to walk onto the stage of the legendary shrine to such famous acts as Patsy Cline, Johnny Cash, Elvis Presley and Loretta Lynn, she took a deep breath and counted to twenty, letting the famous faces of the past skitter through her mind like a slide show.

Finally, she tapped the worn, scuffed wooden stage with the toe of her boot, waited for the crescendo to build after the emcee announced her, then trotted out into the spotlight, where she bowed reverently to the audience and waved to those in the upper balcony. She moved to the grand piano, sat down and wiggled her fingers. For a fleeting moment, she wondered what her parents would think of her performing on such an iconic stage. Whether it would make them forgive her for chasing *her* dream and not theirs and whether it would make them overlook her great *sin* of being gay. No, she decided. If they only loved her for her success now, it wasn't love at all.

"Hello, Nashville!" she yelled into the mic, summoning her stage persona. "Are you ready for a little R & B? A little blues? A little rock? Are you ready for little ol' me?" The audience stamped and clapped, yelled out a collective yes. "Good, 'cuz I'm ready for you!"

She launched into a spirited version of "Am I the Same Girl (You Used to Know)?" Audiences never grew tired of old R & B songs, she'd discovered, because they made you feel good, made you feel like you wanted to get up and dance. When it was time to slow things down, she decided to take a leap of faith. Departing from her set list would give Dayna a cow, but to hell with it. She wanted, needed, to feel Dess right now. Dess had played in this very auditorium two or three times during her career, and Erika so wished she could talk to her about it, share what it was like with her, what she was feeling, smelling, seeing, thinking about. Performers always listed the Ryman as one of their favorite places and said the experience remained indelibly stamped in their memories. Erika could understand why, as she imagined decades of live music coating and infiltrating every crevice and surface in the place, like thick dust.

On the piano, she began playing the opening notes to the ballad she and Dess had crafted together last spring. When she sang the words "*you are the song in my heart,*" she felt her throat clamp up. Her voice cracked and she stumbled over the next line before she could sufficiently recover. Would she ever be able to sing this song without dying inside? Without tears welling in her eyes? Would she ever be able to forget the swell of joy at having discovered real love, then the profound, soul-busting sorrow of losing it? Matters of her heart aside, it was simply too good a song to bury forever. She would always miss Dess, always feel her loss with every breath she took. But singing about their love gave her the strength, somehow, to keep moving forward. She *needed* the sacrifice to be worth it.

She'd closed out her portion of the show when Dayna, breathless and flushed, cornered her backstage. "What the hell was that song?"

"Something I wrote a while back. With Dess."

Dayna's eyes narrowed to slits. "Well. It's fucking spectacular. I want to talk about recording it."

Erika sighed. She was too spent to talk business. "Whatever. We'll talk on the plane tomorrow."

She retreated to one of the rooms in the basement, which was not much bigger than a broom closet and smelled like one. The stage was above her head, the boot stomping of the next performer tapping out a staccato beat. Looking in the dusty mirror, she tried to tell herself she didn't care that Bethany hadn't shown up. Bethany hadn't exactly promised, but she'd said she'd try, which Erika should have known was a euphemism for I-can't-be-bothered. Bethany was in Nashville for a couple of weeks, shooting a cameo appearance for the television series that went by the same name. A faint *ding* drew her attention to her phone. It was a text from Bethany instructing her to come to her penthouse suite downtown for a small party she was throwing for the show's cast and crew.

Erika's guitar player, a giant of a man with a soft-spoken voice, had asked her if she wanted to join some of the performers for a late dinner at the Wild Horse Saloon. She was tempted to take him up on his offer and teach Bethany a lesson but politely declined. She hadn't seen Bethany in more than three weeks. Not that she missed her, really, but she did miss sex. Sex between them was fast and furious—hot, but in a mechanical way devoid of all emotion except for the need to get laid. And tonight, she was ready for some sexual release.

A short cab ride later, she entered Bethany's suite unnoticed. Small clusters of people milled around, stiff drinks in their hands.

The room buzzed with laughter and gossip, the way it did when lips had been loosened by alcohol. At least two people were fall-down drunk, with several more well on their way, Erika noticed. Three of the actors from the television show were among the guests, and Erika stopped one of them to ask where Bethany was. The man, who gave Erika only a fleeting look of recognition, pointed toward what appeared to be the bathroom door, which was slightly ajar.

Impatient at having to go on a treasure hunt for her lover, Erika stalked to the bathroom and pushed open the door. There, bent over the vanity counter snorting lines of coke, were Bethany and her lapdog Raymond. This time he was dressed in lemon yellow pants and a bright red shirt.

"Jesus Christ," she said, too exhausted and unsurprised to work up much anger.

Bethany, her eyes hooded and red-rimmed, produced a lazy smile. "Hey, lover. 'Bout time you got here. Come join the fun."

"As if," Erika snorted. Bethany knew damn well she didn't do drugs and that she didn't approve of others doing them in front of her. Bethany's drug use was the only true wedge between them, because Erika simply didn't care enough to let the daily challenges of trying to maintain a relationship disturb her in any other consequential way. She had long accepted that their relationship was a house of cards, ready to collapse at the least provocation.

Raymond, his hip jutting out defiantly, winked at her but directed his comments to Bethany. "Your girlfriend would be so much more fun if she took that stick out of her ass and stuck some of this up her nose."

Erika had had enough. She turned to leave. If Bethany preferred drugs and Raymond over her, then fine. It was no great loss. She was stopped cold when Bethany mumbled, "Go ahead and leave. See if I care."

Erika walked back to Bethany, pointedly ignoring Raymond and his bitchy scorn. "If you pulled your head out of your ass for once—or out of your goddamned coke and Oxys—you might actually give a shit that you and I are through."

Bethany shook her head, smiling that stupid coked-up grin. "We're not through, baby. We've barely gotten started. And I know you aren't going to leave me, 'cuz I got something you want."

"Oh, stop sounding like a badly written song. The only thing I get from you, I can get from a million other women."

Bethany wiped her nose on the sleeve of her very expensive blouse and glared at Erika. "All except the one woman you really want it from."

"You," Erika hissed, "don't get to talk about her."

Bethany's laugh was iced with vindictiveness. "You know something? Raymond's right. You are no fun. Even that washed-up old singer you're pining for probably realized that."

Erika raised her hand to slap Bethany but stopped herself. She'd never hit anybody before. *And I'm not going to start with someone as pathetic as this.*

She left the suite without a glance back. Pining alone for Dess was far preferable than getting a synthetic high with worthless leeches and hangers-on. Her only regret was that she hadn't dumped Bethany sooner.

In the cab back to her hotel, Erika watched raindrops slither down the window and imagined it was how her soul felt—weeping, gray, cold, lonely. So terribly lonely. She and Dess had made a pact to talk to each other if either of them ever felt despondent or overwhelmed. She could use a good heart-to-heart with Dess right now, but it was a pointless fantasy. Their so-called pact had been nothing but a delusion.

CHAPTER TWENTY-SEVEN

Dess silently prayed that her heavy makeup would continue to soak up the persistent beads of sweat forming at her hairline. She hadn't produced this much sweat since that hot summer night onstage in Madison, the night that had changed so much for her and Erika. She had to practically sit on her hands now to keep them from shaking, but she offered a tranquil smile to the interviewer—*Good Morning America's* Robin Roberts. She'd given thousands of interviews over her career, which made her an old pro at it, she supposed. Except that she hadn't done one in seven years, and this one had all the butterfly-producing hallmarks of her first.

Robin was smooth—and nice, which made all the difference. Once they'd gone through the formalities and a review of Dess's career and her illness, Robin homed in on the most pertinent question, the one Dess was fully expecting: Why the sudden desire to go public again after all these years?

The answer wasn't simple, and she paused to collect her thoughts. It was time, she explained to Robin, that she began embracing life again, living in the light instead of the dark, and that meant dealing with her fear of the media and the public. What early on was a quest for privacy had blurred into something much more harmful and debilitating. So this was a baptism of sorts, she joked.

"Does this make you afraid, appearing on camera?" Robin asked. "Are you nervous right now?"

Dess laughed stiffly and held out her trembling hand. "Does that answer your question?"

Robin asked her what had changed her mind, what had been the catalyst to make her want to change her life now.

That one was easy, but she treaded carefully as she answered. She realized, she said, when she began anonymously playing music onstage again this past summer, how much she missed connecting with people. How much she missed sharing music, even if she couldn't sing anymore. And her bandmates, she added with a smile. "They were special. It was a special time, and it made me see there was so much joy out there that I was missing out on."

Robin began gently pressing her on whether love had anything to do with her new attitude. "Oh, gosh," Dess answered, warmth crawling up her face. "What happens on the road stays on the road, doesn't it?"

Robin winked. "I think that's Vegas."

As diplomatically as she could, Dess explained that since any loving relationship involved two people, it wasn't up to her alone to talk about it publicly. But she did find someone very special last summer, she conceded. And yes, "that person made me want to be myself again, made me begin to really question how I wanted to spend the rest of my life. And my sister kicked my butt too. They were both right. It was time to stop hiding, to stop moping and feeling sorry for myself. It's time to do something with my life again."

"What will that be? Any ideas?"

"It will have to involve music," Dess replied. "Because that's such a big part of who I am. But it won't be in the capacity people knew me in before. That life is over. So no, I'm not sure yet. But I think I'm actually ready to embrace something new and challenging." She looked at the camera and took a deep breath.

"I'll be slow and sure about it, but I'm ready to take it one step at a time."

Emotion thickened her voice, and Dess was eternally grateful when Robin changed the subject to something else. Carol had been right. Doing a television interview was cleansing, emancipating, and it was the first step to changing her life. Laying bare her thoughts, her emotions, opening up her very life, had been her greatest fear. But failing to wrestle that fear down would forever paralyze her into a life only half lived. Now she was on record saying her life was going to be different, leaving her little choice but to follow through.

Dess held little back. She talked about her terrifying battle with cancer, how losing her voice was devastating at first, then became the least of her worries when her very survival was at stake. She talked about how music—playing it, writing it—had saved her life as she recovered from the cancer. And how more recently, music had once again pulled her out of the muck and mire of her life. She admitted she feared her fans and others would forever see her now only as someone who had had cancer, that it would always be an asterisk beside her name. It was a risk she was prepared to take, however. Finally, she asked for forgiveness from her fans for letting her fears get the best of her. She had abandoned people—her fans, other cancer survivors. She'd even abandoned herself, she admitted, as tears trickled down her face.

There really was only one person whose forgiveness she needed, Dess knew, because that was the gaping wound that cut the deepest right now. The truth was that she'd sent Erika away because she didn't love herself enough. And because she didn't think she deserved anyone else's love. It was simple psychology, the most basic, really. She couldn't love anyone else—and couldn't accept anyone else's love—until she loved and accepted herself. Until now, that terrain had been too rough to traverse.

It might be too late to love Erika, but it wasn't too late to start loving herself.

* * *

Erika settled into the soft leather seat of the private jet that was on loan from a record company trying to woo her. Her head pounded mercilessly. After dumping Bethany's sorry ass, she'd gone back to her room and downed a pint of Jack. But not because she was hurt by the breakup. Bethany was a publicity stunt that had gone too far, and any pain from losing her was merely a payback for having taken Dayna's advice to heart.

No. What really hurt, day after day, hour after hour, was the loss of Dess. How was she supposed to get over her first and only meaningful love? How was she supposed to do any of this alone? And how was any of this shit supposed to mean a single thing when there wasn't anyone to share it with? The stage was fun—fulfilling, rewarding, energizing, a real hard-on. But the rest of it? *The rest of it's bullshit.*

Erika flipped on the small television in front of her, needing a distraction from her pounding head and her bleak thoughts. Surround Sound negated the need for headphones, but she kept the volume low, not wanting to attract the attention of Dayna, who sat at a table at the back of the plane with her nose in her laptop.

Dayna had turned out to be exactly as Erika had expected—a first-class bitch. But that was the driving force that seemed to be getting Erika places. By unspoken agreement, the two women never talked about Dess, because it was the one subject each seemed to recognize would instantly set a match to their business arrangement.

Dess. Why does every thought, every subject, always circle back to Dess?

Erika clicked through the channels until she settled on *Good Morning America*. *Good morning hangover was more like it*, she thought. The weather guy was showing off his colorful digital maps, and then Robin Roberts was on the screen. Erika could barely hear her, but for some reason, Robin was talking over photos of Dess on stage. There was one of her on a Broadway stage, another of her singing at Yankee Stadium, one of her shaking hands with the queen of England. A close-up of her singing showed the ropey muscles in her neck engaged in pushing out the sweet notes Erika had first heard back when she was in high school and had really begun appreciating great voices, great songs, and had begun casting about for singers she could look up to.

Jesus Christ, she thought with a sudden panic that drove a stake through her hangover, instantly sobering her. *They only do this shit when people die!* Fumbling, she cranked up the volume in time for Robin to introduce Dess as her guest this morning. *Oh, thank fucking God!*

She watched Dess, adorable in her nervousness, and knew instantly she still loved this woman as much as ever. Hearing her voice, being able to look into her eyes—even if it was just a two-dimensional version of her—was like a warm hug that Erika felt all the way to her toes. She longed to be able to reach through the small screen and touch Dess, to hold her again in her arms, to spoil her with kisses and caresses, to make love to her all night long. She longed for the whispered conversations that came at the end of their lovemaking, their newspaper reading over morning coffee, their idle chitchat, their heartfelt conversations. She wondered if Dess missed any of it too.

With effort, she pulled her attention back to the interview. Dess was warm, engaging, funny, relaxed and surprisingly open. She didn't look anything like the woman who had shunned everything related to journalists and the glare of public attention. Dess looked entirely as though this interview was her own idea, and the realization came as a shock to Erika. What had happened? What was she *doing* exactly? And why?

Robin was trying to coax her to talk about her love life, and Erika was on the edge of her seat. A dreamy look came over Dess's face. Her eyes were gone, lost, and Erika hoped it was because of memories of *her*. And then Dess was shaking her head, smiling, saying it wasn't up to her to discuss something that belonged to two people. But "this person" Dess was saying—and Erika knew she was talking about her—had helped inspire her to be herself again, to want to live again. It was a triumphant moment for Erika, as close as Dess was likely ever going to come to admitting she loved her. But Dess's words, her tone, seemed to imply that she had gotten everything she needed from their relationship—the will to live again and the desire to move on.

The relationship had served a purpose for Dess, like the bridge in a song that was meant to transition back to the verse and chorus. Back to the beginning. The bridge was important in any song, but it was short and served a fleeting purpose. *That's me*, Erika thought with a new level of disappointment. *I'm a fucking bridge in her life. Not a verse, and certainly not a repeating chorus.*

"I'm not surprised she wants back in the limelight now," Dayna said in a tone that matched the perpetual scowl on her face. Erika hadn't heard her sneak up behind her. "I suppose her money's running out, although God knows, she had more than enough to ever spend in her lifetime."

Erika bit the inside of her cheek to keep from telling Dayna to go fuck herself. "I don't want to talk about Dess."

"Well, I'm afraid we need to." Dayna reached over Erika for the remote and clicked off the TV. "Because Dess holds the other half of the key to that song you sang last night."

"Yes. 'The Song in My Heart.'" Erika closed her eyes, remembering when they'd written the words, the music, and how her heart had swelled with love for Dess then. So much that it was going to burst if she didn't scratch out some lyrics and sing it from the top of her lungs. She couldn't contain her love for Dess, and the song, the song Dayna wanted her to record now, was proof of that. What hurt, for her at least, was that absolutely nothing about her love for Dess had changed or diminished.

"She needs to sign off on it," Dayna snapped. "Fifty-fifty. She should go for that."

Erika wavered. "I don't know."

Dayna sat down beside Erika. Her eyes were uncompromising. "I don't care about whatever lovers' spat you two had. That song is a gold mine. You need to fix it with her so that she'll sign off on it."

Everything was a business proposition to Dayna. It set Erika's blood boiling. "I'm not going to force her or beg her to do anything. I agree it's a great song, and I agree it could be a hit. But it's up to Dess to give her permission. Or not."

"Oh, that song is more than a hit. That song is your ticket to everything you want."

No, it's not, Erika thought. *Because it won't give me back Dess.*

Dayna harrumphed. "Anyway, she certainly won't want to talk to me about it. I'll set things up for you to meet with her lawyer in Chicago. Who also happens to be *your* lawyer, as I recall. That might work in our favor."

Distilling her relationship with Dess down to a mere business arrangement sliced a new gash into Erika's heart. It was all they had left to show for their love. A song. A souvenir. But it was something, at least. And just maybe, she thought with the first ray of hope she'd felt in a long time, if Dess loved her, she'd let her record that song. If Dess loved her—had ever loved her—she too would want to share something of their love with the world. *Wouldn't she?*

It was only a moment before Erika relented. "All right. Set up the meeting and I'll be there."

CHAPTER TWENTY-EIGHT

Dess had tried to avoid making the trip to Jennifer Parker's office, employing her usual suggestion that anything needing a signature could be done via courier. But when Jennifer insisted, Dess found herself giving in. She needed to make changes in her life. She had told the world that she was going to make changes. *She* needed to change. And that meant getting out of the house, seeing people, keeping her mind and body active, rejoining life. She'd even begun to mentally entertain some of the many offers Jennifer had received lately on her behalf. There were requests for more talk show appearances, newspaper and magazine interviews, a health-product company looking for her endorsement.

The most intriguing had been an offer from a top book publisher to write her memoirs. "But I don't want to talk seriously to them until after Christmas," she'd told Jennifer over the phone. She wanted to go slow, make sure she was committed to the idea. Mostly, she needed to feel confident that anyone out there wanted to read an entire book about her.

"We'll talk a bit more about the book," Jennifer had promised over the phone. And then she dropped the bomb on her. Told her

that Erika and Dayna wanted the rights to record the ballad she
and Erika had written together.

A flat refusal had been Dess's first impulse. She laid out all
the reasons why she shouldn't sign off on the song, but Jennifer
picked them apart like a trial lawyer pouncing on the testimony
of a weak witness. When it came down to it, Dess had no good
reasons to refuse the song, other than it was a way to stick it to
Dayna, Jennifer said. But sticking it to Dayna would only hurt
Erika, and Dess didn't want that. She didn't want to feel used
either.

Now, as she sat in Jennifer's office, the contract in front of
her, Dess stalled.

Jennifer raised an eyebrow. "Still having second thoughts?"

"This whole process just feels so...cold. And that song. It's...
it's..."

"Anything but cold."

"Yes."

"Perhaps," Jennifer said, tapping a pencil on her desk, "there's
someone who can help you through this...*process*...a little more
productively than me."

She rose and strode to the door, turning back to Dess with a
wink. "I'll be back in about thirty minutes."

"What? Jennifer, what are you—"

But Jennifer was gone, the door closed firmly behind her.
Great, Dess thought. *I'm supposed to sit here and cool my heels for
thirty minutes? How is that supposed to help me make a decision?*

The door clicked open. Dess turned in her seat, then nearly
fell out of it. Erika stood frozen in place, a mild look of shock on
her face.

Dess could barely push the words from her mouth, which was
suddenly full of cotton. "Erika. What are you doing here?"

"Wh—what are *you* doing here, Dess?"

"I..." Oh hell, what did it matter now? They'd been set up,
and Erika was here. Alone. In the flesh. Right in front of her.
And looking ridiculously gorgeous in a tan-colored linen suit
and burgundy blouse. Her hair, still so dark and luscious, was
a bit longer, and it suited her. Confidence was growing in those
brown-black eyes that were so emotive. Dess had dived headlong

into those mesmerizing orbs each and every time they had landed on her, and she did so again now, losing herself to the point where she barely comprehended if she were standing or sitting.

"Dess." The easy way Erika said her name, the sure way she walked toward her, melted Dess's insides. "God, I've missed you."

Erika stood in front of her, pulling her out of her chair and pressing her to her body in one brisk movement. Her mouth was in Dess's hair, against her ear, and she whispered over and over how much she'd missed her. Dess had no defense against the onslaught of feelings Erika's presence unleashed in her.

Oh God, I'm going to faint, Dess thought as Erika's perfume, citrus and something mildly herbaceous, pleasantly tickled her senses, reminding her of their many—and yet not enough—nights together. Dess deepened their hug, clutching Erika hard, so hard, as though to keep her from slipping out of her life again.

It was another moment before Dess realized she was crying. *Oh Christ,* she thought, *I don't want her to see me cry. I do not want to cry. I'm supposed to be the strong one.* And yet crying in front of Erika somehow seemed the most natural thing in the world.

"Oh, baby. Sweetheart. Don't cry."

Dess only cried harder at the soothing plea. She tried to apologize but couldn't squeeze the words out. The tears continued, and the longer they went on, the more troubling it became. Where was stoic Dess? The one who had declared it was best that they went their separate ways? Where was the Dess who didn't need anyone else? Who didn't like to feel so weak, so needy? The Dess who had admitted to no one how much she loved Erika?

Well, she knew exactly where that Dess was. That Dess was long gone. The sight, the sound of Erika's voice, her touch, had vaporized the old Dess in a flash. In Erika's arms now, Dess didn't know who she was anymore, and for the moment at least, she didn't care, because it simply felt so damned good.

Erika guided her to the leather sofa. They sat down, Erika placing her arm solidly around Dess's shoulders, and Dess fell against her. She was so soft, smelling of that perfume—and she thought how wonderful it was to be home again. To be sheltered, safe, to be loved. Erika, she realized, had always made her feel loved, and now Erika was patiently caressing her back, letting her cry herself out. Dess pulled a tissue from her pocket and dabbed her eyes, trying hard to stem the tide.

"I'm sorry," she said. "I don't know what—"

"Please. Don't apologize or try to minimize. I needed this, Dess."

Needed to see me in such a blubbering, weakened state? Needed to see that I'm a mess without you? That you're actually the one with all the control? Fine. You can have my admission.

"I love you, Erika Alvarez. I always have. And I always will. That's what you wanted to hear, isn't it? That's why you came here in person? To hear those words? And for the song, of course."

Stunned, Erika pulled away, her mouth frozen open. "I—"

"You can have the song. And you can have what you always wanted to hear from me. Everything I have is yours. It always was."

Without waiting for a response, Dess hurried to Jennifer's desk and signed the contract for the song. She'd get fifty percent of the royalties, but she couldn't care less. If it gave Erika the number one hit she wanted, then fine. It would be Dess's parting gift to her, because she could see in Erika's eyes how badly she wanted that song. How much she wanted it to be her conduit to superstardom. Erika had that hungry look about her, the same look Dess had once possessed when she could think of nothing but her desire to make it to the top. When making it to the top had become her entire raison d'être. That, she realized, was exactly the way Erika looked at her now.

When she turned around, Erika was behind her. Gently, she gathered Dess into her arms. "Dess, please don't act like this song is some battle trophy."

Battle trophy? Is that what she thinks? "It's not a battle trophy. It's half my heart, and you can hang it on your belt like a scalp, if that's what you want."

"Dess. Don't. This isn't about the damned song now, and you know it."

"The hell it isn't." She understood the music business all too well. Erika needed that song, and now she'd gotten what she wanted, including turning the tables on Dess's heart.

Erika's hand had crept up to her chin, and she pulled Dess's mouth to hers. The kiss started out hard and uncompromising, as though it could mend all the things wrong between them. But it quickly deepened into something that could never be explained in a song, never be defined adequately with words. The kiss had taken on the aura of their bond, their connection, leaving Dess gasping for more. Her desire for Erika had only intensified over the months apart, and she was horrified to hear herself whimper. She simply couldn't be in the same room with this woman and not want her to rip her clothes off and have her way with her.

She also realized that impulsive sex would solve the insistent throbbing between her legs, but little else. It was her heart that was grievously injured and so full of need.

"Do you know," Erika said huskily, "how badly I want to make love to you?"

"No," Dess pleaded. *Oh God.* "Please don't." If she allowed herself to think about it any more, she'd end up begging Erika to make love to her. And Erika would do it, too. *She'd make love to me and then take the song. How's that for feeling used?* "Just. Please. Take the song and go."

"Dess, wait."

"No." Tears began filling her eyes again, but this time, she wasn't going to let Erika see her cry. Or comfort her. She'd gotten what she'd come for, and as far as Dess was concerned, their meeting was over. The necessary reasons for their breakup still remained. "Please just go."

* * *

Erika had a ready excuse for her swollen, red eyes and runny nose. "I'm coming down with a cold," she planned to tell Dayna when Dayna picked her up at the LA airport. But Dayna wouldn't care. All she'd care about were the signed papers in Erika's satchel.

She'd been tricked at Jennifer Parker's office. No one had told her Dess would be there and that they'd be left alone together. She was simply supposed to retrieve the signed papers and add her own signature, then do a short guest appearance on a Chicago radio station. She'd blown off the radio station, her face and voice completely trashed after the emotional meeting with Dess.

Memories of the anger and hurt in Dess's face came rushing back at her. *God, she thinks I'm a ruthless bitch, caring about nothing except the rights to that song.* Her mission had been to secure permission from Dess to use the song in exchange for half the royalties, and she'd done that. But if she'd known Dess was going to be there, it would have changed everything. She would have slowed things down. Talked to Dess, although, of course, all she'd really wanted to do was touch and kiss her. Make love to her again. Convince her that nothing was right since they'd parted.

Erika turned to the jet's window to watch the approaching city and its wreath of smog. It had wrecked her to see Dess so distraught, and yet it was proof that Dess had truly—*finally!*—loved her. Now she couldn't get Dess's admission out of her head. And probably never would. *"I love you, Erika Alvarez. I always have. And I always will."*

Erika smiled, although she felt like crying again. She should have danced with joy. Should have been ecstatic at hearing the words she'd wanted to hear since the first time they'd kissed and again the first time they'd made love. How many times had she fantasized about hearing Dess say she loved her? How many times had she nearly begged Dess to say it and to mean it? But when the words finally came, they'd sounded harsh, almost cruel, like Dess was doing it to punish her. It hurt too that Dess had fallen straight into a defensive posture, not allowing Erika to explain her feelings, to change the course they were on. That had knocked her completely off balance. *I should have gotten down on my knees and begged her to take me back.*

Erika shook her head in self-admonishment. She should have torn up the contract for the song. Should have told Dess she was and always would be more important to her than a song. Seeing her again, holding her, smelling her hair, her skin—it was like nothing had changed between them. All the old feelings were new again. Even now, her pulse quickened at the memory of kissing Dess again. She'd been blinded by her desire for Dess. Still was.

The wheels hit the runway with a thump, and the engine roared as the plane began to slow down. Somehow, she had to fix this. She wasn't going to let Dess slip out of her life again. Not like this.

As the plane taxied to the gate, Erika switched her phone on and pulled up Sloane's name from her contact list. Furiously, she began typing. After that text, she quickly drafted another to Jennifer Parker.

"Ah, there you are," Dayna said, greeting her moments later as Erika and her fellow passengers streamed out of the gate. She held out her hand, not to shake Erika's, but for the damned contract, Erika knew. She pulled the papers from her bag, angrily tossed them at Dayna's feet.

"What the hell?" Dayna sputtered, bending to pick them up.

"We'll record the damned song, but that's it," Erika ground out.

"What do you mean, that's it?" Dayna clamped her hand on Erika's elbow and guided her to a quiet corner before they began drawing attention.

"Get me in the studio later this week. Next week's Thanksgiving, and I'm going out of town."

"Fine, go out of town. But what's the big hurry to get into the studio?"

Erika surprised herself by speaking so calmly. She should have been hyperventilating, and yet, the rightness of what she was about to do gave her the most serene feeling she'd ever encountered. "I'm going to get new papers drawn up for that song."

Dayna's face began to turn three shades of purple. "What the hell are you up to?"

"That song," Erika said, forcing a mechanical smile, "is going to be a hit. You know it and I know it. We're going to record it this week, and it's going to make *you* a crapload of money."

"You're still not making sense. Are you high? Are you taking a page out of Bethany's book?"

"Dayna, listen carefully to me. I'm going to sign my half of the royalties over to you immediately. You'll get the other half within a couple of weeks, which means the entire rights to it—

and all the money that song earns—will be yours." There was still the small matter of getting Dess to sign over her share of the royalties to Dayna as well, but Erika was confident she could convince her. Already, ideas of how to persuade her were beginning to take shape.

"In return for what?"

"For letting me go."

"Oh no. No way." Dayna's mouth twisted into a hateful smirk. "That song will make you a star, and if you think I'm going to let you go the minute you make it big, then you're delusional."

Erika forced herself into Dayna's space, towering above her. "You," she snapped and pointed a finger, "are going to let me go, or I'll never do another thing for you. I'd sooner sabotage my career, be a one-hit wonder, than continue under contract with you." She stepped back, schooled her voice. "You let me go now or I ride out the remaining few months of our contract without doing another single performance, interview, recording or anything else. At least this way, you're getting something out of it."

Dayna shook with fury. "You met with her in Chicago, didn't you! Dess talked you into this. She hates me, and so do you, it seems, because she wants you to end up a washout, just like her."

Erika retreated a few steps, refusing to be drawn into an argument. She kept her gaze fixed on Dayna. "We record the song as quickly as possible. After that, any communication between us will be done through my lawyer."

On the taxi ride to her apartment, Erika checked her texts. She had a plan now, at least. *Her* plan. Not, for once, Dayna's. And soon, she thought as a smile tugged at her lips, she'd be done with all this shuttling around. Planes, taxis, limos. Her life these days consisted of moving around from one city to the next, one concert to the next, one meeting to the next, one hotel room to the next. The so-called glamorous life was ninety percent shuttling around in cars and planes, going to and coming from strange places that would never feel like home.

She glanced at a palm tree as the taxi swept past it. *Good riddance, LA.*

CHAPTER TWENTY-NINE

The smell of the turkey in the oven had been making Dess's mouth water all afternoon. A glass of Riesling and Carol's two young daughters vying for her constant attention failed to take her mind off the food. It would be wonderful to eat a lavish, home-cooked meal, and she was starving. Too often lately she'd been eating out of cardboard containers.

Sloane, a regular at Hampton family dinners, sidled up to Dess. "You look like you're about to rip the oven door off and start munching on that turkey."

Dess sipped her wine, watched Sloane do the same. "That obvious, am I?"

"Yes, and it's wonderful to see you getting your appetite back. Especially in time for Thanksgiving."

Dess made a face. For months, friends and family had sounded like a broken record about how she needed to gain weight, how she was going to make herself sick if she didn't. They were always watching her, nagging her. She still couldn't get used to having gone from the superstar that everyone—including her family—treated like royalty to the poor lamb who needed constant tending. The breakup with Erika and the injury on that Wisconsin stage had, in her family's eyes, made her once again in need of protecting. Just like when she was recovering from cancer. And some days, their constant attention pissed her off, but only a little. She understood how lucky she was to have such loving and generous people around her. And, of course, how lucky she was to be alive. She wondered, for not the first time or even the hundredth, who was looking after Erika. Who was cherishing her. It wasn't Bethany Dunlop anymore, according to the latest gossip websites and magazines, and that gave her reason to smile.

She turned to Sloane. "I promise you that I can wait along with everyone else. But did you see that pumpkin pie my mom made from scratch? I might *not* be able to wait for that."

"I did, and you know what occurs to me?" Sloane sipped her wine again. She was easily on her third glass by now. "That we're getting to that pathetic age where food matters more than sex."

Dess nearly dropped her glass. "Oh, that'll *never* happen to you, my friend."

Sloane considered, before breaking into an impish grin. "You're right, it won't."

The doorbell rang, and Carol poked her head out of the kitchen. "Would you mind getting that, Sis?"

Dess shrugged at Sloane. "This better not delay dinner, whoever it is."

"Do you want me to grab a baseball bat and come with you? Scare off whoever dares to interrupt our Thanksgiving dinner?"

"No, better not. We don't want any lawsuits."

"Good point. On the other hand, if it's a hot woman, by all means, invite her in. We could put our theory to the test." Sloane wiggled her eyebrows, and Dess slapped her shoulder on the way to the door.

This better be good, she thought. *Like a flower delivery or something involving food.* She pulled open the heavy door. Her heart stopped.

"Hi." Erika stood before her, holding a bouquet of flowers.

Dess could form no coherent thought. She couldn't seem to speak either. Or move. So she stood there stupidly, as though her feet were nailed to the floor.

Erika leaned in, smelling faintly of jasmine and sandalwood this time, and gave her a peck on the cheek. Dess's knees went weak.

"Sorry. I keep popping up out of nowhere, don't I?" There wasn't the slightest hint of anger or hurt in Erika's voice from their falling out last week.

"Erika!" Sloane nudged Dess aside and gave Erika a big hug, crushing the flowers between them. "It's great to see you, kid. Come in."

Dess stood back, feeling strangely like the outsider as Sloane tugged Erika along. Carol had come running from the kitchen and gave Erika a squealing hug. "Yes, please, come in, Erika. Join us for dinner, won't you?"

"Okay, but only if you accept these flowers."

Erika's smile was slightly apologetic, but her happiness at being around Dess and her family was clearly evident. It only made Dess want to cry at the futility of it all. Why was Erika torturing her this way? And how could she possibly sit through an entire dinner with Erika in the same room, smelling the way she smelled, looking more beautiful than she had ever seen her, looking like she belonged here? It was all so hopeless. Nothing had changed between them. There was still the white hot desire, the canyon of yearning and need in Dess's heart. But also present was the same fractious issue that kept them from being together— Erika's desire for success and Dess's desire for a quiet life. *We're trapped in a horrible, vicious circle that has no resolution.*

In the kitchen, Dess pulled Carol aside and whispered, "Did you know about this?"

Carol shrugged. "Maybe. All right, fine. She wanted to see you. Said it was important, and she didn't think you'd agree to meet with her if she approached you directly. So I told her to come by."

Dess rolled her eyes. "What is this, high school?"

Looking back to the living room she watched her mother press a glass of wine into Erika's hands. "I hope you've come to sweep my daughter off her feet," she deadpanned.

Dess's mouth fell open. "Mom!"

Erika was playing it cool, thankfully. "I have some business with your daughter, Mrs. Hampton. As for the other, well..." She shot a mirth-filled glance at Dess. "That depends on Dess."

"Well, pleasure first. You can conduct business after dinner. And please, call me Victoria."

"All right. And thank you, Victoria."

"Come," Victoria said to Erika, "and meet the rest of the family before the turkey gets cold."

Wow, Dess thought, *my family acts as though she's already one of us.*

"This is good," Sloane whispered beside her. "Always best when the family gets along with the future in-law."

"Jesus, Sloane!"

"Bull's-eye." Sloane laughed. "When are you going to understand that some things are just meant to be? Come on, let's get first in line for the food."

Erika was perfectly charming over dinner, as if she'd been the scheduled main attraction all along, regaling them with stories from the road, gossiping idly about other celebrities. Carol's young daughters were smitten. So was Carol, her husband, Rob and, of course, Dess's mother. Victoria never once dropped her smile, even while cramming her mouth full of food.

"Dessert's another hour away," Carol announced. To Dess, she said, "You and Erika are welcome to use my study to talk business." She handed her a half bottle of Riesling and two glasses and capped the gesture with a wink. "You might need this."

"Thanks. I think."

Dess closed the door behind them, set the bottle and glasses down on a side table. She didn't want to be alone with Erika, no matter what the reason. It was too damned hard.

"Do you really have business to discuss?" she asked, skepticism creeping into her voice. What kind of game was Erika playing, anyway? Had Dayna finally rubbed off on her?

"Yes," Erika said, sitting on a corner of Carol's desk and casually crossing her arms. "It's about our song. I know this is going to sound completely out of left field, but I want your half of the rights."

Blood thundered in Dess's ears. "Dayna put you up to this, didn't she?" She began to pace in front of Erika, trying not to go out of her mind. "She convinced you somehow that the song should be all yours? Well," she raged, "you both can forget it."

"No. This wasn't Dayna's idea, but it has everything to do with her."

Dess desperately reached for the wine bottle and filled her glass to the top. With a trembling hand, she took a giant gulp. Maybe she should just sign over the damned song and be done with it. Be done playing these games with Erika. And Dayna. *Ha*, she thought. Dayna was as ruthless a bitch as ever and probably knew that Dess could not say no to Erika. About anything. They were playing her, and she was falling straight into their trap.

From behind, Erika's hand snaked its way around her wrist and guided her glass down to the table.

"Turn around," Erika whispered, her breath tickling Dess's ear and sending a hot tremor down her spine.

Mentally bracing herself to give Erika a piece of her mind, she reluctantly obeyed. She took a deep breath, intending to give Erika both barrels, when Erika's mouth was suddenly on hers. The crushing heat of their lips undid her with an eruptive force that nearly lifted her off the ground, made her dizzy with a want she thought she could control but knew she never would. They fit together so perfectly. Not only their mouths, their lips, but their entire bodies. Fit together and belonged together. She slid into Erika's embrace like a hand into a custom glove, and thought, *I could die here never needing or regretting a single thing ever again.*

Erika deepened the kiss as her hands slid up Dess's belly, her torso, until they brushed the underside of her breasts. Dess shivered with pleasure. She remembered how those hands felt on her breasts, on her skin, and she ached for them to touch her all over. But it would be a mistake, came the tiny pinprick of conscience. *She's here because she wants something and I can't damned well say no.*

"Wait," Dess said, breathless and placing a hand on Erika's chest to create some distance between them. It was her last scrap of strength. "You can't kiss me like that."

"Why not?" A defiant little smile flickered at the corner of Erika's mouth, and it was annoyingly sexy. Those damned dimples were alive and well too, Dess noticed.

"Because I have no resistance against it." Dess swallowed. "It makes me want to give you anything."

A single eyebrow rose. "Anything?"

It was true. She'd give Erika her body, her heart, her money, anything she wanted. But she'd be damned if she'd give in quite so readily. "Tell me why you want the song."

Erika reached for Dess's glass of wine and took a sip from it. "I want us to give it to Dayna."

Dess's heart pounded like a jackhammer. "You what?"

"I've just recorded the song, and I told Dayna she could have it."

Shock and anger left Dess trembling. "That is our song, Erika. Yours and mine, and it's not for *you* to give away. Especially not to her. How dare you!"

"I have a good re—"

"I thought that song was special to you, that it had special meaning." Dess's voice cracked, and tears weren't far off. "It was special to me. I couldn't have written those words, that music, with anyone but you. How on earth could you do this?"

Erika reached for Dess, but she swatted her hand away. "Don't."

"Jesus, Dess, let me explain. If we give Dayna the rights to that song, which I know is going to be a hit, she'll cut me loose. Let me out of my contract six months early." Quietly, she added, "I'll be free of her. Forever."

"That doesn't make any sense. What about your career?"

"My career will go on, but in the ways I choose it to. And living out of a suitcase and traveling to so many cities that I can't even remember where I am is not how I want to live my life. I'm done with that."

"But…" Dess couldn't afford to yield her trust so quickly, to risk Erika changing her mind down the road. "I thought that was what you wanted…I mean, you're just getting started."

Facing her, Erika took Dess's hands in hers. "I thought it was what I wanted too, until I began to understand some of the realities. And when I realized I couldn't bear the loss anymore."

Dess shook with anticipation. And fear. "What loss?"

There was unmistakable love in Erika's smile and something deeper that could only be devotion. Dess's heart swelled, even as Erika replied, "You, sweetheart. Nothing is worth losing you over. There is nothing else in this world that truly makes me happy. Not the concerts, not the song charts, not the glamor and certainly not the money."

"But…are you sure about this? It might mean more of those small festivals like we did last summer. And venues of hundreds of people instead of thousands. It might mean perpetual obscurity. I mean, do you know what you're giving up?"

"Yes. I do. I tried it, Dess. And it doesn't come close to filling my heart. Not the way you do. And there's more."

"There is?"

Erika's jaw tightened. "I don't want to be my parents. I don't want to be obsessive and single-minded about music to the detriment of everything else. They lost their daughter because of it. But I won't lose the love of my life because I'm too blinded by my aspirations. I didn't see that before, but I do now. And I don't ever want to be like Dayna and Bethany and all the rest of them…so damned lonely and empty inside and miserable. It's not how I want to live my life, Dess."

"Oh, honey." Tears choked her voice, and she threw herself into Erika's arms. She could have told Erika all about the price and sacrifices of fame—most of all, the bitter, empty loneliness that made you doubt everything and everyone, including yourself. But hearing those things and coming to know them for yourself are two completely different things, Dess knew.

"I love you, Dess. And I want to be with you. Period. Anything else in my life is just gravy."

She'd always known Erika loved her, but not like this. Not the kind of love where Erika was willing to renounce—or at least severely alter—her dreams and goals and future. Now, she knew, it was up to her to offer the same gift.

"I love you too, Erika. With all my heart. And I'm sorry I didn't tell you that a lot sooner. I was afraid to. I—"

"No, it's okay," Erika said with a smile that made Dess's heart ache. "You needed to set me free. I understand that now."

"Then know this too. I'm ready now to walk with you, side by side, wherever you want to go. Whatever you want to do. Okay? I wasn't willing to change my life for you, but I am now. And I will."

Erika smiled, mischief glinting in her eyes. "Good, because I saw you on that talk show, you know. And I was thinking, now that you're comfortable being on television again, we could, you know, do a reality show together. What do you say?"

Dess playfully tugged Erika's ear with her teeth. "No reality shows, sorry."

A hand reached under Dess's blouse and crawled up to her breast. "Then how about our own sex video?"

"How about the sex without the video?"

Erika laughed. "Deal. What are you doing the rest of the evening?"

"It so happens I'm free."

"Good." Erika kissed her. "Let's make a run for it."

"It might be hard getting a cab, it being Thanksgiving and all. Can you handle a twenty-minute walk?"

Erika stroked her nipple through her bra, nearly sending her through the roof. "I can handle it if you can."

"Keep doing that, and I'm going to pull you to the floor in about two seconds."

Erika's eyes glinted with hope. "I wouldn't say no."

"Come on, let's go."

"We're skipping dessert, you know."

Dess grinned, never so happy to skip her mother's pumpkin pie. "No, we're not. I have a feeling dessert is going to be at my place."

* * *

Snow fell in the form of a soft dusting from the sky, and it was beautiful, the way it coated everything with a fine, white, glittery blanket. Erika held Dess's hand tightly as they strolled and thought how clean the snow made the city look. And how festive. Shops along the Magnificent Mile were decorated for Christmas with miniature twinkling lights and dazzlingly adorned trees in their window displays. She wondered what she might get Dess for Christmas, then covertly tapped the small box in the pocket of her wool peacoat. It would have to do, although waiting for Christmas to give it to her would be a challenge.

"You know," Dess said. "I never did give you an answer about signing over our song, did I?"

A finger of panic crawled up Erika's spine. "Oh, shit. You'll do it, won't you?"

"If it means getting that witch out of our life and giving you back control over your career, then yes, absolutely."

"Thank you." Erika squeezed Dess's fingers, which were cold. They hadn't brought mittens or gloves. "I didn't ask lightly. But that song will always be ours, Dess. No matter what."

"I know. And I have a feeling we're going to write more together."

"You do, do you? We could start tonight, you know."

"Oh no, we can't. I have other plans for us. You're going to be kept very busy."

Erika kissed Dess's cheek, warmed by the vision of what was to come. "I like being kept busy, as you know. Especially when you and a bed are involved."

"Ooh, now you're getting me hot."

"And wet, I hope."

"Oh yes. Definitely wet."

Erika tugged Dess's arm until they were running. By the time they got to Dess's condo building, they were breathless and laughing and kissing. In the elevator, Erika said, "God, I love you. I may never stop smiling again."

"I wish I could freeze-frame this moment." Dess paused beside the big oak door, and Erika flashed back to the first time she'd waited for Dess to open that door. How nervous she'd been, and hopeful and awed until she was almost dizzy. *I was a scared kid then*, she thought. *Now I'm a woman with absolutely everything I've ever wanted.*

"You've made me so happy, Erika. Happier than I've ever been."

"Good. But I plan for you to be even happier in about ten minutes."

Dess licked her lips. "Care to elaborate?"

Erika licked, then playfully nipped Dess's earlobe. "I could, but I'd rather show you."

Dess shouldered the door open. Maggie galloped up to them, tail wagging a mile a minute, body squirming with barely restrained energy.

"Maggie! How are you, girl? I've missed you." Erika knelt so the Labrador could lick her face. "Oh, you're such a good girl, aren't you? But your mother and I have some pressing business, so you'll have to excuse us, okay? We'll catch up later, I promise."

Dess had already disappeared into the bedroom. Erika shed her coat and rushed to join her. "Ah," she breathed, at the sight of Dess stretched out on the bed, naked. "The most beautiful woman in the world, and she's all mine."

"Funny, I was thinking the exact same thing about you. Now come here."

Erika only had time to slide off her slacks before Dess was pulling her onto the bed.

"Sorry, I can't wait another second for you to be on top of me."

The softness and smell of Dess's skin was instantly familiar. Every contour, every tremor, every breath brought Erika back to all the other times they'd made love. It was as though no time had passed, like their time together was an endless circle, always bringing them back to each other.

"I've missed you," Erika whispered. "So much. I love you."

"I love you too," Dess whispered, her face flushed, her breath quickening. "Please…"

Erika smiled against the silky skin of her neck. "You don't have to ask twice, sweetheart."

She slid her mouth down to Dess's breast, anxious to taste its supple, salty sweetness again. Anxious to stroke the hardening flesh with her tongue. Her fingers stroked her other breast, and she had to remind herself to go slow. Her need to make love to Dess raged and tore through her with hurricane force, but she'd leave bruises if she didn't relax.

"You don't have to, you know," Dess said haltingly, desire thick in her voice.

"Don't have to what?"

"Go slow."

Erika moaned. "Sweetheart, you read my mind."

"Good." Dess began guiding Erika's head lower, trembling with a need that Erika understood all too well. And was happy to alleviate.

"Oh, you greedy woman, you. I love it."

"Where you're concerned, yes, I'm greedy, because I can never get enough of you."

Making love with Dess never grew old, Erika thought, just as a classic song never grew tiresome. Anything pleasing to the senses only deepened the more familiar and more attuned you became with it. Learning every nuance, every movement, every hitched breath, every moan of Dess's was a cherished discovery that made Erika hungry for more.

Taking Dess into her mouth, Erika moaned her delight, noting the corresponding swelling of her own desire. She tasted, toyed with the soft flesh, felt it harden beneath her tongue. Felt Dess's hips rise up to meet the strokes her mouth meted out. Her mouth rocked in time with Dess, and she plunged two fingers inside her. Dess tightened around her, then bucked beneath her as her body absorbed, then released the violent pulses of orgasm.

"I love you," Erika said, joy bursting in her heart. She crawled up the length of Dess, kissed her thoroughly.

"Oh God, I love you, Erika. I don't ever want us to be apart again."

"We won't be. I promise you." She wiped a tear as it crested in Dess's eye.

"Please. I need that to be true."

"It's true, baby, so true." Erika thumbed her cheek, her wet eyelashes. "We're meant to be a duet, not soloists." To make Dess laugh, Erika began singing the old Peaches & Herb song, "Reunited." "*And it feels so good…*" she crooned, sliding her body softly against Dess's.

Laughter bubbled up from Dess's throat—a sweet sound that Erika wanted to hear every day for the rest of her life. But right now, she needed to come.

"I need you to love me slow. Deep," Erika whispered, looking into Dess's eyes and going breathless at the adoration reflected back at her. "I need you inside me. I need you deep inside."

They flipped, and Dess's body was warm as it covered Erika's, glided over it, ground gently into it. Lips, soft, reassuring, swept across her chest, her nipples, her abdomen, back up to her shoulders, her neck, her throat, her mouth. Eyes closed, head back, Erika wanted to cry at the swelling of her heart and the frisson of their lovemaking. When Dess entered her, a light show erupted behind her eyelids and her heart pounded thunderously. She rose to meet the strokes...so deep, so languid, so full of tenderness. She was filled with Dess, and Dess whispered sweet things to her, but all Erika could focus on was the pounding of her heart, the crowning of her need.

"Ohh," she moaned as the tremors tore through her, leaving her a throbbing mass of expended desire. But Dess was inside her, caressing her, kissing her, reassuring her.

"I love you, baby," Erika said, still breathless. She held Dess tight to her and rocked with her, determined to keep this feeling in her heart forever.

* * *

Dess went dizzy at the sight of the small jewelry box sitting on the breakfast bar. Erika must have gotten up in the night and put it there. She looked back at the bedroom, where Erika was still asleep. A tiny peek. An infinitesimal one. What could it hurt?

As the coffee brewed, she tried to talk herself into snooping. Then, when she finally persuaded herself, she worked on talking herself out of it. Maybe it wasn't even for her. And if it was for her and it was something big—really big—like an engagement ring or something, what would she do? There was no question she wanted to spend the rest of her life with Erika. Just as there was no question in her mind that Erika wanted the same thing. And there was no question they'd make it as a couple. But wasn't it a little too soon for an engagement ring? Wouldn't a little more time together, to get used to each other, to figure out some plans, be the practical thing to do? And yet...

She was pouring the coffee when an awful thought occurred to her. What if she had it all worked out in her mind that it was an engagement ring but it was something else entirely? Erika would see the disappointment and confusion on her face. And that simply wouldn't do. *I'll have to take a peek*, she told herself. *So I'll know how to react.*

"Good morning, beautiful."

Dess jumped at the sound of Erika's voice. Her hand, fortunately, hadn't yet started creeping toward the little velvet box.

"Am I making you nervous, darling?"

"No, but that little box is. Coffee, my love?"

"Yes, please."

Erika was intermittently smiling and yawning when Dess set a cup of coffee in front of her.

"Sorry, I didn't mean to make you jumpy. Wait, I didn't get my good morning kiss yet."

Dess leaned forward and gave Erika a soft, lingering kiss. "Good morning, lover."

"Good morning." Erika smiled, then tilted her head toward the little box. "I decided I didn't want to wait until Christmas to give you this. I meant to get up before you and sneak it into your scrambled eggs or something."

"Ooh, I like that idea."

Erika's eyebrows danced suggestively. "We could start the morning over. In bed. Eating a breakfast of champions."

Much as the idea appealed, Dess was dying to know what was in that damned box. "Oh no. Now that you've got me curious about this, I don't want to wait."

Erika reached for the box, cradled it in her hands, her hair marvelously sleep-tousled but her dark eyes sharp with seriousness. Dess loved the idea of waking up with this gorgeous, wonderful woman every morning.

"I got this made for you just before I flew in. Because I wanted you to understand that you will always be the song in my heart, even with Dayna owning the rights and earning all the royalties from it. It's still about us, Dess, about our love and it always will be."

"Yes," Dess answered, trying not to sound disappointed that it wasn't an engagement ring. Oh hell, she thought, why should she sit around waiting for Erika to give her an engagement ring anyway? Why couldn't she be the one to ask Erika to marry her? Once it came to that, of course. "Nobody can take that song away from us."

Erika slid the box over to Dess. "Open it."

Snapping the box open, Dess gasped at the contents. It was a gold necklace with a pendant comprised of an eighth note encrusted in diamonds and surrounded by a heart made of rubies. "Oh my God, Erika. It's perfect, but it's too much. It must be worth the price of a new car."

"Nothing is too much for you, Dess. Nothing. I love you, and I love the magic we make together. That's what this necklace represents."

"Oh, honey. It's absolutely beautiful. And it's perfect." Dess jumped into Erika's arms and kissed her in a way neither would ever forget. She tangled her fingers in Erika's hair, held her face firmly. "I love you more than anything, Erika. But I have a question for you."

"Ask me anything."

Dess toyed momentarily with the impulse of asking Erika to marry her, right then and there, in their sleep shirts and their messy hair and their growling stomachs. But no. She *would* ask Erika, but she would wait and do it in the most perfect, romantic way possible.

"What if you'd come all this way, with this gorgeous necklace in your pocket, and I'd said no to signing over the song?"

Erika shrugged, but she was smiling with her typical self-confidence. "I would have given it to you as a bribe."

"And if that hadn't worked?"

"Then I would have sneaked it into your coat pocket as a goodbye gift. Or kept trying to convince you until Christmas." Her grin faded, and in its place, her chin trembled. "Oh, Dess, I was so afraid you'd say no. To everything. I can't believe you've given me—us—a second chance. I'm so grateful. And so happy."

Dess pressed Erika into her, inhaling the scent of her hair, her skin. "Sweetie, I love you so much. I'm the one who's grateful that you never gave up on us."

"Remember, I told you months ago that we weren't finished yet?"

"Yes." Dess smiled at the bittersweet memory. "And you were right."

Erika's lips found hers, and they kissed until arousal began burning a trail down Dess's thighs and deep into her belly.

"I want to make love to you while you're wearing that necklace," Erika said in a low voice that was husky with desire.

Dess closed her eyes, her own desire pulsing between her legs. She couldn't get enough of Erika, in bed and out, but they should talk. There were things...plans...stuff they should talk about, shouldn't they? Logistics and whatnot. *Oh shit, I'm losing my mind.* Erika's hands were all over her, under her sleep shirt, stroking her skin, lighting a fire in her belly. And all rational thought quickly ebbed from her mind.

"Take me to bed," Dess demanded, grabbing the jewelry box as Erika tugged her toward the bedroom.

"You read my mind."

Afterward, Dess commanded Erika to stay in bed, told her she'd be right back. She returned with a box full of the private binders of songs she'd written—songs she'd never shown anyone else, but she was ready to now. She set the box down on the bed.

"What's this?" Erika said sleepily, sitting up.

Dess joined her on the bed, extracting one of the binders. "An early Christmas present from me."

"Oh my God, Dess, these are your binders! Your songs! Are you sure you want me to look at them?"

Dess smiled. "Yes, I'm sure." She wanted to share everything with Erika. The good times, the painful times and everything in between.

"Thank you, my love. This means everything to me." Erika kissed her, then eagerly flipped open the binder.

EPILOGUE

Dayna had been right about one thing, Erika thought with satisfaction as she and Dess walked the gauntlet otherwise known as the red carpet outside the Grammy Awards ceremony at LA's massive Staples Center. Those in the business who last year had thoughtlessly shunted her aside—or had refused to even acknowledge her existence—were greeting her now like old friends. Perfectly straight, white teeth flashed pleadingly at her from all sides, almost as brightly as the endless camera flashes. Words, obsequious and dripping with artificiality, burbled at her and Dess like fountains gone wild.

Whatever, Erika thought as she tightened her grip on Dess's hand. She didn't care anymore because she had everything she needed. Thanks to "The Song in My Heart," the world now knew of her talent and had become reacquainted with Dess's—this time as a songwriter. Dayna was reaping the truckload of money the song's number-one status on Billboard was bringing in—the royalties from CD sales, digital sales and radio play. There was even talk that an upcoming Nicholas Sparks' romantic movie wanted to use the song. Erika had no doubt that Dayna would pull it off and make another truckload of money.

As it turned out, if she and Dess had retained the rights to it, their song could have made Erika a millionaire in her own right. But what she had now was worth so much more than that, she knew in her heart. Being with Dess, creating more music over a lifetime together... *That* was priceless to her, even if they never had a hit song again. She was exactly where she wanted to be.

Taking their seats in the second row from the stage, Erika leaned into Dess and whispered, "I love you, sweetheart."

"I love you too." Dess smiled, stroking the knuckles of Erika's hand. With her other hand, she lovingly stroked the necklace Erika had given her, which she wore for special occasions. "Nervous?"

"Why? Oh, you mean because we're up for Song of the Year?" Erika laughed, suddenly calmer than she'd been all day. "I'm not nervous, honey. I've already won everything I need. Which happens to be sitting right beside me."

"Then that means we're both winners." Dess shifted in her seat. Her eyes twinkled, but her smile faltered. "To be honest, I'm a little nervous. Actually, a lot nervous. Sorry."

"No, I'm sorry. I know being in the spotlight like this is difficult for you, but you're doing awesome. And you look gorgeous, by the way." The sleek, silver, black-and-white Gucci gown she was wearing fit Dess like a glove.

"It's not that," Dess mumbled, turning coy when Erika tried to press her. "But as long as you keep looking at me like that, I'll be fine."

"Looking at you like what?" Erika couldn't keep the smile out of her voice.

"Like you want to eat me," Dess whispered, her eyes ablaze.

"Ah, but I do want to eat you, my dear." Erika winked at her. "And I plan to do just that once we get back to the hotel."

Erika felt eyes lasering her back. She turned in her seat enough to glimpse Bethany Dunlop, who quickly looked away, nose in the air. She looked gaunt, pale, and Erika guessed her drug problem had worsened. *I'm so glad to be away from all that,* she thought. She had escaped without ever developing a problem, and although she and Bethany hadn't remained friends, she didn't wish her ill.

The lights dimmed, the murmuring of the crowd crescendoed until it sounded like a billion bees buzzing around, and then Ellen DeGeneres strode out onto the stage to the wild cheering of the audience.

"You two must have gone to the same tuxedo shop," Dess joked.

"Nah. Mine's better."

Dess went to kiss her cheek, but Erika turned into her so their lips met. "I think you just wear yours better, darling. Because you look absolutely smashing."

"Thank you, my love."

At the halfway break, Erika led Dess backstage to prepare for their performance of "The Song in My Heart." It had taken a lot of convincing to get Dess to even consider accompanying her on guitar, and then, to Erika's surprise, Dess had done a complete about-face and, without further discussion, agreed to do it. It was a great honor for them to have been asked to perform it at the Grammys, Dess said by way of explanation. It would be their first time onstage together since the storm in Wisconsin had injured Dess. And this was no pre-fab stage in the middle of a field. Dess was game, and for that, Erika was grateful. Life, she realized, was so much better with Dess beside her.

"Okay?" she asked Dess as they were flashed the two-minute warning by one of the headset-wearing stage managers.

Dess, guitar slung over her shoulder, shot her a thumbs-up and then they were being rushed through a makeshift corridor of plywood and two-by-fours, up a few steel steps and to a door that led directly to the stage. Erika could hear their introduction by Ellen, and just hearing her name uttered by one of the most famous entertainment celebrities in the world and to her largest audience by far—if you counted the television viewers—shot a thrill through Erika. For the briefest of moments, she wanted to puke, before she harnessed her nervous excitement.

"Come on," Dess said, tossing a wink at her, the picture of calm and cool. The Grammys were nothing for Dess, Erika reminded herself. She'd ruled these awards for years.

She took a deep breath and barreled after Dess. The audience erupted in cheers as they stepped onto the stage, hand in hand, and a second later, rose to give them a standing ovation. The salute, Erika knew, was for Dess, and the love and support it represented brought tears to her eyes. To hell with their song's award nomination. This was Dess's coming out. She was back. Not like before, nothing like the insanity of before, but her presence tonight signaled to her fans, to the industry, that she had nothing to fear anymore. Erika was so proud of her. And so humbled.

They sat down on matching stools, staring into each other's eyes, and played their hearts out. Erika sang the lyrics, her voice brimming with the depth of emotion she felt for Dess. And Dess let her guitar be her voice—soulful, stirring, alternately fervent and tender. The audience went nuts, and as they stood for a bow, Dess set her guitar on the stage and made a grab for Erika's microphone.

She glanced nervously at Erika before addressing the audience in a steady, clear voice. "Thank you so much, everyone. You've made my return to the stage something I'll never forget."

On their feet, the audience clapped and whistled, but Dess tried to shush them.

"There's just one other thing that I'm hoping…" Her face began to pink, "will make this night the most important and most memorable night of my life."

Oh shit, Erika thought, wondering what Dess was doing. Her voice, the adorable blush on her cheeks, the slight tremble in her hands indicated some sort of announcement was forthcoming. And she had absolutely no idea what it was. They hadn't discussed any solid offers recently, hadn't mapped out what—

"You see," Dess was saying to the crowd, "I developed a pretty bad case of stage fright in my years away from music. A debilitating case of it, actually. But tonight I need to prove, not just to all of you, but to the woman I love, that I'm over that now. That not only am I okay, but that I'm happier than I've ever been."

Erika, who'd taken refuge on her stool, felt faint. Who was this person who looked so much like Dess but was talking to a crowd of more than twenty thousand people like they were her best friends?

"Erika Alvarez," Dess said calmly, turning to Erika and taking her left hand. She dropped to her knees.

Oh, God. A thousand butterflies zipped around Erika's stomach. Her vision dimmed against the massive overhead stage lights and her ears began ringing. She could hear nothing, but she could see Dess's mouth working, could see Dess looking at her expectantly. Smiling. Then not smiling. Then worried.

"Erika? Sweetheart?"

"W-what?"

"Um, I kind of asked you a question."

The audience laughed. A joke Erika didn't get. "You did?"

More laughter.

"Whew," Dess said to the audience. "She didn't hear me. Okay. I'll just pick my heart up off the stage and try again."

Oh, crap. It was like daydreaming in class and ignoring the teacher's question. Only worse. *Much worse.* "I missed something important, didn't I?"

"Um, kinda."

More laughter erupted, reverberating through the upper levels and around the bowl that surrounded the stage. Ellen ran onto the stage, grinning, holding her microphone and stopping in front of Erika and Dess. "Erika Alvarez, will you take Dess Hampton as your lawfully wedded wife? To have and to hold and all that cool wedded stuff?"

Slack-jawed, Erika looked questioningly at Dess, who was still on her knees.

"Erika Alvarez, would you do me the great honor of marrying me?" Dess repeated.

Erika's free hand flew to her mouth. She hadn't seen this coming, not for a second. *Dess asking me to marry her? And here, on this stage, in front of, oh, about thirty million people?* The dizziness was back, but she pushed through it, her heart climbing to a height she never knew existed. *Oh my God! Dess wants to marry me!* Incredulous, she giggled, then sucked for air that didn't seem to want to enter her lungs. *Dess wants to marry me*, she kept repeating in her mind. She was suddenly a child again. The child she wished she had been—happy, loved, cherished.

Dess handed her microphone to Ellen. "Um, Ellen? You *are* the best woman, remember?"

"Oh, right." Ellen pretended to search the pockets of her tuxedo. "Darn it, I had it here somewhere. Oh, wait, did somebody send this suit to the dry cleaners?"

The audience was laughing, but Dess's face was turning three shades of red.

"Oh, wait," Ellen amended. "I think I found it." She produced a small, black velvet box from her pants pocket and handed it to Dess, adding a wink for luck.

Dess held the box up to Erika and flipped it open. Inside sat two simple, white-gold rings, each topped with a clear, heart-shaped diamond.

"Oh, Dess, they're beautiful. And yes! A thousand times yes, I'll marry you!"

Erika fell to her knees too and they held each other. She could hear the crowd clapping and whistling, but Erika could see nothing but Dess and the tears of joy in her eyes.

"Oh, Erika. My darling. You make me so happy. I love you so much."

Tears came to Erika's eyes too. Her heart was still pumping a mile a minute. "Oh, sweetheart, I love you to the moon and back. Thank you for choosing me to share your life with."

"You ain't seen nothing yet," Dess shouted over the ear-shattering applause.

She didn't know how they got back to their seats. They floated, Erika guessed. She was still thinking about the proposal—the sheer surprise of it, the tumult of emotions that continued to rumble pleasurably through her—when the presenters began announcing the nominations for the Song of the Year award.

"That's us," Dess whispered.

They clutched hands that were suddenly clammy, simultaneously drew nervous breaths. Erika stared at the matching engagement rings on their left hands and felt like giggling again. No award was ever going to match *this*. Not even close, she thought, unable to contain the smile spreading across her face.

"And the winner is…"

"The Song in My Heart"
Music and lyrics by Elaine Dark

V1

      A
Send me your love
 Bm
Make it fast and make it right
C#m
I don't think I can take
 D
Another lonely night
       A
Come take my hand
 Bm
Won't you spend some time with me
     C#m
Let me really get to know you
D
As you get so close to me

V2

      A
Show me your eyes
Bm
Oh those deep and darkened eyes
C#m
How they capture my emotion
 D
Make me quiver at the sight
     A
I'm on my knees
Bm
And I'm beggin' darlin' please
    C#m
Tell me I'm not dreaming
 D
I'm not blind to what I see

CHORUS

    A
Last night I had the sweetest dream
  A7
You were here just loving me
        D
It must be written up there high
   Dm
So high amongst the stars
       Bm
You're my muse when I need you
 E
You are the song in my heart

V3

        A
Send me your love
 Bm
Keep me near when you are far
  C#m
I know that you've been lonely
     D
And you nearly fell apart
     A
Now that I'm here
     Bm
There's no need for you to cry
    C#m
We can take this world together
E
All we have to do is try

CHORUS

Last night I had the sweetest dream
You were here just loving me
It must be written up there high
So high amongst the stars
You're my muse when I need you
You are the song in my heart

BRIDGE
(possible instrumental bridge: E C#m F#m B)

  A
You're the sultan of symmetry
     F#m
You've got everything that I'd ever need
    Bm
You're so beautiful I try to explain
    E
How the touch of your hand just drives me insane

CHORUS

Last night I had the sweetest dream
Don't you know you are the sweetest
You were here just loving me
(Yes by far you are the sweetest)
It must be written up there high
So high amongst the stars
You're my muse when I need you
You are the song in my heart
     D7
The song in my heart
     A7
The song in my heart
     D7
The song in my heart
     A7
The song in my heart

Bella Books, Inc.

Women. Books. Even Better Together.

P.O. Box 10543
Tallahassee, FL 32302

Phone: 800-729-4992
www.bellabooks.com